Jack Polo

The Partners

Black Rose Writing | Texas

ISBN: 978-1-68433-178-9
PUBLISHED BY BLACK ROSE WRITING
www.blackrosewriting.com

Printed in the United States of America
Suggested Retail Price (SRP) $19.95

The Partners is printed in Palatino Linotype

For my partner Hillary, who's always had
my back standing by my side.

THE PARTNERS

"I would not wish any companion in the world but you."
– William Shakespeare *The Tempest* • Act III, Scene I

ONE

"EYE OF THE TIGER! REALLY?"

Zoey Martine shook her head. "I'm not Rocky."

"Yeah, but you are the champ," said Nat Munroe. Nat was Zoey's personal assistant, and like all those who serve, Nat knew that stars could never hear too much about themselves. "Nothing wrong with cheesy if it works," he said. "And all those rich women see you float in? Rocking those Maugham dresses? Ka-ching! Sales will go through the roof."

"What I want is to go through this damn traffic."

Nat jammed the shiny red Jaguar I-Pace HSE into a lane. Behind him the driver he'd just cut off blasted his horn.

"Nat! You're manhandling eighty-five thousand dollars of car," Zoey warned. "Be careful."

"You can afford it."

He didn't wait for a rebuttal, checked his side mirror and hit the accelerator again. The all-electric 394 horses under the hood galloped – or actually *jolted* Nat thought – the vehicle forward.

"This pony's better than any Audi Q5 or an X3 Bimmer."

Zoey checked her Cartier La Dona watch, its white gold glinting in the sunshine beaming into the car from its open roof.

A watch, Nat thought, that's about twice the cost of this Jag.

Jesus, some people. He loved his job as Zoey's assistant. He'd lucked into it when he'd gone to the wrong address for an interview and showed up on the exact morning when Zoey's other assistant, some wonk named Justin, had confused his three-years on the job as freedom to speak his mind. Zoey had ripped him a new one, and Justin had left in tears – freakin' tears from a man! – and Nat had sauntered into the room, thinking he was there to tell this hot-looking chick why he'd be great as an Uber driver.

"We're already twenty minutes late," Zoey said.

"Next block," Nat said. "I'll pull you right up … Hey!"

Nat slammed on the brakes as a grunged-out, faded yellow Toyota Corolla cut right in front of them, huge billows of exhaust fumes rising like a nuclear mushroom cloud from its rattling tailpipe.

"Asshole!" Nat yelled. He pounded the Jag's horn.

And he immediately thought that road rage *was* an actual and dangerous life issue even here at the beach.

And that like Alice, he and Zoey had fallen down the rabbit hole.

Because the Toyota's passenger and driver's doors flew open and two men, enormous men, stomped back for the Jag. Their faces hidden by Guy Fawkes masks.

Those are not guns!

But they *were* guns. Big, nasty-looking automatics with the black opening of the barrel dark as eternity.

Zoey screamed.

Nat tried to get the gearshift into reverse, but the two men were at the side windows before there was time. Goddamn, they were fast!

"Open up, yes?" The man on Zoey's side said, an incongruously polite request coming from the stylized face with its oversized smile and red cheeks, its wide mustache upturned at both ends and a thin, vertical pointed beard; and above it a shiny and shaved bullet-shaped head.

But that politeness vanished in a second when the man decided she wasn't obeying fast enough and slammed the gun against the glass, spider webbing it. He motioned for Nat to slide down the window; which Nat did immediately. As it was sliding down, Zoey slid her left hand down in the narrow opening between her seat and the center console, hoping they wouldn't see the Cartier.

The V-man on Zoey's side yanked open the back passenger door and checked inside. He saw the half-dozen Maugham dresses laying on the back seats and tossed them to the floor.

Zoey started to protest but immediately abandoned that idea. They were just dresses. A quarter-million-dollars of dresses, yes, and that was just wholesale, but not worth your life.

The man stomped back to the rear, hit the button and waited while the deck lid pneumatically lifted. He checked the carpeted area, then lifted it up to look beneath the lid at the spare tire area and saw just the tire and jack.

"Fock!" he snarled. Definitely an accent, maybe Russian.

"Where's money?" the V-man on Nat's side said.

"What money?" Nat said and gestured with his empty hands.

"Keep focking hands quiet," the man said and jammed the weapon into Nat's cheek. Hard, too: Nat winced from the impact.

The man on Zoey's side flung open her door and thrust his automatic into the interior. "Supposed to be two hundred thousand in this Jag. Where is? You drop it off? Maybe not pick up yet? Tell me. I am not focking 'round here, you unnerstand?"

"Yes, yes, we understand," Zoey said. "But we don't have any money. Except what I have in my purse and you're welcome to that. Take it, please."

She could see the man's dark eyes appraising her behind the mask.

"I take it vhether you say please or don't say please. But we here for money. So stop bullshit."

"We're not bullshitting," Nat interjected. "We ... AWWWW!"

The gun barrel slammed into Nat's nose, and even in the searing white-hot pain, he knew it was broken. He felt blood flow from both nostrils and was about to grab his nose but remembered, just in time, about not moving his hands. The blood streamed over his lips and splashed his once brilliant white shirt with crimson drops.

"I ask you one more time," the man on Zoey's side said. "And only one more time."

"Can I... may I talk?" Zoey asked.

Her man nodded his head.

"I'm... Zoey Martine." She waited for some reaction, some recognition. Jesus Christ, she was the number one movie star in the world. And not just females, but all of them – men, dogs, cartoons. If one of her films didn't gross a hundred million box office within the opening two weeks, it was a flop. And these two idiots didn't seem to have a clue who they were robbing.

"You... you may have heard of me? I starred, and directed, 'Bone Dry,' you know, that ... movie about two women that..."

"No, I hate movies. Vaste of time, making and watching, okay? Now, vhere's money?"

Zoey stared at Nat, the panic rising in her face quickly changing to wide-eyed horror at the red tide of blood that was now coursing freely down his shirt. The gun must have ruptured a capillary. Her eyes went down to the leather seats, checking to see if he'd bled all over that supple calfskin, she couldn't help herself, that material girl side of her would always remain.

"Vot's in your hand?" Vhy you holding it down there? You hiding something? Maybe gun?"

"No, no. Nothing."

Zoey brought her hand up slowly, palm up, to hide the gleaming beauty of the watch and showing just the unadorned links.

"Give me watch."

"Take my purse," Zoey said, and yanked it up, "here, it's got over..."

The .350-grain bullet ripped like a cannonball through Zoey – coring her ribs and heart – and buried deep in the driver's door.

The bullet's power sent Zoey's head like a bowling ball into Nat's skull, moving her body so hard that the seat belt became a webbed garrote that bruised and purpled her neck as they later discovered in the post-mortem.

Just before he fell into the black abyss of unconsciousness, Nat heard:

"Igor, vot fock you did?"

TWO

"NOTHING ELSE, YOU'RE SURE?"

Detective Mollie Simmons looked at Nat's bandaged nose and bruised eyes and cheeks. Poor guy was a mess.

"That's it," Nat said, nodding his head. He winced as the pain raced through his swollen face. Nat turned to the other detective and saw himself in the small medicine cabinet mirror of the ER. "Jesus, I look like Nicholson in Chinatown." He gingerly touched the bulbous assembly of gauze and tape that held his nose in place.

"Hey, Simmons and Trane! I need to see you."

Mollie turned and saw Lieutenant Jack Riley standing in the doorway.

"Ten seconds," Mollie said.

"Trane?" Nat said after Riley had gone. "That's your last name, Trane?"

"Yep."

"And your first name's really Cole?"

"Really."

"Cole Trane? Your folks into jazz, huh?"

"My grandfather used to sit in every now and then when John was in the neighborhood. My dad's favorite song was *My Favorite Things*. Anything else?"

Nat studied the detective and decided he liked him. He was good-looking, but not pretty. A slightly-bent nose that must have been painful when it happened took care of that. His Levis weren't pressed or tight, just casual. He wore black Nike Air Max 97s – the same shoe

Nat had back home in his closet. His Armani jacket had a few seasons on it but still held its classic lines. But in the end, Nat decided it was the gardenia that stuck up out of Cole's breast pocket jacket. A perfect white creation that gave off such a wonderful aroma that Nat could smell it even through all his bandages.

Mollie was from central casting for a Beach Boy song.

Lithe body, with curves. Shiny wheat-colored hair that belonged in a shampoo commercial. Luminous, too – as if all that California sunshine she'd absorbed as a teenager was still inside her and radiated out. And her face could send a priest to confession for carnal thoughts.

"Excuse us," Cole said.

He and Mollie walked out of the ER to a small, private room where Riley was waiting for them.

Jack Riley was a career lawman. He had started out, like every cop, walking the beat as a rookie. But even back thirty years ago crime in Ciudad de Los Reyes was as rare as a gloomy day. Rich people came to stroll the beautiful beaches and ended up living there. Maybe you rounded up a couple of drunk surfers or convinced an airline pilot and three flight attendants, although they were called stewardesses back then, to take their naked bodies away from the beach and up to their motel.

And with the new money had come new crime, but still, it happened in the bedroom or Boardroom, not on its streets.

This was Cole and Mollie's first murder.

"Anything?" Cole asked Riley as he and Mollie walked into the room.

"We found the masks a few blocks away, but that's it. We'll run prints and DNA profiles, but that's gonna take time. And who knows whether these guys are in the system. Her assistant have anything?"

"No," Mollie said. "Same MO he told Levendowsky and Hartman when they responded to the 9-1-1 call."

"Anything going on between this Nat guy and Zoey?"

"You mean like romantic?" Mollie said.

"Yeah," Riley said as if Mollie's question was more out of left field than the idea that a personal assistant and his boss, a beautiful, sexy boss, could be exchanging bodily fluids. "I mean he seems pretty broken up over this."

"Probably more in shock than in love," Cole said.

"Don't rule it out."

"Got it," Cole said.

"I'm having profiles run on any Russian or eastern Europeans that might be connected." Riley's cell buzzed, and he checked the caller ID. "Christ, just who I need."

He nodded goodbye at Cole and Mollie and marched from the room, "Hey, Matt!" he said into his phone, his unctuous, smarmy tone over the top.

"The King's not in his Counting House, counting all his money," Cole said.

"But he is making sure the cash flow will continue," Mollie said.

The King was Mayor Matt Gaylord. A ruthless five-term puppet master who pulled strings, greased palms and made sure the city council voted *his* way; especially when it came to real estate and zoning laws. The Mayor didn't own all of the town, just its most expensive parts.

"That's why he's calling," Mollie continued, "get this solved and fast. Crime rate goes up, property values go down. And property values can never go down."

"My guess is we're next on his call list."

"You buying what he was saying? That Nat and Zoey were lovers?"

"Anything's possible. But I don't see her risking her brand in exchange for some sessions between the sheets."

"So, this is just a robbery gone bad?"

"Yeah."

"Which means we start with where'd the V-men get the idea that there was a quarter-million in cash in the Jag?"

"Who told them? How'd they know? Beyond the starting point that it had to be somebody that knew Zoey."

"Or Joelle and Michelle Maugham."

"The question is, how does a quarter-million in dresses become a quarter-mil in cash."

"The perps are stupid."

"Maybe it was a set-up from the jump," Mollie said. "Maybe somebody wanted Zoey off the board. So they sent those two, knowing they were stupid, had nasty tempers and were quick on the trigger."

"Too many combinations have to hit on that idea to make it work. It's a five-cushion bank shot."

"Yeah, this was FUBAR pure and simple."

THREE

"IT WAS OVERKILL."

Medical examiner Tony Rivers adjusted his green gloves, although he wouldn't be coming near Zoey's body since he had a long steel pointer.

"In every sense of the word."

Cole and Mollie had gone to city hall the next morning and brought Winchell's doughnuts and coffee as covert bribes, to get advance information on the shooting.

Tony was early 30s, tall and lean as a human thermometer with a shiny head of dark red hair, and easily the smartest human being Cole and Mollie had ever met.

"Start with the entrance wound," Tony said and pointed at Zoey's breasts. He positioned the pointer several millimeters away from the body. "Relatively small going in," he moved around to the other side of the cadaver, prudently arranged the sheet on her right side and again used the pointer, "but large upon exiting. Because even after shattering her number six rib, going right through her heart, being slightly deflected as it exited between ribs seven and eight, it still had enough mass ..."

He went to a white porcelain tray and used a set of tweezers to pluck a dark, misshaped hunk of lead and held it out to them, "... that it weighed 275 grams."

Tony squinted at the distorted bullet.

"A 300-grain bullet can drop a moose. A hundred-and-seventeen-pound woman? It eviscerated her."

"Enough of the bullet to get striations? Cole said.

"Luckily, yes. My guess is this came from a Desert Eagle, 50-calibre."

He dropped the mass back unto the tray where it clinked loudly in the quiet of the room.

"Fires a bullet at 1814 feet per second. Which is goddamn fast."

Cole couldn't remember the last time he'd heard Tony curse; so it was clear he was angry over this senseless killing.

"This massacre over a wristwatch?" Tony said.

"I don't think the watch was their original target," Cole said.

"Oh?"

"I think things went south, they shot Zoey, maybe by accident, maybe out of anger or frustration, and then just took whatever they could get away with."

Tony nodded, his brain whirling through the permutations of the crime.

"Any ideas on what they were after? I mean a half-dozen designer dresses don't sound like the score of the year. Unless they had girlfriends or wives with *avant-garde* taste."

"They thought there was going to be a quarter-million in cash," Cole said. "Anything else, Tony?"

"Yeah. She was pregnant."

FOUR

"I NEVER HAD SEX WITH THAT WOMAN."

Nat was doing his best Bill Clinton imitation, mostly in disbelief.

"And why am I giving blood? I don't think I have any left."

"Part of the investigation," Cole said.

He turned as a nurse entered the room and watched while she tapped Nat's left arm for a vein, then his right. She went back to the left, swabbed it with alcohol, then slipped a needle into the crook of Nat's elbow. She filled a small vial, pulled the needle and pressed a cotton ball on the entry point. "Keep pressure on that," she said, then unwrapped a small circular band-aid and put that over the tiny hole.

Cole waited until the nurse was gone before he said, "You sure you weren't fucking Zoey?"

"I'm sure. It's not like having sex with Zoey would have been something that I didn't remember."

"You tell us now, we're cool," Cole said.

"We find out later you were fucking her," Mollie said, "we'll bust your ass for withholding. Now, last chance, Nat. Which door's it going to be: Freedom or jail?"

"I never had sex with her. Not that I wouldn't have loved to; but it never happened. Why are you asking? I mean I'm not a suspect, right?"

Cole and Mollie looked at each other. Mollie nodded for Cole to deliver the news.

"Zoey was pregnant. Fourteen weeks."

Nat looked like he'd been tasered. His eyes blinked rapidly, he shook his head and winced at his unconscious physical reaction. "God, really?"

"So, who was she seeing?"

Nat's mouth opened, then closed.

"We aren't going to do this again," Mollie said. "Tell us, or we take you on a short ride to the jail."

"Oh, man, this is gonna blow up her world. And *his*, too."

"A name."

"Sid Kent."

It took a moment for the name to register.

"Sid Kent that lives here?"

"Yeah."

"How does that happen?" Mollie said. "And I don't mean because Sid's married with three kids. Or because he's worth a couple hundred million."

"They met at some Hollywood red carpet event. Five, six months ago."

"She have a father complex?" Cole said. "Sid's in his fifties."

"May-December thing," Nat offered. "I don't know. Only way I found out was by accident. One morning I arrived early to pick her up, and Sid walks out of her bedroom, his hair wet from the shower. You should have seen his face. I act like I didn't see anything and just turned around and went to wait in the car."

"And Zoey followed you, right?"

Nat nodded, surprised: How'd you know that?

"Yeah. She came up, and as I opened the door, she slammed it shut. 'This is private!' she says. 'You're clear on that, yes?' And I said yes. And that was it. Although two days later she had me sign a confidentiality document."

Nat shrugged.

"That's why I wasn't so sure about saying something. But I guess it won't matter too much now. Right?"

He looked at Cole and Mollie for confirmation.

"Don't worry. You're not a person of interest."

FIVE

"WE'RE SUSPECTS?"

Joelle Maugham was stunned. "Really?"

"No," Cole said. "But your connection to Zoey has to be explored."

"This is just what we needed," Michelle Maugham whined. "I told you this was a bad idea, Joelle. Right from the start. Having a diva like Zoey as a model." Then she caught herself and said, "No disrespect intended."

"Oh, right," Mollie said. "None inferred."

Cole knew from Mollie's tone that she meant exactly the opposite.

It was a sign that only Cole and Sophia, would have noticed. Sophia was Mollie's lover, had been for the last three years. It was a relationship that seemed headed for the altar.

A significant change in Mollie's love 'em and leave 'em romances.

Cole had been one of those romances.

More than six years ago. It had been a brief, but red-hot secret affair; made even hotter because it was against every department rule. But that hadn't stopped them.

There had been sparks before, but when Riley made them a team, that had ignited the fuse. And a week after they'd solved their first case and were celebrating with drinks, things exploded. Five intense months of sex at least twice, sometimes three times a day.

On the job, off the job.

In every place, one could imagine.

And several one shouldn't imagine:

Stopping the elevator in-between floors of a building too old to have security cameras.

A blow-job in the bathroom of a Seven-11 where there'd been a break-in, and the owner was up front talking with his insurance agent.

And the most dangerous, in their squad car parked on a dark street while they were on a stake-out: Mollie watching the street while sitting on Cole's lap, as he pounded her from behind.

Puberty-stricken teenagers with raging hormones unable to keep their hands off each other had nothing on them. Then one weekend, Mollie went to San Francisco to see her father who'd fallen and broken his foot.

"Something happened back home, Cole. I ran into a girl I knew from high school."

And then she'd gone on to explain how she and Annie had finished a bottle of some cheap red wine and become lovers. And that it was like nothing she'd ever known.

Cole went through his macho denials and disbelief, but in the end, he knew they were over.

"Do you want to still be partners?" Mollie had asked.

"Do you think we can?"

"Do you think you can get past your resentment?"

"I'm not resentful."

"Hurt?"

"Wouldn't you be?"

"Are you kidding? I'd be a basket case."

"We're still Trane and Simmons."

"Great. Although we've got to work on the order of the names."

They'd bumped fists and never talked about it. They'd blossomed as partners, but they'd blossomed into friends even more.

A beautiful Asian woman named Sandi was Mollie's first intense relationship. A relationship that didn't end well.

"Part of my learning curve," she told Cole in a teary confessional night. An Alexis came next, then a Jacqueline, a Babs, a Karen, another Karen, a Marika, who lasted a year, and finally, Sophia.

Each time, Cole had patiently listened to Mollie's laments, her heartache and talked her through the night. There was one time when

Mollie was confused and told Cole that maybe she'd made a mistake with chicks. And then she'd kissed him so fiercely that his lips were sore for a couple of hours after, but the spark was gone, and they continued as if that aberration had never happened.

"So, Joelle and Michelle," Mollie said, bringing Cole back to the present, "any idea who would want to steal your dresses?"

"Nobody and everybody," Joelle said. "They have spies everywhere with amazing software. This happening on the night of our premiere has just delayed them. Whenever we redo the showing, a week later, copycat versions will be in stores across Japan, China, and Korea."

"Eastern Europe?" Cole said.

"The Italians and French are too good or too snobby to bother. And the eastern Europeans are so inferior, we don't even bother if they do steal. We wouldn't want to be associated with anything that bad."

"This would have never happened if she'd have listened to me," Michelle said.

"What do you mean?" Cole said.

"I was supposed to help her get dressed, make sure everything fit."

"You weren't going to do that in the car, right?"

Michelle looked at Cole as if he were the stupidest man on the planet. "Of course not. We were going to do it here in the dressing room."

"So, what would you have accomplished by being in the Jag?"

"I don't know, I could have been there to keep her focused, to remain calm. She wasn't totally sure she could do this. I would have been there to show her that she could. I would have been her mentor."

"You could have also been something else," Cole said.

"What?"

"Dead."

SIX

"I'D LIKE TO KILL EVERYTHING."

Mayor Matt Gaylord stared at Cole and Mollie. He waited for an answer.

"We're checking out the eastern European link," Cole said. "But that's a long shot. Hard to believe anybody would send two mooks, over-armed and under-brained, to steal some dresses. Even Maugham originals."

"Okay, so it went bad from the jump. The quarter-million was in fabrics, not cash. And these two morons killed Zoey, concussed her driver and took her watch. Why? Because they got angry? Or maybe an accident? Doesn't matter how it ended, you two have got to find out how it started."

"Yes," Cole said. "Somebody knew what Nat was driving and when he and Zoey were scheduled to arrive."

"We're tracking their route from Beverly Hills through the state's traffic cameras; see if anybody was following them," Mollie said. "Accord to Nat, the Toyota was a carbon-monoxide bomb. Smoke blowing out the tailpipe like a fog. It's a wonder they didn't get pulled over for pollution."

"Yeah, where's a cop when you need one?" the Mayor said.

"We've got the word out for the possible sale of the watch," Cole said, ignoring the Mayor's dumb joke. "Piece that expensive, going to be hard to unload."

"Anything on the masks yet?" the Mayor asked.

"I wouldn't count on that for a couple of weeks," Cole said. "You've got to get in line with the labs, and I hear they're way behind on their rush jobs, and then you've got to hope that the two perps are in the system. If they're not, strike three."

"Not like what you see on TV," the Mayor said. "They get blood, they get an answer before the next commercial break."

"Yeah," Cole said, "that's pretend, this is real."

The Mayor's hooded eyes-cobra-smile told Cole he just been put back on the politician's shit list. Matt Gaylord didn't like being one-upped.

Cole didn't care. He made that list whenever the Mayor decided you didn't agree with his vision of life in his City of Kings. And then you were swept off it with a flourish when you broke a case.

"One of the biggest movie stars in the world was murdered in my … our town, detectives. Do you understand how bad that is?"

Cole knew that the Mayor's bad reference was about everything that mattered to him – the town's image, its property values, his career. And zero for Zoey.

Which is why he decided to zoom to number one position on the enemies list.

"I do. But as bad as it is for us, it's nowhere near as bad as it was for Zoey."

SEVEN

"YOU ALWAYS HAVE TO MAKE IT WORSE?"

Mollie shook her head as she and Cole headed to their car.

"You just can't avoid pissing on his shoes?"

"I could. I just choose not to. Fuck him. Zoey was twenty-three years old, she was going to be a mother, she was loved all over the world. Her whole life was still ahead of her, and it was snuffed out by some Russian dickhead named Igor, and all Matt Gaylord can think about is his own personal shit. He's the beach version of Donald Trump. A narcissistic asshole who's the center of his own universe."

"I know, but it just slows us down, having to give him report cards."

"That'll be my job. I'll be designated kiss ass. I'll keep Riley in the loop, then he can relay it to the Chief and to his Honor."

Cole bumped fists with Mollie: done deal.

"Well you did win the Flying Donut Contest as a rookie."

"Of course," said Cole and laughed. "It was a chocolate-glazed."

The Flying Donut Contest was an inside joke they shared about Mayor Matt Gaylord. As a requirement for employment, the mayor would toss a Winchell's donut into the air and the candidate who could kiss its center three times before it hit the floor was hired.

After they waited fifteen minutes, the Mayor's secretary had come out and said, "I'm so sorry, but Mayor Gaylord has been called away suddenly. But his personal assistant Charles Patterson is on his way."

"What do you think Chuck's got for us?" Mollie said.

"I hope not another problem. This one's going to take everything we've got."

But when Charles entered, that's exactly what he brought: another problem.

And not a small one.

"First, I want to convey the Mayor's confidence in you, Mollie and Cole. He wants you to know, and I echo his sentiments, that you two are the only detectives he feels he can entrust with this responsibility." He grasped first Mollie's hands and then Cole's with both of his. The freakin' two-hander.

Definite trouble coming on.

If the Mayor was the sand and surf Donald Trump, Charles Patterson was his Rudy Guiliani – a mongrel who'd bark or bare fangs when it was time to attack, or a lapdog when a favor was needed. This was definitely Benji time.

"Something's come up. Something sensitive."

Big Trouble. With a capital T.

"Jon Gaylord's fallen in love."

Charles waited for Cole and Mollie to say something. But they remained silent. What the hell was there to say? Jon was the mayor's 19-year old son, and the fact that romance had come his way wasn't news, it was trivia.

Which meant, Cole thought, the love object is the problem.

"And Matt doesn't like the girl."

Charles squeezed out a smile. This was going to be difficult.

"Uh ... and excuse me for phrasing it this way, Detective Simmons, there's nothing pejorative either implied or inferred and ..."

"Chuck!" Mollie snapped. "Do not go there. Seriously."

"Whoa," Charles held up his hands. "Don't shoot the messenger, okay? I don't agree with the Mayor's views, but I got stuck with the job."

"Jon's gay," Mollie said. "It's not about the girl, it's about the boy."

"Yes, yes. I'm sorry, but yes, that's the... the problem. Not that I think it's a problem, but..."

"Can you believe this shit?" Mollie said.

"Fuck them, let's go."

"No, wait, please wait. I can explain."

"Explain what? That the Mayor's a discriminatory hypocrite, who mouths equality for all but secretly hates same-sex love?"

"What exactly does Matt think we could do?" Cole asked. "Beat the shit out of the other guy?"

"No, no. He just wants him investigated. Checked out to make sure he's not after money."

"You've got to be kidding me," Cole said. "What money? Jon gets an allowance, a new Corvette every year and trips to Europe or the Bahamas or wherever his little trust fund takes him. But that's chump change for Matt."

"The Mayor thinks this guy may try blackmailing them."

"Blackmail how?" said Mollie. "You mean sully the mayor's golden reputation, besmirch the Gaylord brand? Because his son…" she held up crossed fingers to ward off the dark forces of evil.

"because his son was gay? Do you have any idea how offensive that is? Not just to me, but to every LGBTQ person in America?"

EIGHT

"INCLUDING HAMZA NEJEM."

"Who?" Mollie said.

She jabbed the push button starter on the Ford Fusion and stomped the accelerator. The RPM needle shot up past the red safety line. It hadn't come back into the white before she slammed the gearshift lever down into "S" and they rocketed off, the front-wheel-drive grabbing asphalt in chunks before it settled into a high-speed departure.

"Whoa, Mollie. Shit."

Mollie took a corner so fast Cole lurched against her, and she nearly lost control of the car. But she corrected against the slide and the black sedan shot down the street.

Parked cars flashed by as she roared down Avenida Del Oro.

"Stop sign coming up," Cole said.

Mollie didn't take her foot off the gas.

Cole checked the speedometer – they were doing 70!

"You're more than three times the speed limit," Cole yelled over the high whine of the engine. "And kids play on the street, Molls."

The stop sign came up, and Mollie slammed on the brakes. The car's rear end came out a notch, but she turned into the slide, and they came to a tire-smoking panic stop.

"Fuck," she snarled. "Just fuck-fuck-fuck."

"You're better than them, Molls. Way better."

"Cole, you know how hard it is? Especially here?"

"I do."

"People say they're enlightened, that they support me or my kind."

"There is no 'your kind.' Period. Whomever you choose to love is your personal business. It doesn't define you or label you."

"Not according to those assholes."

"Right. Assholes. So, do you want to ass-o-ciate with ass-holes?"

Mollie looked at him and tried to stay mad. But lost the battle. She smiled and nodded.

"So, back to Hamza Nejem."

"Who is...?"

"Jon's boyfriend. That's his name. Hamza Nejem. In Arabic it translates into Lion and Star."

"You Googled that pretty fast."

Cole waggled his fingers. "Prodigious digits."

And for a moment his mind flashed back to when and his fingers did their own special kind of typing on Mollie when they were lovers.

NINE

"VORLD'S MOST LOVED STAR."

Fyodor Bezrodney was livid.

"And you kill her. And for that ve get vot? Vristvatch. And police after us, Pytor vants kill us. Focking great."

Igor Petrak shrugged. "I look up vatch on internet. Is Cartier. Vorth hundred thirty-seven thousand dollars."

"Is worth nothing. Who's going to buy? You know anybody?"

"Maybe Pytor?"

"Pytor?"

Vladimir kicked the coffee table; the empty remains of the McDonalds cartons flying and Igor's cola spraying the floor.

"We are hiding, now from Pytor. Because you fock up this entire job. Or you forget?"

Igor stared at the mess on the cheap carpet. Better the floor than Vlad's face. Because everything Vlad said was true and Igor was ashamed. But the more important reason was that he thought if he looked into Vlad's eyes and saw contempt, he might kill him.

"Look at mess you make, Vlad. Vhy you got be so angry all the time? I focked up, yes. But has got to be vay out of this. Somebody vill vant vatch. Maybe ve get fifty thousand."

"Maybe we get three hundred fifty-grain-bullet instead. Although somebody shoot you in head, they miss your brain, because it is in your ass."

Igor turned the table back upright, scooped up the Styrofoam containers and his waxed cardboard cup. There was one last swallow left in it, and he let the cold cola slide down his throat. He went to the cheap motel dresser and withdrew the Cartier watch.

"Vere the fock you going?" Vladimir yelled.

"To sell this."

"Not alone."

Igor turned around to face Vladimir.

"You don't trust me? Ve are together since we are twelve-years-old and you say this? To my face?"

Vladimir saw the dark blood rush to his cousin's face. That was always a danger sign. Over the decade since he and Igor had started out as common runners for Pytor Gusarov, back in Belgrade, Vladimir had watched Igor change from a sweet, naïve kid into a sadistic killer who was as mentally stable as nitroglycerine – one wrong bump and he exploded.

A couple of times it had saved their lives. None bigger than when they'd walked into a trap with one of Pytor's enemies. Igor had sensed it and pulled out the KBP PP-2000 hidden under his trench coat and sprayed the room. The 9x19mm Parabellum bullets blew holes in the two advance guards like human Swiss cheese. Igor didn't take his finger off the trigger, shooting through the drywall and killing two men waiting in ambush. But the shootings had escalated.

After Igor had gunned down two bodyguards for one of the higher-ranking members of the Solntsevskaya Bratva Mafiya, there was no turning back. And because Igor worked for Pytor, the minor Mafiya boss's life was now in danger too. Pytor had escaped to America, taking six young men with him, including Igor and Vlad.

They'd landed in Brighton Beach. But Little Odessa was closed territory. And after a year of frustration and threats that had ended the lives of the other four men, Pytor, Vladimir and Igor had fled to the west and found less competition under the sunny skies and palm trees of Los Angeles; so many of the younger Russians deciding beautiful, easy women and the amazing climate more alluring than the threat of violence and death.

Pytor had learned his lessons in Belgrade and Boston and took new positions and new territory in a carefully controlled and orchestrated campaign. Three years after arriving on the ancient Super Chief train, Pytor was a man to be reckoned with in Los Angeles. He was happy.

Igor and Vladimir weren't.

They felt like they'd been pushed aside, out of the mainstream of action and money. Their loyalty didn't seem to get them the rewards and movements up the ladder that they felt they'd earned.

But they didn't know anything else. And for all their youth, they clung to the old methods. They still believed that force was the only way to stay in power. But in the United States, there were too many reprisals waiting for you from citizens with cell phone videos. And a city filled with police and government security cameras.

Which is why they'd been given this supposedly simple snatch and go job: They couldn't screw it up.

Except that there was nothing to snatch because somebody *had* screwed it up. There was no money. Just some dresses. And the watch that Igor thought they could sell.

"Don't get panties in twist, okay? You go alone, how do you know stranger isn't cop? Or maybe has his apparatchik come in behind you? And they not only take vatch, but maybe take you out?"

Vladimir knew it was a bullshit line, but Igor, for all his violence, was still naïve. And he still hungered for approval and praise.

"Okay," Igor said. "We go find somebody vit money."

TEN

"MAUGHAM EMPLOYEES MAKE PEANUTS."

"Really?" Mollie said.

"According to Joelle they work there because it looks good on their resume," Cole said. "And for the experience."

"You wonder how long that can last. This Amanda Cullen's been with them two years. Cynthia Hoak and Dee Legee both about a year. The only long-term staffer is Irikina Pevac, five years."

Mollie and Cole hadn't gone through channels to get official permission to hack the Maugham's computers, but would if they found anything. It was against the law, but sometimes the law was just something you used as needed.

And the last thing they needed now was being slowed down. "Only long shot and it's really long, is Irikina."

"Because she's Russian?" Mollie said.

"Why not? Nat remembers hearing the name Igor and that his partner Ivan sounded Russian."

"Ivan?"

"Seems as good a Russkie name as any."

"When you go racial, you go all in."

"In for a ruble, in for a pound."

"Zoey was going for her wallet. Hardly a reason to shoot her."

Mollie hit the print button and checked to see that the printer's light had gone on. Once it had, she said, "Maybe Igor's a rookie."

"Or a hothead."

"Any possibility it was an accident? Gun went off?"

"Remote. You don't put your finger through the trigger guard unless you're intending to pull it."

The printer whirred, and the pages slid into the tray.

Mollie picked up the documents and handed a set to Cole. He flipped through the pages.

"Not too much detail on Ms. Pevac. Other than current and past addresses, DOB, past employment history and her SS number, it's a wash."

"They aren't screening for nuclear codes security clearances."

"Smart ass."

"Okay, let's check them all."

An hour later, Cole and Mollie had cross-checked all the information on the four women. Nothing jumped out at them. Not even Irikina, who was born in Glendale, had graduated from the prestigious Art Center in Pasadena and left every day at two o'clock to go pick up her twins from daycare.

"She's named after her grandmother," Cole said. He'd contacted Jax Robinson, his special computer analyst for the data. "Russian emigre back in early part of last century. And her husband's a veep at Merrill Lynch. I doubt she's selling dresses for the money. She'd probably do it gratis, just to make sure her degree didn't go to waste."

"You take Dee," Mollie said. "I'll take Amanda and Cynthia."

ELEVEN

"I GOT ZIP."

Mollie clicked in her seat belt and looked at Cole. "Amanda and Cynthia are clean. Or their connections to anyone who's Russian or from eastern Europe are so well-hidden that they're too smart to mess with a puny quarter-million-dollar hit."

"Same for Dee," Cole said.

"That's all?"

"You were expecting more?"

"Yeah. I saw Dee's picture. She's hot. Unless that photo's ten years younger and she's put on some tonnage."

"And they say men are chauvinistic."

"You still haven't answered my question."

"Yes, she's still beautiful. No, she hasn't put on any weight. And no, we aren't going to be having dinner or coffee or any further contact; unless she turns out to be Igor in disguise. I'm not looking for a date."

Cole headed north on the coast highway, the slow-rolling waves of the ocean on their left. "How's your mom?"

"She's amazing. Evans said they're going to release her tomorrow."

"Really? That's great, I guess."

"What'd you mean?"

"I would've have thought that they'd want to keep her there for a few more days; just to be sure."

"She seems to have passed the crisis. So, as long as she takes it easy, she'll be okay. Whatever the hell 'okay' means."

"I'm sorry, Molls."

"Thanks."

Cole noticed Mollie looking at him intently.

"What?"

"You're slick, Slick."

"About what?"

"I ask you about Dee, and you flip it around to my mom."

"I didn't flip anything around, I love your mom."

Mollie pursed her lips and settled back, but Cole could see her glance at him sideways.

"Why all this noise about Dee?" he said.

"How long's it been since you and Amelie ...?"

Oh, shit! Here we go again.

"Broke up, you can say it. Three months."

Three months and twelve days.

But who's counting?

Amelie François had come to town for a photo shoot. She was one of three models for the new line of summer cardigans and loose knits from France's hottest designer, Alice Limoine.

The shoot had drawn crowds of people on the silky sands of the beach. Which was highly unusual since most of the locals went out of their way to be out of the way: God forbid you ever showed excitement. Keeping your cool was the most admired quality of all. But by the second day of the shoot, fans had doubled, and Mayor Gaylord assigned special teams just for crowd control.

On the last day, several TV stations had sent news crews. It was worth millions of free publicity to the Alice Limoine house and even more in profits since the new line-up sold out. Back in France, they were scrambling to get back into production.

Mayor Gaylord loved it too. He made sure he got face time on every channel and went into full publicity mode on every one of them, explaining that the "film crew" had fallen in love with the city when they'd gone out to capture local "color" and were blown away by, "Our beaches, our amazing weather, our incredible safe reputation as one of American's cities with the lowest crime rate and, of course, one of the most solid property value investment values in the nation."

That third night, Cole was grabbing a cheeseburger at "Burge's Burgers" when Amelie strode up to the take-out window and checked the menu. She and Cole were the only two customers.

Amelie frowned and turned to Cole.

"I heard this was the best place in town to get a cheeseburger," she said, her French-accent husky and silky.

"It is," Cole said.

He couldn't take his eyes off her face – that even without any make-up was stunning: high, angular cheeks framing the most luminous green eyes he'd ever seen.

"So, where is everybody?"

"Out looking for you."

"Me?"

"You and the other models. So they can take a selfie or watch how the truly beautiful people live or maybe go the other way and say, 'Oh, they're not that terrific, it's all make-up and lighting.'"

"It *is* all cosmetics and photoshop."

"Not in your case."

Amelie studied him for a long moment and then smiled; which added a vulnerability and sweetness to her that made her seem approachable.

And to Cole, irresistible.

She was old, for a model: 28.

TWELVE
BUT SHE PHOTOGRAPHED
A DECADE YOUNGER.

And projected vitality and youth in person.

And sex.

God, yes, sex.

Cole didn't think he'd ever met a woman who radiated so much carnal heat with such innocence.

"So, what are you having," Amelie said.

"Cheeseburger, fries and a Heineken."

A teenager came up to the window to take her order.

"I'll have what he's having?"

The kid looked at her and frowned.

"Is something the matter?" she said.

"I'm sorry, but I gotta check your ID."

Amelie's hand went to her mouth, but she couldn't stifle her laughter which pealed out, surprisingly indelicate for all her femininity.

"Oh, thank you, really, thank you."

She handed over her Paris license and passport.

The kid studied them and frowned again.

"She's good Timmy," Cole said.

"Works for me."

Timmy returned her documents and went back to give the order to the cook.

"Thank you." She extended her hand, "Amelie François."

"Cole Trane."

"Like the saxophonist."

Cole nodded; then noticed Amelie waiting for more.

"What?"

"What is your first name?"

"Cole. And Trane is my last name."

Amelie looked at Cole: Was he putting her on?

"My father played sax a long time ago when he was very young. And he'd sit in on sessions with John and the others."

"Your father must have been very good."

"I've heard his old tapes. He was. But as he used to say, 'Good ain't genius.'"

They took their food and beers and sat on the park bench in front of Burge's. Below their high perch on the bluffs, the waves rolled black and then shattered into white, phosphorous fragments lit by the full moon.

She went home with Cole that night, never went back to France with the models and crew, and stayed with him for three years, five months and nine days until she did leave.

It was the best three years, five months and nine days he ever had.

But who's counting?

Followed by the longest three months and twelve days of his life.

THIRTEEN

"THIS IS FOCKED UP KIND OF LIFE."

Vladimir slammed the cheap motel sofa and then had to fan away the dust that rose from the lumpy cushion.

"Ve are like hunted animals."

Their search for a buyer for the Cartier watch had turned up nothing. They'd driven around south-central L.A., but every time they found a group of young black men hangin', a patrol car would appear before they could even establish there might be a buyer in the pack.

The one time they had managed to start a conversation, Igor, who was on full alert, noticed a tall, muscular banger who wore a red do' rag on his shaved head, reach behind him and Igor's automatic was pointed at the leader before any of the Bloods set could react.

"Whoa, what the fuck?" the banger said, both hands coming up. "Be cool."

Vladimir floored their junkie, and they drove off in a blue cloud of smoke and noise. They'd stopped at a Seven-11 on the way back to the motel, and while Vlad bought sandwiches and drinks, Igor stole two cell phones.

Igor used the throwaway phone to call Oleg, his last friend in their group.

"You fockin' crazy, calling me?" Oleg shouted.

"Last time. Just tell me, how bad is it?"

"I hope you calling from Canada or Japan. Because you and your cousin are Pytor's number one enemies. He has put out five-thousand-dollar reward."

"Five thousand? Fock, ve worth ten times."

"Igor, I like you, okay? And nobody knows ve talk. But this is last talk ve ever have, okay? I give you advice: Get hell out of L.A., because I know you still there. Goodbye."

As Igor listened to the silence on the line, he knew all hope for him and Vladimir was gone. He pretended to be absorbed in a black and white episode of "I Love Lucy" because he didn't want to talk to Vladimir and he didn't want to risk switching channels because every other channel was filled with the brutal murder of the "World's Biggest Star!"

"Ve already saw this," Vlad said and took the remote and flicked through the channels. He stopped at CNN when he saw a promo for John Walsh's "The Hunt."

"Hey, maybe you become famous? Killer of best-loved American movie star in fifty years."

"Vhy only me?"

"Because you pull trigger."

"You thinking turning me in? Collect reward?"

"Fock. You crazy?" Vladimir held up a thick index finger, a finger that had the Cyrillic eight-pointed star tattooed at the top knuckle. "One, we cousins, but we more like brothers, okay? And you don't give up family. And two," he held up his middle digit, so the two fingers formed a V, "And two, "...who's going to give us money? Fockin' Pytor? He would throw us in pit of mesquite and gasoline and watch us burn. This TV guy, Walsh? He puts men in jail, not give them money."

"So vhy you say I am guy?"

"Because, fock, we talking in circles. What we should be doing is talking about vay out of this mess."

"I don't think there is, Vlad."

"No, no. There is always vay."

Igor switched back to "I Love Lucy," and they both watched in silence until the credits rolled and then Igor turned off the television.

"Maybe we don't try and sell watch here."

"Oh? Where we going?"

"Ruskin. Is in Canada. I remember my mother has third cousin live there."

"And vot we do in Ruskin?"

"We pay her surprise visit. Everybody happy for old times' sake."

"You remember her name, this cousin?

"I'll think of it."

"While you think of that, also think where we get gas to make this drive? Since we out of money. And maybe car, too."

"We got to where they have money. Bank."

Igor rose and grabbed the keys.

"Where you going now? Banks aren't open."

"No shit. I am driving see vhich one looks best for famous criminal to rob."

FOURTEEN

"ROUND UP THE USUAL SUSPECTS."

"That was a terrible Claude Rains," Mollie said. "Didn't work in Casablanca, because by then Louie and Rick were flying off to Marseilles. And it didn't work for us."

Mollie stirred her coffee, then asked "What's previous?"

"We could go to the funeral."

"You're kidding, right? That is going to be such a circus of national hysteria and bullshit. Every actress will be in tears with their make-up running about such a tragedy and how everybody loved Zoey."

"Molls, she was the number one star on the planet."

"I know, but every network, cable outlet, internet wank, you name it, will be there broadcasting. It'll be a flood of tears and boo-hoos. And you want to subject us to that in person?"

Cole signaled the waitress, "Nan! No more coffee for Mollie, she's already over-caffeinated."

"Seriously, though, you're not thinking the perps might show up?"

"I don't know. But somebody might that was connected to Igor and Ivan."

"Or maybe Igor and Ivan themselves."

"Them too."

"We have another day to think about it."

Nan came by with the coffee urn and the check.

"Give me both," Mollie said. "My turn to buy."

"I accept. Quickly and unashamedly."

Cole gazed around the restaurant. "Nan's Table" was one of their favorite local spots to grab a great breakfast and lunch. Nan didn't serve dinner. The place was filled with locals and several couples that could only be tourists, judging by their matching swimsuits and tops.

The front door opened, and a refrigerator-sized man stood at the entrance and scanned the restaurant. He had a shiny, shaved head and a glossy black suit that had to have been custom-made, not for styling, but for size. He was one of the biggest men Cole had ever seen, and he and Mollie had done security work for the L.A. Rams.

The big man entered and was followed by a man that could have been his twin in terms of size. His head wasn't shaved, but extremely close-cropped. And his suit was a muted grey. Tamara, the hostess, welcomed them with a big smile and led them to a table in the back.

As they passed, Cole noticed one of them had a newspaper.

"Ready to go?" Mollie said.

When she saw Cole's eyes, she said, "What?"

"Those two guys."

Mollie turned casually, as if she was stretching, clocked the two men who'd sat down in a booth and filled the bench seat all by themselves.

"Healthy."

"One of them's carrying a newspaper. And I think it's Sovyetskaya Rossiya."

"Which is…?"

"'Soviet Russia.' It's the most prominent daily news for orthodox Communists and hardcore Russian nationalists."

"Was that a question on Jeopardy?"

"I couldn't sleep last night and was on the computer for a couple of hours."

"How much of that was porn?"

"Jesus. None. Well, I mean unless you count 'Cock To Face.'"

"Hey, there are ladies present!"

"Actually, the official name is Obraz Petelin. That's Slovenian. And I got there from starting with the Russian mob, Solntsevskaya Bratva Mafiya, who are into money laundering, prostitution and porn, and every other criminal activity you can think of."

"I'm impressed."

"I'd rather have been asleep."

FIFTEEN

"YOU DREAM THIS UP ALL BY YOURSELF?"

Lieutenant Riley shook his head as he looked at Cole.

"Big Russian guys, Russian newspaper, killer's name was Igor, I get it. But other than the JFK conspiracy theory, I can't think of a wilder idea."

Cole held his cell away and took a deep breath. "All I'm saying is can't we have a patrol car stop them? Get their IDs, a friendly chat?"

"No. I'm not having my men and women harassing people. For all you know they're just tourists." Riley broke the connection.

Cole looked at his phone as if it had betrayed him.

"Didn't even say goodbye, did he?" Mollie said.

"He says maybe they're tourists." Cole pointed at the entrance to "Nan's Table" where the two Russian Mastodons exited, looked around and headed towards one of the town's most famous attractions - the Ciudad de Los Reyes Pier.

The pier had been built in 1910 when the Pacific Electric Red Car trolleys ran from the downtown station in Los Angeles all the way to the Strand. Thousands of people, men in their straw boaters, women with parasols, would come down and spend their Sundays on blankets on the soft sands, inhaling the clean ocean air and basking in the brilliant sunshine.

The pier jutted two hundred yards into the ocean and ended in a round, railed lookout point, where still for a quarter, you could gaze through one of the six telescopes west towards Catalina, north to Santa Monica and Malibu and south towards the bluffs. There was also a Sea

Museum that had live fish from the local waters.

"Maybe he's right," Mollie said.

But just before they reached the Pier, the men turned around a corner. Mollie and Cole followed.

They're going to the Shrine," Cole said.

Zoey's fans had come in droves and placed flowers and movie posters and mementos of her career at the site where she'd been killed. It was now a huge collection that flowed along the sidewalk for at least fifty yards in either direction. People kneeled and reverently placed their gifts to her memory and stayed there, heads bowed, some of them tears streaming down their cheeks, for ten, twenty minutes; some diehards for several hours.

The two men stopped and checked out the crowd.

"Maybe I'll pay my respects," Cole said.

Mollie watched Cole stroll past the two Russians, saw him casually "clock" them, then stop five feet away.

Cole kept his attention on the memorial as if it was the most important thing in his life. Then he sidled closer to the Russians.

"Such a tragedy," he said, loud enough for the two to hear him.

The man nearest Cole said, "You going to arrest me?"

"What?" Cole said, pissed that the Russian had "made" him so fast.

"You cop, no?"

"Detective."

"Ah, you young. You must be pretty sharp guy."

"Beach town. Pretty low key, not much competition."

The other man smiled, and the Russians nodded as if they were in on the joke together.

"But not as sharp as you. When?"

"I saw you look little too long as ve passed."

He held out the Russian newspaper. "Here. You read Russian?"

"No."

"You call me sometime, maybe I translate."

"So, you're visiting our little town on vacation?"

"Ve are thinking of maybe living here. But I see this, I don't think so. Too violent for us."

"Not like Brighton Beach."

If the Russian was surprised at Cole, he covered it well. "You been?"

"No."

"Nice place. Great food, good people. Of course, weather there can't compare to this…" He spread his massive arms wide, and his jacket gaped, and Cole saw a black nylon holster below his left shoulder and the black embossed grips of an automatic weapon.

Cole motioned for Mollie to get here fast without looking back to make sure she saw him. He backed away from the two men.

"Okay," Cole said. His voice was quiet but hard. "We do this nice and easy."

The Russian glanced at Cole, then dropped his arms.

"I have permit. So, does Mikhail." He pointed his chin at the other man. "We have private security company. I will get ID from back pocket, slowly, okay? Then I will get permit from breast pocket. Also, slowly."

Mollie stood to the right of the two men. So far, everything was cool.

"We're copacetic?" she said.

Cole nodded.

The Russian's eyes cut towards Mollie, and he smiled: An aha moment – your partner. Cole took the man's wallet with his left hand, his eyes never leaving the man's face.

"Aleksander Prokhanovich."

"In person."

Aleksander turned to his partner, "Mikhail, give the detective your ID. Unless you vant partner check?"

Cole motioned for Mikhail to wait while he checked Aleksander's data.

"You live in Hancock Park?"

"Hudson Street."

"Private security pays better than I thought."

"Yes. Is very good. You should consider."

Cole examined Mikhail's ID.

"Mikhail Zhirov. Date of birth, 2/5/84."

"Yes. I am Aquarian." Mikhail smirked at Cole.

Cole handed back both men's wallets. He checked Mollie: she'd never taken her eyes off the men.

That's my partner.

"What're you carrying?" Cole said and nodded at Aleksander. "Tell, don't show."

"Understood. GSh-18. Is similar to famous Makarov PM pistol. But, I think, better. GSh stands for Gryazev and Shipunow. Chief designers of pistol, who are heroes for their aircraft cannons. Can you imagine? Men who design cannons on jet fighters do little handgun?"

Cole looked at Mikhail. "You, too?"

The giant nodded.

"What's the eighteen for?"

"Magazine capacity."

"Eighteen rounds? What caliber?"

There was a long moment while both men stared at each other. Aleksander looking down from his four-inch height advantage, Cole staring straight at him.

"Aleksander, I want you to reach in, with your left hand, extract one of the extra rounds and give it to me."

Aleksander awkwardly reached in with his left hand. He was right-handed and favored the cross-body draw, which Cole had picked up when he first saw the holster. Aleksander's body only exacerbated his problems. His chest was so massive and thick and his arms bigger than the average man's thigh that he didn't have enough flexibility to reach his left side with his left arm.

"Turn to your partner," Cole ordered.

As Aleksander complied, Cole reached in and plucked a cartridge. Its brass cartridge had a pointed black nose.

"Private security needs armor-piercing rounds?"

"Is holdover from overseas job. I keep forgetting to update. These are first versions of nine by nineteen Luger-Parabellum round. Developed to defeat body armor."

"I'm not sure these are legal in California."

Aleksander and Mikhail looked at each other. A private signal passed between them.

Mollie caught it, stepped up behind Mikhail and jammed her automatic into his spine. "This is a Beretta 92 SF."

"Vot you vant me to do?" Mikhail said.

"Just stand there, Mickey, you mind if I call you Mickey?"

"No. Anything else, lady detective?"

"Yeah. Don't focking move."

SIXTEEN

"IT TRAVELS 600 METERS PER SECOND."

Darryll Remington held up one of Aleksander's bullets. Remington was the department's ballistics expert. He wasn't related to the Remington arms family, but he knew more about guns and ammunition than anyone Cole had ever met.

"This ammo can penetrate 8mm plate steel at 20 meters."

"But it's not connected to Zoey."

"And neither is the weapon."

Remington held up Aleksander's gun.

"These are wicked cool. This GSh-18 is a recoil-operated, locked breech pistol. Lightweight and rugged. Polymer frame with steel inserts and slide rails. The trigger's like a Glock. Ejection port located at the top of the slide, so the empties pop straight up and back."

Remington's eyes had a holy glow. This was religion to him.

Or gun porn!

"And I heard they didn't protest when you confiscated their weapons?"

"I think they wanted us to see them. Show them off."

Cole and Mollie had called for back-up. Three patrol cars and six cops pulled up and quickly secured the area. Cole read Aleksander and Mikhail their rights, then the cops put them in separate cars and went to the station.

Riley was ballistic over the bust. "You could expose us for entrapment."

"Not a chance. Mr. Prokhanovich and I were discussing our town's wonderful weather when his suit jacket flared open, and I observed he was carrying a concealed weapon. Despite his claims that he was fully licensed, upon further discussion, my partner, Detective First Grade Mollie Simmons and I decided this had potentially dangerous implications for our citizens, and we brought Mr. Prokhanovich and Mr. Zhirov in for further questioning."

"You ever decide to go into politics, Gaylord should be worried."

"Thank you. I guess."

"So, you had Remington run ballistics? On what grounds?"

"Possible ancillary connection to Zoey Martine."

"They lawyer up?"

"Soon as we got to the station."

"But, unfortunately, due to both Mr. Prokhanovich's and Mr. Zhirov's accents," Mollie said, "we had a difficult time understanding their pronunciation and couldn't contact their attorneys until after five o'clock." "Who's coming in for them?"

SEVENTEEN

"I AM BORIS YANAYEV."

Wow! Nothing like I was expecting.

It took Cole several moments to process that he'd racially profiled Aleksander's and Mikhail's attorney in looks and speech.

Instead of a deep, guttural accent, the Russian's voice was smooth, his diction perfect, and had the high polish of an Oxford graduate. Instead of the dark, swarthy look and bulk of Aleksander and Mikhail, Boris was, maybe five-six, looked like he'd just graduated high school and had a perma-grin fueled by super-caffeination or some Tony Robbins affirmations.

Boris enthusiastically pumped everyone's hand.

"So, I am hopeful that we can come to a satisfactory understanding of the events relating to my clients."

"Absolutely," said Riley.

Boris glanced at his notes and smiled at Cole and Mollie.

They were looking at a baby-faced assassin who didn't need notes or a gun to take you out.

"You detained Mr. Prokhanovich and Mr. Zhirov on a weapons possession charge. Weapons that were holstered and out of sight from any citizens."

"Yes, that was the problem. They were out of sight."

"Would you have preferred to have their weapons visible for everyone to see?"

Cole decided silence was the best defense.

"When asked about his weapon, Mr. Prokhanovich immediately

answered that he was legally permitted to carry a weapon in accordance with his professional employment as a private security operative. And offered to show you this license. As did Mr. Zhirov."

"The issue wasn't just the weapons," Mollie said, "but the 18-rounds of ammunition loaded into them."

"Were your concerns based on the number of rounds?"

"No. The type and grade. They are armor-piercing."

"And the laws of Ciudad de Los Reyes, a lovely town in my opinion, but nonetheless, I am compelled to ask: Do the town's laws permit such subjective determinations on the merits of arrest?"

"Neither Mr. Prokhanovich or Mr. Zhirov were formally charged."

"A technicality, no?"

Cole and Mollie remained silent.

"As I understand it and certainly please correct me if I have reached an erroneous conclusion here, but the single witness to the tragic shooting of America's beloved star, Zoey Martine, has stated that the killer's name was Igor."

How the hell did he get this? It wasn't publicly-shared yet.

"Am I correct, so far?"

"So far," Riley said.

"Excellent. And from that unsubstantiated statement, given that there were no other witnesses to corroborate Mr. Munroe's statement, your department, which I again should say, has an outstanding record of public service, made the cognitive leap of faith, if you will, was that since Igor was Russian, and Mr. Prokhanovich and Mr. Zhirov are Russian; you, therefore, had cause."

No one said anything for at least thirty seconds. Boris gazed at the police officers, his smile firmly in place, then said, "I am reticent to remind you that while Igor is, indeed of Russian derivation, it is also Polish, Slovene, Croatian, Serbian and Macedonian."

Cole had reached his limit.

"Are you going to be suing us?"

"What? No, no, of course not. We have no reason to embarrass the city's finest, nor do Mr. Prokhanovich and Mr. Zhirov wish to prolong what was clearly a simple misunderstanding."

"So then what's this meeting about?"

"Mister Prohanovich said you were very intelligent Detective Trane. And once again, I diverge, but I must tell you that I am absolutely fascinated by the origins of your name and your parent's boldness in choosing it."

"It was better than Choo-Choo."

It took Boris a second to get the joke. And Cole's implied warning. But he handled it smoothly.

"So, this meeting: Our firm would like to interview the Maugham sisters. Under your supervision of course."

"What?" Riley half-rose out of his chair. "Are you kiddin' me? Why?"

"It is a rather sensitive matter, but if I could have your assurances that what I am about to divulge remains strictly within these walls."

Riley shrugged and accepted with a dismissive wave of his hand.

"Excellent. Our firm represents several international investment and financial consortiums. One of them had expressed an interest in assisting the Maughams, who are among the most creative artistes today, with both an infusion of capital and marketing acumen. Of course, this was before the terrible tragedy. And yet, the head of the group still believes in Mmes. Joelle and Michelle and wants to analyze the impact of this terrible event and their potential going forward."

"Why would a Russian business group want to own them when they can wait a couple of days and just steal their designs like every other manufacturer?"

EIGHTEEN

"I'M STEALING MONEY."

The bank teller stared at Igor as he pushed a note toward her.

"And you focking sound alarm, you are dead voman." He looked at her name plate, "Nancy D'Angelo."

Nancy D'Angelo was the definition of a survivor. At forty-nine years old, she had already endured a double mastectomy. She'd also raised her daughter Andrea as a single mom from the time she was twenty-seven when her husband Ron had fallen overboard on a sailfish excursion and somehow wasn't found until the next morning. So, while she knew Igor was serious, she wasn't afraid. It wasn't her money.

Which is what she told Igor.

"It's not my money."

She reached down into her till and withdrew cash from the drawer.

"You didn't read note."

"What? Oh, okay."

She read the note. "'Give me all money.'"

You forgot the article, she wanted to say but knew this beast of a man would never understand proper grammar.

So instead she said, "Where's the 'the?'"

"Vot?"

"Nothing."

Igor pulled back the note, read it.

"Give me pen."

Nancy looked at him like he was nuts. Which he was.

She handed him the pen and watched Igor draw an arrow between "all" and "money" and insert "the" above and in-between the two words.

He shoved it back, smiled.

Nancy smiled back. Her hand hovered over the tens. "You want the tens?"

"How much there is?"

"I don't know, about a thousand."

Igor nodded. "Better have thousand and not need than other vay around no?"

"I agree."

But my guess is you'll never get to spend any of it, you dumb shit.

She forced herself to not look up at the security cameras that were recording every second of the robbery.

Igor's big left tattooed fist came under the window and left a crumpled plastic bag. "Put in there."

It was a Seven-11 bag.

Nancy almost laughed. But she carefully slid the loose bills into the bag, and then the banded packs of the larger bills.

"That last money? They have exploding things?"

"Are you kidding? Look around, we're small potatoes. Our manager wouldn't spring for that."

Igor searched her face for any telltale signs that she was focking with him.

"How much?"

"Every teller gets thirty-one thousand, five hundred. But I've had a busy morning. So, you're getting about forty thousand or so. I haven't zeroed out my drawer."

"No," Igor said, smiling, "I did."

NINETEEN

"THAT'S HIM! THE GUY ON BOLO."

Nat couldn't believe his eyes.

"That's Igor."

The robbery of the small savings and loan in Culver City had gone off like a movie heist. Igor strolled out, the Seven-11 bag bulging with cash tucked under his arm. Vladimir pulled up in a new Chevy Impala, courtesy of an Uber driver who was gagged and bound and squeezed together like a concertina in the minuscule trunk.

Nancy had counted to a hundred, as Igor had ordered, before she sounded the alarm button. By then, Vladimir was rolling up the entrance to the 405 north.

The cops and the Feds stormed the little savings and loan. It made for great television, but lousy police work. Nancy became a media star for a couple of days, regaling the audiences with her droll recounting of Igor's dedication to correct his grammar. The FBI got excellent photos of Igor and put it out on the Be On the Look Out, BOLO list.

Cole had watched the news while eating an omelet. The photo and Nancy's description gave him hope that they'd hit a longshot. He'd called Mollie, who called Culver City and they exchanged information. But before they could call Nat, he called Cole and was jumping up and down with excitement.

"That's freakin' him. Goddamn Igor."

"Okay, Nat. Sit tight. Mollie and I will come over to, and we'll go through some additional information. It's not secret, but it is privileged."

"Hell, yes," Nat said, his voice ramping up in volume and excitement. "I'll do anything to catch that sadistic fuck that killed Zoey."

"So why rob a savings and loan?" Mollie asked Cole later as they rode to Nat's house in Westwood.

Cole checked his mirrors and switched lanes. "They need money to get out of town. I doubt if they can unload the watch. And they must know that somebody, I'd say their boss, sent Aleksander and Mikhail after them."

"Where do you think they're headed?"

"Accents like Nat said? Not south. They're having that much trouble with English? Spanish isn't the answer."

"Canada?"

"They're desperate, but yeah. They go there, maybe find somebody give them ten cents on the dollar and then they disappear."

"You think Boris would tell us who he works for?"

"Only if he wants to or it's expedient. Nothing gets past or out of Boris."

"It took him a moment to get your joke about Choo-Choo."

"That's probably more cultural than intelligence."

Cole pushed the car into the right lane and got a loud blaring of the driver's horn for his efforts.

"I was going to say Night, but I didn't think he'd get it, being from Russia."

Mollie's silence told Cole she didn't get it either.

"C'mon. Dick Night Train Lane? Hall of Fame defensive back played in the 'fifties. He was married to singer Dinah Washington."

"That from your internet searches?"

"My dad. He loved football, knew all these insider stories about the players."

"Night Train because of the song?"

"No. Because when he laid a hit on another player, he derailed them."

Cole remembered that Derailed was also one of the nicknames his father had endured as a kid when in one of the few times in his life, he'd resorted to violence to solve a situation.

"Freakin' amazing," Nat said as he opened the door for Cole and Mollie.

"Check this out."

He'd downloaded a photo of the Russian; then photoshopped a V-mask onto it. He'd printed it out on his laser printer and had it ready for them.

"I'd recognize that shaved bullet head anywhere. But I hope I never see it again; except when he's in an orange jumpsuit headed for a life sentence."

"Can we have this?" Cole said.

"Absolutely."

Cole showed Nat photos of Aleksander and Mikhail.

"One of these guys Igor's buddy?"

Nat immediately shook his head. "No, he was big, but these guys are like houses. They his comrades?"

"We think so," Mollie said.

"This some kind of Russian mob hit? On Zoey? That doesn't make sense."

"We don't think it started out that way," said Cole. "But somehow, they're involved."

"Zoey say anything about people who were giving her grief?" Mollie asked.

"Zoey? Who didn't love her? I mean, yeah, every star has her detractors, but for her? I've never seen so many fans who absolutely adored her. I mean you saw the shrine in your town. And they're all over the world."

The outpouring for Zoey across America and the world *was* phenomenal. In countless small towns in every state, her fans had gathered together for tributes with flowers and gifts, singing, and poems. Same for big cities like New York, Chicago and San Francisco. In Paris, the base of the Eiffel Tower had been strung with white tea roses, Zoey's favorite flower, and then thousands of candles were lit.

"Enough candles," one besotted woman said to the reporter, "that it'll be seen from space and by Zoey in heaven."

In London, Rome and a dozen other capitals across Europe, similar tributes and shrines were created. In Tokyo, seventy-five thousand Japanese fans had gathered at the Edo Tokyo Museum in tribute to the place where in her highest- grossing film, "Sayanora Love," Zoey had died in her lover's arms.

"I mean," Nat said, "what kind of guy shoots someone like her?"

TWENTY

"HE IS FOCKIN' IDIOT."

Pytor shook his fist at the TV. He and Oleg and Misha were watching the news of the robbery.

"He thinks I von't run him down like focking rodent he is and kill him?"

Goddamnit, Oleg thought. Just what we need, to go on a wild goose chase.

Because when Pytor said he would run down Igor and Vladimir, it would be Oleg and Misha doing the running. And Igor and Vlad had outmaneuvered and outsmarted a state-wide manhunt, so what the hell did Pytor expect they'd be able to accomplish?

"He and Vlad are still in L.A.," Pytor said. "Trying to sell watch. And looking for pussy."

Pytor shook his index finger at them; an act that always infuriated Oleg because it sent him back to his days at school when his teachers were always lecturing him.

"I vant you go down Compton and South L.A., and ask around."

"Afroamerickej muža, "Oleg said, reverting to his native Slovak for African-American men, "not going to have that kind of money."

"I know that," Pytor barked. "They down there looking for pink chocolate."

But Igor and Vladimir were three hundred miles north in a cheap motel in Fresno. And they weren't looking for sex but staring at the banded bundles of money. And looking at the unfortunate man they'd kidnapped, Bruce Dillon, the owner of the Impala.

Bruce was terrified. He also smelled bad, having pissed his pants bouncing around for over three hours in the trunk.

"You want me to take off the band?" Bruce said.

"Yes. And make sure you point it away, into shower."

Igor and Vladimir were outside the tiny bathroom while Bruce was inside, his back against the rusted and chipped sink.

"Okay."

Bruce held a band of cash and aimed it at the fiberglass shower stall. He slipped his finger under the band and ripped.

Nothing happened.

"Yes!" Vladimir bellowed. "We good now."

Vladimir moved to grab one of the packets of fifties, but Igor held him back.

"Let him do all. Just in case."

They waited and watched until Bruce was standing in a small pile of ripped money bands, Igor and Vladimir gathered up all the bills, closed the door on Bruce and went into the small bedroom.

"Vot you vant do vith him?" Vladimir asked. "Can't shoot him."

"Vhy? Better not leave vitnesses."

"Guy has vife and two kids."

"Ve can do anything ve vant. But guy is okay. Doesn't vine. Except maybe vhen pull tape from mouth."

"And he only piss pants because ve don't stop," Vladimir said. "And he doesn't complain."

But twenty minutes later, the duct tape was back across Bruce's mouth. It was also wound tight across his chest, hands, and feet to the toilet and stretched across to the sink. His pants had been pulled down.

"So, next time you have to go, you are okay," Igor said.

He put his meaty hand on Bruce's neck where it connected to his shoulder.

"And when you wake up..."

Igor compressed the vegas nerve in Bruce's neck and held him in place with his other hand until Bruce's eyes rolled up into his head and he went limp.

That would only give them a head start of fifteen minutes or so, but

Igor knew that when Bruce regained consciousness, he'd feel like absolute shit. His head would pound with the worst headache in his life. He'd be nauseous, have no strength in his muscles to try and work himself loose. Those symptoms would last well into the night.

Igor had paid for three days rental in advance so the motel manager wouldn't be around until Friday. He'd left a Don't Disturb sign on the door and told the manager he didn't need the sheets changed. The manager was a cheap bastard, Igor could tell, so would comply. But even if he didn't, or his Mexican housekeeper didn't get the message and went inside to clean, she still wouldn't find Bruce until tomorrow.

And by then they'd be in Washington.

TWENTY-ONE

"THE WORLD IS YOUR OYSTER."

Boris's perma-grin was at full wattage.

"Everybody just adores the Maugham Sisters."

Joelle and Michelle were sitting in the Presidential Bungalow at the five-star Beverly Hills Hotel on Sunset. The Mediterranean-influenced room with the hotel's signature touches of pink and green went for over $7000 per night. Joelle could look through the wide sliding glass doors to the secluded patio and see the turquoise- water private pool lit by the underwater lights, surrounded by high fencing and lush palms and vegetation.

But her eyes and attention were on the tall man just to her left, Nikolai Voronov. Voronov was too rugged to be called handsome, but there was something so compelling about him that Joelle knew he could be dangerous.

Voronov had shaken her hand, his ice-blue eyes locked on her deep brown eyes and said in a mellow voice, devoid of any accent, "We should have met years ago."

Joelle wasn't sure what he had said to Michelle and didn't really care. Michelle was the more beautiful one, but she was the magnetic one. Joelle knew that in a competition for a man, she could blow her sister out of the stadium.

She'd done it once before.

But Gregg Zanders was one of those guys.

He was an amazing designer.

And he wasn't gay.

Michelle had been in heat for Gregg, so Joelle kept her distance. But as Gregg did more freelance work for them, she looked past his stunning good looks and saw his deeper qualities, his casual charm, the way he made both sisters laugh, his impeccable taste and style and her desire sparked.

One night when Michelle had flown to New York and Gregg had come by late on his way to drop off a new idea, it was, to use her father's old expression, 'Gloves off.'

Actually, it was bra and panties off, Gregg's jeans and boxers off, as in some fascinating moment of spontaneous combustion, they'd slammed into each other, their mouths locked, hands groping, parts pressed so hard together, they could barely stand. They spent the entire weekend in bed, consumed by a lust Joelle had never experienced in her life.

When Michelle returned from Manhattan, Joelle and Gregg acted like the event had never happened. A week later, Gregg got an offer from Dior and moved to Paris. When he was in Los Angeles, he would see Joelle in secret, and they would resume their affair as if they'd been apart just a few hours instead of so many months.

The third year of their on/off romance ended when Gregg met Chloe Bissette, a brilliant French mathematician and in less than a year had married Chloe and helped deliver their baby girl they'd named Blaise, taking the first name of one of France's most famous mathematicians and child prodigies, Pascal.

Joelle glanced again at Nikolai Voronov and was surprised to see that he'd been staring directly at her while she'd been thinking about Gregg.

"You don't think that's a good idea?" Nikolai said.

"I'm sorry."

Boris's perma-grin increased its wattage, and he waved his index finger gently.

"Ah, Mademoiselle Joelle has already started negotiating, Mister Voronov."

Everyone laughed politely.

Nikolai sensed that Joelle's thoughts had been elsewhere, so repeated his question: "I had asked if the idea of global expansion, with the very highest returns on investment, was an idea that you and your sister had entertained?"

Before Joelle could answer, Michelle jumped in: "We're not giving up ownership."

Nikolai put up a well-manicured hand.

"And we are not proposing *that*, I assure you."

"What do you want?" Michelle said.

Nikolai's dark brown hair, cut in the latest style, caught the soft lights of the room as he nodded at Boris.

"V-12, Mister Voronov's company, actually just one of his companies, represents his international investment and financial interests. V-12 is prepared to offer you a significant infusion of capital. We will also give you access to the company's worldwide marketing acumen. This latter point of marketing? While Mister Voronov is reluctant to say it since he is so modest, but of which I have no reservations, includes some of the sharpest and most intellectually sophisticated minds on the planet."

Boris' perma-grin, impossible as it seemed, actually increased.

"We rock 'n roll!"

Boris glanced at Nikolai as if to ask: 'Too much?'

The Russian oligarch merely smiled. A Cheshire cat smile that was open to interpretation.

"We are the most avant-garde fashion line in America," Joelle said. "That seem like we're slouching to you?"

"Not at all," Nikolai said. "And we never intended to imply anything but our highest admiration for your success." He paused a moment as if to gather his thoughts, but Joelle knew was part of his sales pitch, "But we see ways to take your base and expand it exponentially."

"And how would you do that?"

"By better control of product distribution, more stringent security safeguards so that pirating is reduced to a minimum. And finally, establishing your own Maugham factories here in the United States and in several strategic plants in Europe."

The news of the factories stunned both sisters.

In their silence, Boris struck – the torpedo arrowing through the waters to slam home the explosive charge – and produced two slim genuine calfskin folders.

"Here is our proposal. I suggest you read it later at your leisure, certainly consult with your attorneys, ask us questions, please, and tell us what you think, if you'd like changes or anything else you deem important or necessary."

"And this proposal," Joelle tapped the leather with a long, pearl-painted nail, "requires no surrender of ownership?"

"Nothing changes," Nikolai said. "You and Michelle own one hundred percent."

"So what does V-12 want for all this generosity?"

"Manufacture and marketing."

There was a soft knock on the door, and one of Vorovov's bodyguards opened it and two waiters entered, one pushing a small cart laden with a small feast; the other carrying a wide tray with frosty green bottles of Krug champagne and iced ones of Stolichnaya Elite Vodka. The waiters quickly set up the drinks and food on a side buffet table and vanished; each pocketing a huge tip from the bodyguards.

"I am not expecting a decision tonight, of course," said Nikolai. "So we thought this would be a good time to have some food and drink and then see what the rest of the night brings."

He said this while gazing at each sister in turn, a subtle smile on his lips.

"There is caviar, Beluga of course," announced Boris. "Which would be an excellent garnish for the egg-white omelets, which I believe, Michelle, you prefer."

If Michelle wondered how Nikolai knew her diet, it didn't appear to dim her enthusiasm.

"Oh, wow," she said and heaped a huge portion of eggs on to her plate, then sprinkled three teaspoons of caviar over the omelet.

Nikolai moved to the table, close to Michelle who was now adding fresh fruit to her meal. Then with his back to Joelle and Boris and with the slightest movement of his hand, made a small plastic bag that sparkled with a white powder magically appear on Michelle's already crowded plate.

No words were exchanged between Nikolai and Michelle, but so much was said in the silence of the moment as his blue eyes bored into hers:

Jesus, how did you know?

I have so much more if you want it.

I'm not fucking you.

Why resist when we can have so much fun together?

Nikolai gave her the briefest of nods and turned to take a plate from the stack.

He's trying to bribe me.

TWENTY-TWO

"THERE IS BUSINESS. THEN THERE IS US."

Nikolai smiled at Michelle, waited for her reaction.

"Monkey business," she said and snorted a small laugh at her own joke.

They were laying together in the king-sized bed of the Paul Williams Suite of the hotel. Nikolai had ordered one of the bodyguards to call down to the front desk and book the room.

There was an advance reservation of course, but Drago's 6'6" size and insistence on paying double the standard $3,700 room rate, as well as paying for the new room for the bumped guests cinched the deal.

"What about the other room?" Michelle had asked.

"That was for our negotiations. This is for our pleasure." Nikolai drew Michelle closer. Dawn was an hour or so away. They had spent the entire night having sex, Michelle fueled by the pharma grade coke, Nikolai fueled by his secret plans falling so smoothly and easily into place.

"So extravagant, and it seems like such a waste of a great room."

"I let Boris stay there. and Drago booked a hooker for him, so he's happy."

"You didn't."

"Why not? Boris needs a little reward now and then. Get him away from his wife and three daughters."

Michelle sniffed, took a tissue from the bedside table and caught the nasal drip from the coke. "That was amazing flake."

"I can get you as much as you want."

"Do you realize how volatile those words are to someone like me?"

"Someone like you? No, you are the one and only Michelle Maugham."

She snorted another laugh and tapped his shoulder with her fist.

"Flirt."

"Seriously, it's not a problem."

"And what's the price?"

"There is no price," he said, an edge to his voice as if he'd been insulted. "It's free."

"Nothing's free in this world, Nikolai. If you think you can get something without strings attached, you haven't looked hard enough for the strings."

Nikolai smiled and nodded in agreement.

Maybe there's more to you than you let on.

"If we are going to work together, consider it part of our deal."

"The loo," she said and sprang out of bed.

She didn't bother to hide her nakedness.

And why should she?

Sleek dancer's body, with voluptuousness in her breasts and that firm ass, she should want to show it off.

When she returned, Nikolai had poured coffee and rested against the pillows.

"So, where's home for you?" Michelle said.

"Boston, New York."

"Originally."

Nikolai hesitated. He disliked even something so innocent as his birthplace.

"Rostov-on-Don," he said.

"Oh, my god," she said, "that's amazing. A couple of months ago we had a young receptionist, very beautiful girl, Oksana something... Oksana ...Kosar, yes, that was it. Oksana Kosar. I'd forgotten all about her; until you mentioned Rostov- on-Don."

"Why did that remind you of her?"

"Because she was from there too."

Michelle's eyes were alive and sparkling.

"Don't you think that's amazing? I mean two people from the same little town?"

"It's not so little, there are over a million people living there."

"But from a city halfway around the world, two people, two very, very different people, are linked to the Maugham Sisters. What are the odds?"

"So where is Oksana now?"

"Don't know. She was with us for maybe two weeks and then she just left. Poof, gone."

TWENTY-THREE

"THEY'VE VANISHED."

Cole shook his head.

"How do two mooks like Igor and Ivan manage to pull that off without help?"

"Maybe they have one of those Invisibility Cloaks from Harry Potter," Mollie said.

"Assuming they could find it."

"What?"

"If it's invisible, how do you know where it is?"

Cole did an overblown English accent: "I say, Ignotus, have you seen the invisibility cloak? I thought I put it over there on the dresser."

"Ignotus? You're a Harry Potter fan?"

"No."

He didn't want to explain, but if he tried to stall, Mollie, then she'd get very interested.

"Amelie used to read it to Vince and Bianca, they're my next-door neighbor Glenn's kids. And Ignotus always stuck in my head, like Ignoramus."

"Okay, back to our own ignoramuses, who seem to be geniuses at avoiding capture," Mollie said.

"Geniuses and goddamn lucky, too."

Extremely lucky.

Igor and Vladimir didn't get a day's head start like they'd planned.

The owner of the cheap motel had rented the adjacent room to a married father of four who was banging his twenty-something secretary.

In their rush to lust, he and the secretary had confused rooms and inserted the key into 106, the room that Igor and Vlad had abandoned and since the locks weren't worth the cheap metal they were made of, the key worked.

The boss was taking his clothes off as they entered, while his secretary hurried to the bathroom. She opened the door and let out a shriek that would have made a dog's ears hurt.

They removed the tape from Bruce, who blurted out his story. The secretary dialed 9-1-1, but her boss cut the call off and bellowed that they needed to get the hell out of there, now.

The secretary refused. "We run, the cops will think we're part of it."

"Fuck this," he snarled, hopped back into his pants and stomped to his car, carrying his shoes and shirt.

"You're a coward."

"And you're fired!"

"You don't think your Madeline's gonna know about this?"

She slammed the motel door and locked it. He banged on the door, pleading with her until he heard sirens in the distance and then smoked his tires getting out of the motel. The cops interviewed Bruce, put out a stolen car notice and a new BOLO for Vlad. After they took the secretary's information, a squad car was sent to interview her former boss.

The motel owner expected television and media blitz and thought all that attention would get his instant fame. And he could raise his rates. But that idea vanished when the police put a lid on any reporting because they didn't want Igor and the newly-discovered Vladimir to know their getaway had been short-circuited.

They promised the owner that in three or four days he could get his 15-minutes of Warhol fame.

Cole and Mollie had just left Lieutenant Riley's office after listening to another of his tirades. Cole had pointed out that a small army of law enforcement personnel was after Igor and Vlad.

"Not just Mollie and me and the rest of the city's own cops, the Fresno police are on his trail. So are the LAPD. And now that they abducted Bruce, they've got the FBI after them."

But it hadn't mollified Riley. He was still unhappy.

"These assassins murdered the number one movie star in the world. Right here in our hometown."

"Matt's turned up the heat, huh?" Cole said.

Riley tried to bluster his way past that.

"I don't give a fuck what the mayor thinks, okay? This is on my watch, my responsibility. And I am disappointed. Very, very disappointed."

"Let me tell you something," said Cole, putting iron in his tone.

Riley looked at Cole, not sure what was coming next.

"You're right. We're disappointed too."

"Absolutely," echoed Mollie. "It's hard to imagine the depths of our disappointment. It's like an abyss of darkness."

Cole subtly signaled Mollie to dial it down. Riley wasn't the shiniest badge in the department, but he hadn't made Lieutenant on just dumb luck.

"We're doing everything we can," Mollie said. "They can't stay gone forever."

But while it wasn't forever, it was now three days; and no sign of Igor and Vladimir.

Then cops had found Bruce's Impala parked at the farthest corner of a Wal-Mart Supercenter on Stacey Allison Way in Woodburn, Oregon. A 74-old man from Eugene, Vincent Rhea, had reported his 2015 Ram Rebel missing, but that was two days later. Asked why he didn't report it sooner, Vincent said he'd had a drink or two and couldn't quite remember where he'd parked it.

Again, Igor and Vladimir's luck held.

Although they looked at it from the opposite end of things.

"We like that focking song," Vladimir said, "you know, by black blues guy?"

"Black blues guy? Vot the fock, only a million of them. Who?"

"Fock, I can't remember. But song goes, 'If wasn't for bad luck, wouldn't have no luck at all.'"

"Oh, yeah, sounds familiar. Look it up on cell."

Vladimir didn't like using his cell other than tapping the presets: his fingers were so big they covered two keys at a time, so he had to be very precise when he did a search; which meant he was very slow.

"Ah," he finally said, "Albert King. Song is called 'Born Under A Bad Sign.'"

"That's us. Poor families. Your father runs away, mine goes to prison. But I say, fock them all. And vhen you think of it, we doing good so far. I mean we get watch, we get money from bank, two cars and we still free."

No mention of killing world's most famous movie star.

Or that Pytor was after them.

Vladimir thought it was best to let those things pass.

"Yeah," he said. "Next problem is how we get into Canada."

"I vas thinking. This Rebel is focking beast. I read on Internet, it is strongest off-road machine around. Chews up land."

"So?"

"So I am wondering if maybe Vashington border has place where no assholes patrol."

Vladimir thought about this for a moment, and a broad grin spread across his Slavic face.

"You focking genius. Crazy, but focking genius. Only one problem."

"Vot's dat?"

"We need expert to show us that place."

Igor tapped the shopping bag with the cash.

"Ve hire tour guide. How expensive can he be? Fock give him some whiskey and tobacco and focker be in shit-kicker paradise."

TWENTY-FIVE

"THE ANGELS IN HEAVEN ARE REJOICING."

Reverend Billy Singer gazed at the throngs of people that stretched from Zoey's gravesite all across the lush green lawns, standing carefully between the headstones and copper plaques embedded deep in the grass, and the hundreds standing in the roads and paths of the cemetery.

"Rejoicing with celestial music and joy."

Zoey's funeral had been a gluttonous media orgy, just as Mollie had predicted.

Actresses shrieked and moaned, actors shed the theatrical tear. Liberal politicians gave speeches about gun violence, the NRA trotted out their bullshit about people killed, not guns. Twitter and the other sites blew up with everybody expressing their anguish. It was a marathon of grief. Even now, after her snow-white casket, draped with so many white tea roses it seemed to be floating on a soft vanilla sea, had been lowered into the ground, people were still mourning.

Reverend Singer got the gig because back in Zoey's junior high days, she had occasionally attended his Little White Chapel in her hometown of Lafayette and requested him in her will. The fact that the last time Zoey had attended the Reverend's house of worship was when she was thirteen was beside the point. Hollywood studio execs, politicians, and several world religious leaders protested. But on that bright, sunny day, it was Reverend Billy was speaking directly to God and probably thirty million people across the planet.

Cole clicked off the TV.

He hated that breast-beating, hysterical crying bullshit. Yet, he'd watched it, because he knew he was stalling. He'd told Matt that he'd talk to Hamza Nejem and didn't want to do it. Cole's research had given Hamza not just passing grades, but high marks for personal conduct. He'd come to America with his parents when he was nine from Mazar-i-Sharif in northern Afghanistan. They'd settled in New York and then after Hamza's father died from a massive heart attack, he and his mother went west to San Francisco, where she had a distant cousin.

Hamza had graduated with honors from UCLA, gone on a full scholarship to the University of Helsinki and graduated summa cum laude in his class with a Masters in Intercultural Encounters. He was currently an associate professor at the Annenberg School at USC, teaching "The Power Spectrum of Life." The fact that he was openly gay in direct defiance of his Sharia religious roots told Cole that Hamza had courage. That he'd convinced Jon to come out despite his father Matt's pig- headed views told him that Hamza was caring. As well as inspiring.

"So does the power spectrum apply to everything?" Cole asked Hamza after he'd told Cole his teaching background. Cole had learned that Hamza liked a new trendy bar near the SC campus called "Hot Rods." And while the owner was into souped-up cars from the Fifties, with murals on the walls, tuck- 'n-roll leather booths, drinks named for engines and hot rods, many gay men went there looking for their own version of a joystick ride.

Cole had managed to find a bar stool next to Hamza and casually started a conversation. After Hamza had told Cole what he did to afford the twenty-dollar drinks, Cole used that as the bridge into his investigation.

Just make sure it's not an interrogation.

And not an inquisition.

"Everything is power. Power is everything. Someone is trying to get power or keep it."

"Like who's in power here?"

"I think you just moved to grab it." Hamza saluted him with his drink.

"I don't think life's black and white. So that kind of a summation doesn't allow for many variables."

"Oh, but it's all variables, and always in flux." Hamza signaled the barkeep for another round. "On me."

"Thank you."

"Let's use me as the guinea pig," Hamza said.

Cole listened carefully. He already knew Hamza's story, but he wanted to see if he would elaborate or improve his history.

"I came out when I was nineteen." That was new. And not an embellishment.

"That must have been terrifying."

"It was. But also liberating."

"How did your parents take it?"

"My mother was very supportive. My father was worried that I would get hurt. There wasn't the stigma back then."

"I thought being gay was punishable by stoning."

"I don't mean that stigma. I meant our current one. You know, anyone from my ethnic background, we of the mongrel horde, who are overcrowding and over- polluting America with so many of our radical, intellectual terrorists or poor, suffering immigrants."

Hamza finished his drink as the barkeep placed their fresh ones down.

"My father, Andalib, which naturally became Andy, feared the Iman and his tribe would come after me. But I wasn't afraid. I was third-degree black belt in Silat Mubai, which is a Muslim martial arts discipline." He gazed at Cole. "And I have a move in that discipline which cannot be defeated. Would you like me to demonstrate?"

"I didn't bring my helmet."

Hamza laughed.

"Okay, first position yourself as if you are going to throw a punch."

"Right or left?"

"Doesn't matter."

Cole shifted and cocked his right hand.

"Now here is my first move."

Hamza crossed his right leg over his left, so his body was narrowed, but still a target.

"Got it?"

"Yes."

"And here comes the undefeatable move."

And before Cole could say anything, Hamza sprung from his right leg into an amazingly fast sprint, and in four steps he was halfway across the floor.

Cole smiled.

So did Hamza as he came back.

"I call it, Cut and Run."

Cole clinked his glass against Hamza's.

"You said you ran sprints at UCLA?" Cole said but knew the answer.

Hamza frowned.

"No, I didn't."

Oops, think fast.

"Okay, busted. When you went to the john, I Googled you."

Cole tapped some keys, and Hamza's bio came up.

"Pretty fast hundred meters time."

"Thanks, but I wasn't Usain Bolt."

"Nobody is. Except Usain."

"You're not gay, so are you taking a walk on the wild side or just visiting the zoo?"

"Neither. I'd heard about their 'Texaco High Octane' and was going to try it."

"But all you ordered was the House Red."

"Once I thought about the drink, which was mixing Stoli Vodka, Coca-Cola and Lime-aid, I thought I'd pass."

"You made the right decision."

"You ever had one?"

"A sip. From a friend's drink. As the Valley girls used to say, Ewwww."

"What about you?" Cole said.

"What do you mean?"

"About coming here. I've seen several men, good-looking ones, smile and try to make contact."

"But, Cole, I thought they were flirting with you."

"Nice try."

"No, you're right. I noticed them. But the truth is, I'm in love."

TWENTY-SIX

"IT'S NOT A MARRIAGE MADE IN HEAVEN."

Stirling Lindsay looked at Michelle.

"As your attorney, I would strongly advise against signing this."

"Well I am signing it," she snapped. "It's too good an offer to miss. We can finally control our business, Joelle."

"No, we can't," Joelle said. "We can register our opinions and whatever the hell we want to say, but the final decision is V-12's."

"Nikolai told me we'd be millionaires within a year, eight figures within twenty months."

"And," Stirling said, "if their sales projections are even remotely accurate, V-12's figures will be thirty percent higher."

Michelle's eyes were glassy, and she kept sniffing. Joelle knew she was doing coke again.

How clichéd can you be? A coke whore? Nowadays?

And at your age and all the shit you've been through.

And put me through.

"I can't believe that," Michelle said. "Thirty percent?"

"Conservatively," said Stirling. "But even if you cut it by fifty percent, it's a sucker's contract."

"How can that be? We're sharing everything?"

"You're sharing everything except the profits. Because the way V-12 has set up this contract, it amounts to piracy."

Stirling loved to sling incendiary words when he was on the attack.

But in this case, his words weren't that inflammatory.

"When you extrapolate the fine print details and sundry clauses, you discover that their so-called 'legendary financial acumen' and 'worldwide marketing' and their 'distribution strategic centers' carry the most expensive fees I have ever seen."

"They don't seem like much when listed as a percentage, but it is percentages on percentages. Maugham is paying for every business conference, meeting, text, memo, telephone call that comes from running the business. Every. Single. One. Plus, supplies. And transportation. And construction of facilities. Governmental and trade ratification approvals, code and regulatory requirements. The list's as long as my arm."

"Well..." Michelle was flustered. This was not going like she'd expected.

She'd thought Stirling would outline the enormous cash flow, how they'd scored a true bonanza that would set them up for life, a life she was sure would include her and Nikolai traveling across the globe, the *bon vivant* couple so admired by the world. And now here was Stirling pissing on everything.

"If we have sales of ten million, how much does V-12 make?"

"V-12 and Maugham would gross the same amount."

"So, how's that bad?"

"Because," Joelle interjected, knowing that Michelle would tune out Stirling, "our net wouldn't be within one percent of theirs."

"I don't understand."

"Because like Stirling said, we pay every expense. Any costs that any of his V-12 companies incur? We pay for them. So his Rocket Manufacturing, or Raketi Tootmine, which is its name in Estonian, since that's where the factory is located; and his Rocket Marketing, Commercialization de la Fusée, just outside Paris; and every single one of his companies that are the fulfillment channels of this deal, will be charging us for their services."

"But that means we're paying him!"

"And handsomely, too."

Michelle's stomach clenched; she thought she was going to vomit right there on Stirling's shiny table.

"Excuse me," she moaned, slid back her chair and fled to the bathroom.

"Clearly, we have to renegotiate," Stirling said.

"Nikolai doesn't negotiate. And neither do I."

Joelle didn't want to even try.

Stirling was one of the best attorneys in Los Angeles. One of the most expensive, too. She knew that Boris would blow so much hot air at them and bury them in a white paper blizzard of counter proposals and new clauses and conditions that would have to be examined again and again, that she'd have to add a second mortgage on her house to pay for it.

"What about Michelle?" Stirling said. "Obviously she wants the deal."

"That's what's nice about being the older sister. And having fifty-one percent."

"We have three more days before we're required to respond. Let me see what I can do."

"Two hours, Stirling. Maximum. We've already spent way too much on this."

Stirling had grown inured to his clients bitching about his rates. They always complained when it came time to pay the bill. But they'd sell their first-born to have him save their asses.

"Sometimes, discovering what you won't do, is more valuable than doing it."

TWENTY-SEVEN

"VOT FOCK YOU DOING?"

Igor shoved Vladimir's hand away from his shoulder.

But Vladimir knocked Igor's hand back and shook Igor's shoulder so hard he bounced him against the headboard.

Igor rolled away, and his knee nudged the empty Sobieski vodka bottle and it fell to the cheap carpet and rolled under the other twin bed where Vladimir had slept.

Vladimir had drunk a half-glass of the cheap vodka, but Igor had emptied the bottle. He was going to be hung-over and nasty. Vladimir wasn't looking forward to the day and their next step at getting free.

"Let's go, we will be late to meet the guide."

Igor squinted out the window at the blue-grey Washington sky that was turning a soft roseate as dawn approached.

"What time?"

"Five o'clock. We have half-hour." Vladimir yanked back the covers and hauled Igor up by the smelly New York Jets jersey that he always slept in. He got him to his feet and wrangled him to the bathroom.

"Stop!"

But in this case, with Igor barely conscious and drunk, Vladimir could manage him. He grabbed Igor's jersey and shoved the ox into the shower, then turned on the cold water full blast.

"FOCK!" Igor bellowed and struggled to rise.

Vladimir shoved him back against the stall. Igor's thick skull bounced off the fiberglass, and he fell on his ass. Vladimir adjusted the spray, it hit Igor in the face and watched as he just lay there slumped against the wall.

"You soaking jersey."

"It stinks, just like you."

Igor moaned and rolled over, so he was flat on his back with the shower hitting him full force. He struggled with the green jersey and got the "Namath" up over his head, but the 12 was too much.

Vladimir grabbed the shirt with two hands and pulled it over Igor's head. The cold water made Igor's blue-tinted body come alive, the dark ink of his tattoos now shiny and wet.

The huge tattoo of Saint Basil's Cathedral in Mosco's Red Square signified not Igor's Russian Orthodox religion, but his devotion to the religion of thieves.

The handle of a dagger was tattooed on the right side of his neck, low enough so that it couldn't be seen under a shirt collar. The sharp end of the blade came through on the left side of his neck. That was a sign to show others that he'd killed in prison, the two drops of blood the number of murders. The rose meant he'd turned 18 in prison.

"I am going get coffee. Be ready when I come back."

Vladimir strode down the parking lot, his boots banging against the asphalt.

We are focked, I know it.

You should just go back, shoot him while he's still groggy, take the money and go the opposite way – head to Mexico.

He'd had these thoughts for days now. And while the news programs hadn't stopped talking about Zoey's death, the law was after Igor, not him. He was clean.

Pytor and his goons were on his trail, but they wouldn't stay on it much longer.

Pytor had his business to run and hunting for two former gang members didn't add to the bottom line. Eventually, Pytor would figure out that his secrets were safe with Vladimir.

The waitress behind the coffee shop counter couldn't have been more than nineteen. She had soft brown hair and eyes. She smiled at Vladimir as he entered.

"We're up bright and early today," she said. "Where would you like to sit?"

"No, sorry, I am just ordering to go. Two coffees, biggest you got."

"Gonna hit the road before the traffic, huh?"

She smiled again, this time over her shoulder as she filled two Styrofoam cups.

"Room for cream?"

"Just coffee, please."

I could take a girl like you, Peggy, that was what her name tag said and settle down someplace.

"We've just gotten a fresh delivery of muffins and rolls. You should try them. They're to die for; especially with our coffee."

"Okay. What's your favorite … Peggy?"

Peggy blushed at hearing her name.

"Oh, gosh … I... well, the blueberries are terrific."

"Two blueberries, please."

Peggy put lids on the two cups, making sure they were on tight. "Why don't I warm up the muffins in the microwave?"

"Okay."

Vladimir put a twenty on the counter while Peggy set the microwave for thirty seconds.

"That'll be eight forty-nine," she said, "out of twenty. And your change is…"

"No change. All for you."

"What? No, I couldn't."

"I insist." Vladimir pushed the bill closer to her with his blunt index finger.

The microwave beeped.

Peggy laughed. "Saved by the bell."

TWENTY-EIGHT

THE WARNING DING-DING WAS LOUD.

The Ram Rebel's open door violated the peaceful stillness of the morning as Vladimir climbed down from the driver's seat, and Bart Williams stepped up and into the cab.

Bart was the 34-year-old son of Randall Williams, the guide that was going to get the two Russians into Canada.

"You sure this is only vay?" Igor asked Randall. Igor's head was still encased in the pincer grips of a Defcon-4 headache, ears ringing, white flashes in his eyes and in no mood, or shape, to hike fifteen miles through the Washington wilderness.

"No, it ain't the only way," Randall growled.

Randall was almost as big as Igor and Vladimir. And while his age gap of thirty-seven years meant he wasn't as fast as them, he more than made up for it in cunning and wickedness.

"You can ride up there in that shiny truck of yours and hope that the border crossing guards are blind or sleepy. But if you expect to visit the great and sovereign country of Canada and enjoy its fine landscape, women, and food, not necessarily in that order, for years to come, it is the only way."

"I thought truck could go through rough terrain."

"Yeah. Terrain that's in some pretty TV commercial. But this country? Not a fucking chance." Randall stared at Igor, then Vladimir. "We clear?"

"Yes," Vladimir said. He took Igor's arm and gave him a gentle push. Igor threw off Vladimir's hand and stomped forward.

"Where you going?" Randall bellowed.

Igor stopped, now thoroughly pissed off. He didn't want to hike. And he didn't want to take orders from some asshole bearded mountain man. But he knew Randall and his sons were his and Vladimir's only hope.

I focking take care of you across the border.

"Just so we're clear," Randall said. "I'm going to tell you this one last time. I lead, you two follow behind. The trail we're going on? Ain't no trail. It's a hard-ass trek through treacherous terrain. One false step and while you may not go off the side, you can goddamn well break your ankle or leg. And I sure the fuck ain't carrying either of your asses out on my back. Got it?"

Randall deliberately waited until both Vladimir and especially Igor had nodded they understood. He then waved Bart over, then called out to his youngest son, "Steve, get over here."

Steve was nineteen, a late-life surprise for Randall and his wife, Betty-Jo. And like every youngest child, over-indulged and held to much looser behavior standards.

But the kid was a natural.

"Steve you're following Bart to Sumas. You both cross over there, then go have lunch someplace, kill an hour or so. Then you drive east on Jones Road, right?"

Both boys nodded they understood.

"By about six tonight, just before sunset, me and our two guests should be coming out of the woods."

Randall shook hands with Steve, then Bart and watched as his youngest son gave him a thumbs up, then jogged over, climbed into his father's ancient and dusty Jeep and pulled it behind the sparkling Ram Rebel.

The State of Washington has 13 drivable border crossings across its 687 kilometers (427 miles) border with British Columbia, Canada. About 32,000 vehicles cross every day; mostly through the Peace Arch, Blaine, Lynden or Sumas ports.

Bart and Steve, as their father ordered, would cruise through Sumas. They'd made this run enough times to know some of the guards, if not by name, at least by face, so they'd be waved through without the guards checking.

Randall knew that his family's familiarity with the guards meant they could have hidden Igor and Vladimir and simply driven across the border. But Randall had been doing this since he was nineteen and had never been discovered.

Never even been suspected. Because he never took a chance.

He'd fallen into this business back in the late '60s by accident. remembered the date exactly, June 1, 1966.

But then it was hard to forget your birthday; especially your 18th birthday right at the height of LBJ's war in 'Nam. Randall felt like Muhammed Ali: They'd never called him names and he'd never even seen a Viet Cong, except on television at night when Walter Cronkite tallied up the number of Vietnamese that the US Army had reportedly killed, a total that eventually was close to the actual number of people living in the country.

And there was no way Randall was going to be drafted for such an evil war.

So at 4:00 am, June 1, 1966, he'd set out for Canada and slipped through the borders like "...a breath rippling by." as the Who sang. He'd done it so easily that after four months of being alone, he came back to his folk's ranch just outside of Nugents Corner, Washington because he missed his parents and Betty-Jo.

His mom and dad were overjoyed to see him but nervous that he might get caught. After four terrific days together, Randall decided no sense pushing his luck and went back, this trip even easier.

The second time he went home and then back into Canada, he took his best friend, Billy MacCauley. The third time he was planning to go back alone, but Betty-Jo showed up and said he wasn't leaving her behind ever again.

Randall couldn't tell you how many times or people he'd ushered into a new life. Over the years he developed a network of other resources, passports and birth certificates, credit cards, a job waiting for you at your new destination. Randall was rich, but that was another rule he never broke: live modestly and you'll live a long time.

Without trouble. Randall had taken all kinds of people into Canada. Same for traffic going the other way. He always researched his clients before he allowed himself to be hired. These two, these Russians had shown up without any references, which went against all of Randall's rules. But he hadn't taken anyone across in a month, and they'd offered double his fee.

"You really think you should help them?" Betty-Jo said.

"I don't know, I'm gonna find out."

It didn't take Randall long to learn that Igor was a fugitive; and while there was nothing on the media about Vladimir, he had to be one too. Randall didn't let his conscience bother him on his clients. If you had the money, you were good to go.

He did draw the line at killers or child molesters.

So far, four of those low-life animals had vanished.

Randall didn't fancy himself in the role of meting out justice, but some people needed to end up looking at the blue sky with sightless eyes before the forest dirt hit their faces.

Three were men.

Mick Lee, a fucking slope who'd had three wives and butchered them all.

Krishna Patel, a small-time drug dealer that had doctored his product with synthetic elephant tranquilizer and had to flee Los Angeles when five of his clients died the same week.

Matt Mullan, a high-tech executive that had a secret life as the ringleader of a huge kiddie porn network.

The fourth was the only woman he'd ever killed, but Dionne Furmanitor was an evil bitch. He'd nicknamed her the Terminator because all four of her husbands had died in mysterious ways. Randall never let his emotions affect his decision, but that cunt had it coming, and he shot her a half-mile into the trip.

Randall wasn't sure about Igor and Vladimir. Igor had robbed a bank. Not cool in Randall's book, but since no one had gotten hurt, not worthy of canceling Igor's contract with the living.

But when Randall had the two Russians change outfits, so they'd be prepared for their trip, he'd seen Igor's tattoos.

He'd had Betty-Jo investigate, and when he learned about the dagger and what it signified, he put Igor's chances at coming out of the woods at fifty-fifty. It just depended on his attitude.

And so far, that sullen face was tipping the scales the wrong way.

TWENTY-NINE

"MY WAY OR THE HIGHWAY."

Nikolai looked at Boris.

"Isn't that the American expression?"

"Yes," said Boris.

"So, tell that to Stirling Lindsay. We are not negotiating."

Boris nodded in agreement but felt that Nikolai was drawing a line in the sand too early.

"I will let him call us. Gives us stronger bargaining position."

"If you think it will help."

"Perhaps there is still a way to get the sisters to change their minds? Given your relationship with Michelle."

Nikolai's head turned and his icy gaze lasered on Boris.

Shit, shit.

Boris' stomach clenched.

"Sorry, I meant no disrespect. I have no idea what your relationship might be, but the young lady does seem to admire you very much."

Nikolai burst into laughter. He loved making his staff squirm.

"She admires my dick, Boris. And my bank accounts."

And the coke – they both left unsaid.

Sex with Michelle was amazing. She reminded Nikolai of some of the best prostitutes that were part of his far-flung empire, an erotic body combined with a dirty mind, a mouth ready for servicing and whispering ideas that would galvanize a man better than Viagra.

Yet, Nikolai was getting bored with her. Sometimes, during their thudding, heart-pounding, body-pounding nights and mornings, even as Michelle was orgasming and he was coming, a small voice inside his head was nagging: Do the deal, bitch.

This was a high-profile venture for Nikolai. Taking the Maugham sisters into wider distribution and into the less expensive, but higher volume and profit margin segment of the market would call attention to himself. Something he never did. But it was within that grandiose, bravado move of using the Maughams as a façade that he would launch his most brazen venture yet: synthetic drugs.

He'd come across Timofey and Ilya Kusnetskov, a set of demented and off-the- charts brilliant twins that defied description. The brothers Kusnetskov had raced through the tough graduate chemistry program at Ivanovo State University of Chemistry and Technology in Ivanovo Oblast, Russia. They'd completed the grueling four-year course in three years; both graduating cum laude.

While they were blowing through the lectures and study halls and chem labs, Timofey and Ilya would wait until midnight, two hours after the last class and sneak into the university labs. They supplied the night guard with drugs, mostly speed, to keep him happy and quiet. Then they would work until 2 am, developing a new special opioid.

Just before their official graduation, they had their own ceremonial event: the perfection of a new wonder drug. A violent, nasty drug, yes, but one that had enormous growth potential; especially in the dark markets of illegal trafficking.

Timofey and Ilya had perfected a synthetic derivative of carfentanyl, one of the most potent opioids on the planet. Carfentanyl's use for animal tranquilizing was wide-spread. And for a brief period, especially in the Midwest, bottom-feeder drug dealers had used it to cut their heroin; to boost the weight as well as the kick.

But those idiots didn't understand potency.

Carfentanyl was close to 10,000 times stronger than morphine. A microgram would knock you on your ass. So when the dealers had added what they thought were small amounts, they'd added murder to their crimes.

Timofey and Ilya had created a hybrid compound that was more controllable, had fewer side effects, and cost about a thousand percent less to produce. Timofey and Ilya would make that rocket ship. And Nikolai would command it into the stratosphere of distribution and control, and best of all, profits.

And the Maughams were the ticket to that star ride.

Nikolai liked Joelle. In fact, when he'd first met the two sisters, Joelle was who he'd wanted. But it was Michelle who'd thrown herself at him. And while he wasn't looking for sex as the entry to the sisters, entering all of Michelle's orifices, the crude thought automatically rising, it was a nice lagniappe to the deal. He just hoped Michelle could convince Joelle that it was in her best interest to sign the contract.

Her life depended on it.

THIRTY

"HAPPY WIFE, HAPPY LIFE."

Cole remembered that motto was his father Ben's favorite.

"It's the secret," he would tell Cole when they were driving to the hardware store for a Fluidmaster repair kit to fix the basement toilet that Aileen complained would suddenly run at odd times.

"It's a lot easier to just do what she wants than to fight it." Then Ben would add. "Not that your mother's demanding."

And Aileen Crane, buoyed by Ben's positive outlook on life and his willingness to help around the house and anticipate her moods or inchoate needs, never complained or harped. His parents shared a life that Cole remembered has without an argument, or at least one he'd ever witnessed.

His father was no doormat, either. Cole had seen him stand up to a burly neighbor who outweighed Ben by forty pounds. And there was a time when they were standing in line to pick up tickets to a Dodger game and two tattooed skinheads cut in line in front of them. And Ben calmly tapped the biggest guy on his swastika tat, which was visible from under his strap T said, "Excuse me, but the end of the line is behind us."

And the dude's shaved bullet head slowly pivoted around, like he was some muscular lighthouse and stared at Ben. They looked each other eyeball to eyeball.

Cole was frightened for his father. But he couldn't say a word. Then the second skinhead looked down at Cole and saw that he was wearing a Mike Piazza jersey and said, "Big Mike. Alright." And he held out his enormous fist, which was nearly blue from tattooed ink, and Cole bumped his fist.

"You think he's gonna hit another dinger tonight?" the skinhead asked.

"Maybe number thirty," Cole said. The year, 1995, when both Piazza and teammate Eric Karros hit thirty-two.

And the first skinhead looked at Cole, then Ben and said, "Sorry. Our bad."

And they moved back past them to the end of the line.

Cole had used his father's motto with Amelie. He doted on her, had his radar set for any advance warnings of possible dark clouds or even a storm, ahead.

So, their time together – those three years, five months and twelve days – had been wonderful.

And then they hadn't.

Maybe because Amelie wasn't his wife.

Maybe because while they'd talked about marriage, Cole had never asked; the question un-popped, a kernel of potential never heated to blossoming.

Maybe, maybe, maybe.

That shit always ran through his head.

"PTAD," Cole said to Mollie several months back when they'd stopped for a drink after a long night. "Post Traumatic Amelie Disorder."

"Yeah," Mollie said. "That comes from too much fuzzy thinking."

Cole laughed and then Mollie joined him, realizing her gay double entendre.

THIRTY-ONE

"TWO SIGNATURES?"

Michelle was confused.

"Yes," Joelle said. "Yours and mine. Both. That's why it's called a partnership."

"It's not fair," Michelle whined. "If one of us doesn't want to do something, she can stop the other partner any time they want."

"Pretty much."

"It's bullshit. I'm amazed we ever get anything done."

"Me, too, sometimes."

"Joelle, this is the opportunity of a lifetime."

"For Nikolai, not us. You read the contract. You heard what Stirling said."

Michelle nodded, faking it. Joelle knew Michelle hadn't read the contract.

Because she never read any of the contracts except for the bottom line numbers. The fine print and all the other significant terms that the attorneys always buried under obscure categories, Michelle never researched their long-term ramifications.

She hadn't done it with their partnership contract signed so many years ago.

The one that founded their company. The one that gave Joelle 51% and Michelle 49%. The percentage split had never come up before because Michelle had always eventually agreed to what Joelle wanted. But this? This might expose the secret to the light. It was the last thing Joelle wanted.

"So I can't sign it by myself?"

"Sure, you can. But it won't mean anything without me signing too. Same way if I signed and you didn't."

Okay, so that's a lie.

"This is a nightmare," Michelle said. "We're ruined."

"We're not ruined. This is a rough patch, but we'll get through it, just like we always have. I mean until Nikolai came along did we ever think of his kind of expansion? No. We were exclusive."

"And we've lived hand to mouth. I'm tired of it. I don't want to give up the money."

"The money? Or the coke?"

The words were barely out of her mouth, and Joelle regretted letting her emotions get the better of her.

Michelle's head snapped back as if she'd been slapped. And, in truth, she had: the accusation sharp and hurtful. Her eyes filled with tears and she spun on her heel and ran from the office.

"Michelle! Wait, I'm sorry... Michelle!"

She heard Michelle's footsteps bound down the stairs, then across the hardwood floors and then the violent slamming of the front door. She walked slowly out and sat down on the top step. From up here she could look down into the salon's showroom, see the plate glass window where two of last season's dresses, failures, were still on the mannequins.

Two young housewives, buffed bodies in biker shorts and halters tops, both pushing custom strollers, appraised the dresses. The blonde pressed her hands to the glass and peered into the salon. Maybe she'd like to come in and try it on? She could easily afford it. Jesus, her baby's stroller cost over a thousand dollars. Her leggings, which looked like Givenchy stretchies were almost double that.

Come in, bitch, spend some of your husband's money.

But then the blonde's baby fussed, and she bent down, kissed the little brat and she and her pal pushed on.

Shit.

Those two had money.

Everybody in town had money.

Except for the Maugham sisters.

And so what if Nikolai made fifty, sixty or even a hundred million? She and Michelle would make close to fifteen. Fifteen million! That was enough for Michelle to get cured. Or fall even deeper into it.

I am not my sister's keeper.

But then her mother's words, whispered through the oxygen mask at the hospital, came to her:

"Promise me you'll look after her."

What could be more cliché or melodramatic than the deathbed request?

Except for the guilt-ridden promise to fulfill it?

Okay, so I am her keeper.

So then why not take the deal? She'd over-ruled Stirling's recommendations before. Twice with terrific results; and that one time, that disaster that almost sunk them. It was money in the bank. Or the promise of money in the bank.

Boris had said that Nikolai would even advance them a quarter-million against future profits once the contract was signed. By both sisters.

"Our signatures are like rocket fuel? Is that what you're saying, Boris?" Joelle had asked during their speakerphone meeting. "Speed things up?"

"And get business booming."

THIRTY-TWO

THE SHOT ROARED.

Crows flapped away, chipmunks dove into their burrows, mice scurried under fallen tree trunks.

Randall Williams thudded into the hard mountain path, his nose breaking as it smashed against a rock, his blood just a small red blotch because his heart had pumped its last as he crashed to the earth and lay still.

Then the forest was still too; the animals listening on full alert.

"Vot the fock, Igor?" Vladimir shouted. "Vhere you get gun?"

Igor ignored Vladimir and squatted down, keeping the small but effective PSM pointed at Randall's head, even though he knew Randall had died instantly.

The Pistolet Samozaryadny Malogabaritny, Russian for "compact self-loading pistol" could penetrate 55 layers of Kevlar, so Randall's skull, no matter how thick and bony, was no match. Igor was sure he'd heard the bullet that had passed through Randall's head, hit a tree twenty-feet down the path, followed by his skin, bone and brains.

Vladimir came up to Igor and pointed at the small automatic.

"You hid this vhere?"

"Could have been between ass cheeks, it's so small."

Igor was joking, but Vladimir knew it was a possibility. The PSM was 21mm wide. Its grip panels were thin aluminum. An average man's hand engulfed it.

Randall had confiscated their weapons. "No offense to you, but this is my number one rule, and it applies to anybody and everybody. And that is – absolutely no weapons."

Randall made a big show of stowing Igor's 9mm and Vladimir's Glock in a special backpack printed in camo fabric and secured with a heavy-duty lock.

Igor pulled the camo pack from Randall's shoulder. "Vhere you think he has key?"

Irog lifted Randall's parka to look in the guide's pockets and stopped.

"Look this."

He undid the leather strap on a leather hip holster and held out a Colt. 45.

"Focker was secretly packing."

Igor handed the gun to Vladimir and rummaged in Randall's pockets and found the key. He released the lock and pulled their weapons.

"So now ve even more armed and dangerous."

Igor rolled Randall over onto his back. Vladimir gagged. The PMS fired a specially-developed new kind of bullet: spitzer-pointed, full metal jacket, steel conical core. It had taken out most of Randall's face as it exited. His right eyeball hung down like some ghoulish caricature from a horror movie. He had no forehead, nose or facial features on his left side. It was pure gore. Gore that didn't seem to affect Igor.

Igor flew through Randall's jacket and front pockets and extracted the dead man's wallet and what he was really looking for: his cell. It hadn't rung on their trek, most likely because making a connection in that remote an area was impossible. But twice Igor had seen Randall slip his phone from a pocket while he was leading them on the trail. He thumbed the cell on and went to the text messages.

This cocksucker's pissing me off.

He scrolled down to the next one.

One more whine and he's toast.

No response from his sons.

Igor trudged a dozen yards up the steep trail to where it took a sharp right turn, and he looked down. He could see a dirt road, empty in either direction. There was a small turn-out area for the rendezvous. The Rebel was parked nose-to-tail with the Randall's Jeep. Bart and

Steve were shooting the shit, from their driver's seats, waiting for their dad.

Igor painfully tapped out a message, making several mistakes before he finally could hit send:

Bring shovels.

THIRTY-THREE

"YOU EVER BEEN BURIED?"

"In paperwork?" Cole said.

Amelie smacked his shoulder.

"No, in the sand. Up to your neck?"

They were laying on the warm sands of Makena Oneloa Beach on the Southside of Maui.

Why they'd had to travel three thousand miles to lay on sand that to Cole seemed just like the sand of Ciudad de Los Reyes struck him as funny, but he didn't mention it to Amelie.

"I think I may have dug a hole and sat in it by the water's edge." He turned his body to her, bent his arm up and rested his head on his hand. "Up to your neck isn't something you can usually do by yourself."

"This is true. When I was nine we went for a family vacation in Majorca; all twelve of my cousins, my aunts and uncles and my Grand-maman. And because I was the youngest, Paolo, who was the oldest, decided I should be buried. Paolo was my uncle Pierre's only son, and just like his father, who I hated, a real bastard. So, Paolo directed the others because of course, he couldn't get his pouf hands dirty, to dig a hole not too far from where the waves broke, and then forced me to sit in it while my cousins buried me up to my neck."

"And then he told everybody to leave you," Cole said.

Amelie looked at him in surprise, then smiled.

"It's that common a story?"

"Hardly. But the bastard part was a big clue."

"You are a natural detective."

"Yes," he said, and with his left hand lifted the small zigzag patterned triangle of her Missoni Mare bikini. "And I am looking for clues."

"No," she said, "people might see."

"We're the only people for about a hundred yards." His hand slipped down.

"Oh..." she gasped softly, "what clues?"

"I am wondering what happened to your hair?" His fingers glided over her naked mons and paused at the top of her cleft.

"A bikini wax for a bikini. Appropriate, no?"

"Dangerous, too."

"Oh?"

Cole's middle finger moved lower and caressed the now-moistened bud of her sex. But Amelie clamped her hand over his and stopped any further movement.

"We cannot do this here." She pulled his hand away and jumped to her feet.

"The hotel?" Cole said.

Amelie didn't say anything and sprinted for the ocean and dove into the water. Cole got to his feet and watched for her head to pop up, moving for the surf as he did, slightly anxious, until her wet, glistening hair appeared fifty yards out.

"I've heard of cooling your heels," Cole said after he'd swum out and joined Amelia who was treading easily, the bottom far below them in the clear water. "But this cools every part."

She smiled and wrapped her legs around his middle. "Are you sure?"

Later, when they were back on the beach, resting on their towels, Cole said, "When your cousins left you there, up to your neck? As the waves got closer, weren't you afraid?"

"No. Because I knew that I could always hold my breath for a single wave."

"But what about as the tide got higher?"

"I could always cry. And every mother since Eve knows her child's voice."

THIRTY-FOUR

PYTOR'S TONE WAS RESPECTFUL.

"I am sorry, Nikolai, no one expected this."

"Successful management," Voronov's voice was calm but with a definite edge as it came through Pytor's cell, "demands anticipation."

Pytor's mind was racing as he listened: How had Nikolai tracked him down?

How had he connected Igor and Vladimir to him?

And as if he was a mind reader, Nikolai said, "Why you have not taken care of Igor like the rabid dog that he is that he is puts your business at risk. And your risky business that has a domino effect on mine."

Pytor didn't like the way this conversation was going. Yes, Nikolai wielded great power and influence. But he was, in Pytor's mind, just like him: another Russian podnikatel. And if another businessman disrespected you, well, they didn't – not if they were smart.

"I will take care of it," Pytor said, sharply. "I have Oleg and Misha out looking for him as we speak."

Which came as a surprise to Oleg and Misha who weren't looking for Igor, but looking right at Pytor as he was speaking to Nikolai. Pytor waved a finger at them to be silent, while he smiled and nodded his head at the phone: fock this guy.

"And if they find Igor and Vladimir, have you anticipated your next course of action?"

The question threw Pytor.

In the few moments of silence, Nikolai said, "Pytor Gusarov, we are approaching, as the scientists say, 'Critical mass.'"

"Vot are you saying?"

"That you need to take your head out of your ass. That you take care of them by taking care how you do it. Do you understand?"

Pytor again wasn't sure what Nikolai was saying but wasn't about to admit it.

"Yes, I understand."

"Then I will expect that their story dies just like they will: quietly."

"Igor and Vladimir who?"

"Precisely. I anticipate an expansion of business within the next few months.

Business that will require associates who know how to do business. Who are smart, trustworthy, and, most of all, able to see the long view."

Holy shit, is Nikolai making me an offer?

"I will make sure I am that associate."

"I look forward then. With anticipation."

THIRTY-FIVE

"HOPE SPRINGS ETERNAL."

"I'm glad somebody's an optimist," Mollie said. "Because we've got bupkes on these guys."

"Sooner or later their luck has to run out."

"We're way past later."

"And sooner can't come soon enough."

"If ever. Now that Zoey's funeral is over, other than shows like TMZ and Entertainment Tonight..."

"Airheads talking hot-air," Cole interrupted.

"I agree," Mollie said. "But except for those and her die-hard fans, she's dropped off the radar."

"You think the Feds have stopped looking for them?"

"No, but I'd bet they're no longer a top priority. You know how bosses are. They want action on a certain case, that's what they're getting."

"Like Riley and us."

"Exactly."

"I was thinking of blocking his number on my cell. Then at least I could call him back when I felt like talking."

"Meaning after you'd had a chance to figure out some bullshit."

"Mollie Simmons. You cut me to the quick."

"Cole, if you block him then he'll call me."

"How do you figure?"

"Because you don't answer? His phone rolls over to me."

Cole looked at Mollie. They were leaning against their unmarked car in the department's parking lot, drinking coffee.

"You have any idea why Matt's so fixated on this? Giving Riley shit, which he in turn passes on to us. I mean like you said, she's dropped off the radar, why keep bringing it up? The sooner people forget about it, the sooner they'll get back to normal. And Gaylord can relax and rub his hands and watch property values rise."

"Which means his value also rises and he's re-elected for another term."

"Well, we still haven't talked to Sid Kent."

Mollie's eyes sparkled – the chase was back on.

"Right. I'd sort of forgotten about him."

"I'd like to know if he knew he was going to be a father," Cole said.

"Holy shit! You don't think?"

Cole tossed the rest of his coffee to the ground. There was a trash can ten feet away. He was going to try his best Steph Curry, but Mollie handed him her cup, so he walked them both over and dumped them into the bin.

"It would solve a lot of problems that could've reared their pointed little head," Cole said as he walked back. "I've heard Tanya Kent is a real ball-buster."

"As only third wives can be," Mollie said. She opened the door and slid into the passenger seat.

Cole got in and started the engine, the Crown Vic's powerful engine roaring to life.

"Let's go talk to a rich man."

"In this town that could be a couple thousand."

"Rich man worrying."

THIRTY-SIX

DEAD MAN PISSING.

That was the trap Igor had set for Bart and Steve Williams. He had propped their father with his back to them leaning against a tree as they came up the trail. He'd wedged Randall's canteen between the dead's man bulk and the tree, the cap slightly unscrewed, so the water dribbled out in a slow stream.

On closer inspection, the tableaux wouldn't have fooled the two mountain men. But they weren't going to get the time to do that.

All Igor needed was two seconds of time while their eyes and brains recorded and processed the scene. Two seconds while their concentration and awareness would be focused on their father and they walked past Igor and Vladimir, positioned on opposite sides of the path, their automatics tracking them from behind.

Igor fired first – two shots so fast they sounded like one. The PSM had so little kickback that the first entered Bart's spine at the Atlas cervical vertebrae, blowing it apart, and the second an inch higher at the base of his skull, splattering bones and brains everywhere.

Vladimir's shot from Randall's Colt.45 sounded like a cannon; the 250-grain full metal jacket bullet obliterating the top half of Steve's head, pole-axing him, the mist of red gore from his brains and skull falling over him as he thumped to the ground.

"Focking life, huh?" Igor said.

"What?" Vladimir's ears were still ringing, and he was in a daze from killing the third man in his life.

"I said life is focking veird. Asshole Randall's own gun kills his youngest son."

Before Vladimir could respond, they heard a muffled song - the Star-spangled banner. Igor yanked Randall's cell from his pocket and checked the ID: Baby.

"Must be girlfriend," he said as the cell went to message. He waited until the cell went back to normal, then hit playback.

"Hey Papa Bear, it's Mama. I hope you and the boys didn't have any trouble with those Russkies. Call me."

Igor clicked off. "Calls his vife Baby?"

A new song, barely audible, came from Bart's body. It went to record mode before Igor could roll Bart over and get his iPhone. He checked that ID: Mom.

"She's checking," Igor said. "Vants to make sure family's okay."

Vladimir went to Steve's body. He was patting his pockets when Steve's cell rang. He pulled the phone and looked at the ID: Moms.

After the recording was over, Vladimir checked and saw that Steve had texted his mom five different times since he'd left this morning. "Her baby," he said.

"So text her," Igor said.

Vladimir read the texts again, to get Steve's style and then typed:
Commie bastards didn't make it. Call you later.

"Vait," Igor snapped, his hand out to Vladimir. "Give me phone."

Igor pressed the keypad, then proudly held out his addition:
Love you.

"Focking funny."

He hit send and laughed and laughed.

THIRTY-SEVEN

"THIS A JOKE?"

Sid Kent stormed around his office, "If it is, it's not funny."

"We look like we're laughing?" Mollie said.

"I'm not answering any questions. And I'm calling my lawyer."
Cole stood up.

"And we'll call our boss, Lieutenant Riley. And we'll see who gets here first: Your attorney or the warrant for your arrest."

"Wait, wait," Sid said. "Just a minute. Give me a second to figure this out."

"Nothing to figure out," Mollie said. "You were fucking Zoey, she got pregnant, you told her to abort it, she refused, and you hired two Russian fuck-ups to take care of the problem."

Sid's face went ashen and seemed to collapse into every one of his fifty-nine years.

"What? What? No, no. Oh, my God! I loved Zoey."

"But you didn't want her to have the baby," Cole said.

He was bullshitting, had no idea how Sid felt, but this seemed the best way to cut into his defenses, get him off-balance.

"It's not that I didn't want it, we... I just couldn't have... I mean, how would ... Jesus, I'd lose everything."

"No," barked Cole, getting into his bad cop role. "Losing everything is losing your life!"

He let the volume of his voice buffet Sid and then said, much quieter, "It's also spending the rest of your life in jail, having your asshole be the receptacle for, maybe if you're lucky, just a single three-hundred-pound deviant, who's your cellmate; but more likely for a parade of rapists, murderers and any other kind of criminal you can think of, lashing you to a bed face-down, no pants, and having at your goodies."

"Stop, please."

"Not to forget they'll knock all your teeth out so when they stick their dicks in your mouth, maybe right from your own ass, that you can't bite them. That happened to me? I'd rather be dead," Cole said.

"Can we take a few minutes here and calm down?"

Sid held up both hands in a stop gesture.

"This description of prison life I've heard before, okay? It would be terrifying if I were guilty. But as I said before, I loved Zoey. I wouldn't do anything to make her feel bad, much less harm her."

Cole nodded slightly to Mollie: Your turn.

"Zoey was fourteen weeks pregnant. We will need all of your phone records, your daily calendar, people who can corroborate your statements of where you were, who you saw, what you did for the last six months."

"She got pregnant right away. After she missed her first period, she told me, but she said it was probably just due to all the strain from all the work promoting her new movie. She didn't seem too worried about it."

"What about you?" Cole said.

"A little nagging. But, Jesus, I'm fifty-nine. And I like to think I'm doing okay for my age. But to father a child that late? I didn't think I had it in me, so to speak."

"I wouldn't speak that way," Mollie said. "It's disrespectful. Makes me think you're trying too hard here."

"Nobody gave me the script on how I'm supposed to act. You two blow in here, accost me, accuse me. Damnit, this is scary. Because I'm innocent. And even having to explain it, other people could get hurt."

"If you're innocent," Cole said, "we can keep this from Tanya."

Sid exhaled a long sigh of relief.

"But if you're playing games or withholding, I'll personally tell her," Mollie said. "And trust me, girl-to-girl dishing is the worst."

"It will take me a couple of days to get all of that material together, but I will do it. Anything else you need?"

"Let's start with your phone records. How many cells do you have?"

"Just two. One for company business, the other's personal."

"We'll need history going back six months for both," Mollie said. "I'm assuming your secretary or office manager pays the bills?"

"Colleen. I'll buzz her and ask to get the records."

"She handle just your business appointments, or she get into the personal side, too?" Cole said.

"Business, but she always checks my personal, so I don't get double booked."

Cole and Mollie spent the next two hours with Sid going over his life for the past six months.

"That the secret to becoming rich?" Mollie said to Cole during a break while Sid went to the toilet, "Meetings? Jesus, this guy does nothing but talk to people."

"Whether he likes it or not." Cole pointed to a line on a page of Sid's printed schedule. "You think Josef Cznarniik knows Igor and Ivan?"

Mollie started to respond, then realized Cole was making a joke, pointing out, the enormity and eventual futility of the work ahead of them.

"Because Josef is the only Russian-sounding name we've found so far?"

"Bingo."

"And who's to say it might not be," she scanned the pages, "Joe Daugherty?"

"Or George Fujita," Cole said. Then his eye caught a name of one of Sid's appointments. He traced it down to another sheet, then another. Mollie saw him staring up at the ceiling.

"What?" she said.

Cole didn't answer, but instead pushed the printouts together, picked them up and tapped them on the table so they made a uniform pile.

Mollie waited for an explanation.

"He didn't do it."

"And you know this, how?"

Cole slid his pile to her. "Check the entry for June 27th, 4:00."

"Monsignor Antonio Galati. He's the head priest at St. Ignatius Loyola."

"Count how many times he saw the monsignor."

Mollie's finger traced and flipped pages.

"Ten entries. He was guilty about something."

"But I don't think it was murder."

"Why not?"

"Because the last time he saw the monsignor was two weeks before Zoey died. You go to confession *after* you commit the sin, not before."

Mollie flipped through the pages. "He's been married three times. You have to assume the second or third wife had started out as an affair. Adultery's one of the big ten no-nos, and now he's suddenly getting holy?"

"Impure thoughts? Cheating a business partner? Who the hell knows?"

Cole pulled the pile back to him and searched the pages.

"What're you looking for now?"

"A memo or an entry about charitable contributions. I'd like to know how much St. Ignatius' coffers increased last few weeks."

THIRTY-EIGHT

"V-12 IS HIGHLY PROFITABLE."

Nikolai waited for Alix Bunin to continue.

"Easily our best third quarter ever."

But all the Russian boss did was nod his head. No sign of pleasure or satisfaction at the phenomenal success of his massive realm. Bunin had been with Nikolai for a dozen years; starting as an accounting intern with one of Nikolai's ancillary businesses, and because he'd quickly grasped Voronov 's all-consuming goal of being rich, richer still, had rocketed through management until he now headed the firm.

"Our weapons-grade nuclear materials increased twenty-six percent alone; thanks to a timely distribution of newly-available product."

That was another reason Alix had advanced: his facile mind for obfuscation. Timely distribution really meant they had hijacked a five-truck convoy sent from Russia's nuclear energy center, Rosatom. Newly-available meant that Voronov's team of armed hijackers struck at the convoy's most vulnerable point on a narrow road in the Ural Mountains.

"And the automatic weapons shipments," Alix continued, "was..."

"You know what I want to hear," Nikolai said.

Alix turned to the last pages of his report. "Youssef and Mohammed topped out their production at eighty-two percent. This was due..."

Nikolai slammed his hand on the table.

Alix took a deep breath and continued, "... this was due to a growth of insurgents in the area."

"They need more weapons?"

"No. They quashed the rebellion, which I am told was internal and led by a field supervisor named Jaxaria, who saw the error of his ways and has reformed."

Saw the error of his ways meant he was captured, tortured and set on fire before the hundreds of poppy field workers.

Reformed meant his body was a charred, ghoulish mass of black flesh that the Rasheed brothers kept on the main road to their fields as a grim reminder just in case any of the laborers missed the barbeque.

"Along with their production and the others, our total tonnage was up thirty-two percent; which is even above last year's twenty-seven percent."

Nikolai nodded.

Jesus, at last, something!

"The UNODC estimates that next year, the world market will be over ninety billion dollars."

"Terrible," said Nikolai. "Perhaps that should be one of the topics I discuss in my speech to them in November."

Alix smiled and could only admire Nikolai's audacity: One of the biggest criminals of the United Nations Office On Drugs and Crime, the drug lord they'd code-named White King, was the biggest and most outspoken champion of the organization.

Talk about the fox in the hen house!

"And what about China?" Nikolai said.

"Getting closer. One of our associates has established a valuable link with Ah Fan that should be most advantageous shortly."

The associate was a fourteen-year-old prostitute that had started puberty at eleven and with Nikolai's Chinese associates administering growth hormones had grown into a voluptuous and rapacious bombshell.

Ah Fan, the Directorate of the province where Nikolai was planning to build the first Maugham factory, was addicted to Howin Qiaohui, whose name translated to her best talents – "loyal swallow" and "skillful."

Two traits that Ah Fan couldn't get enough of in his fifty-fourth year of life, thanks to an accelerated ingestion of special Chinese herbs including yin yang huo, ginseng, Devil's Thorn, Shilajit and enough additives to make a big pharma company drool.

China was going to be Nikolai's first factory for the most pragmatic of reasons: it was the biggest market in the world. There were over 2 million heroin users in China and their addiction to it was even more ingrained than their craze for gambling, pornography and every other vice on the planet.

China had the world's largest population that would only get bigger.

"Chinese fock like rabbits. More rabbits, more users."

Most of China's heroin supply came from Myanmar. It was Nikolai's goal to supplant that with his own product.

"Construction starts within the next three months, so Ah Fan's timetable needs to be accelerated."

"Good. The contracts were signed and..."

The look on Nikolai's face told Alix that he'd erred on the side of enthusiasm.

"I want Ah Fan under control *now*. Your timetable does not depend on other contacts. I want him so tightly bound that he can't wipe his ass without asking permission. Tell SW to get busy."

SW was Nikolai's derogatory term for the young prostitute. It meant Super Whore.

"I want her to have more swallows than Capistrano."

THIRTY-NINE

"VHERE FOCK ARE VE?"

Igor slammed the dash of the Rebel. "Doesn't look like national park. Looks too groomed."

Vladimir saw a sign on the right. "That's because is golf course and country club. See sign? Ve lost."

"Ve are not lost."

"Vell, this doesn't look like Sumas National Park."

"Can't be too far away." Igor had decided that they should drive the Rebel until they could steal another vehicle. And after laboriously checking his cell, he'd found the Sumas National Park and figured there'd be numerous families there on vacation or camping or just sightseeing, so they'd have their choice of vehicles to use for the next stage of their escape.

"Goddamn cell," Igor said and shook his phone as if the violence would bring the service back. "You got anything?"

Vladimir didn't even look at his cell. He knew there wasn't any connection.

And that was how they'd gotten lost. Their cell phone service didn't have any towers out in this less-settled and mountainous region of Canada, and without the phone's GPS, they had no idea where they were going. For a few miles, the Rebel's navigation system had worked, but then it too went dead.

Igor stomped the accelerator, and the mammoth SUV roared ahead. "Vhere you going?" Vladimir barked.

"Rich fockers got cars. Maybe we roll up to my cousin's house in a

Ferrari." Igor had finally remembered his cousin's name, Annushka Orlov. He'd Googled and run it through several sites, but she didn't come up in Ruskin or any other Canadian city. But Igor figured like everything else, keep charging forward, something will happen.

"Who knows?" Igor said. "Maybe one of rich fockers vants to buy his vife or girlfriend amazing vatch."

Igor slowed down and turned onto the smooth road of the county club, and the Rebel's big engine coughed.

Vladimir knew what the problem was before Igor could think to look at the fuel gauge.

"You didn't check the gas."

"Vot? No... I..."

He pounded his fist into the Rebel's thick steering wheel, almost veering off the road.

Then Igor started laughing, and laughing loud like he'd just heard the funniest joke in his life.

"Luck holds again."

"How is running out of gas lucky?"

"Ve are done vit it, so who cares vot happens? By time cops or Mounties find it, they have to tow it out."

Vladimir didn't follow Igor's line of reasoning. He just knew Igor's behavior was getting more bizarre and unpredictable.

As the Rebel rolled into the country club parking lot, a young man in a golf cart immediately turned and accelerated for them. He had a big smile on his tanned face. He took off his red Titleist cap, smoothed his blonde hair and then adjusted it, just so.

"Help you, gentlemen?"

Vladimir put a hand out and touched Igor's arm, unseen by the young man.

"We are going to have lunch, Lance," Vladimir said as he read the man's ID badge.

"The Chef's special is fabulous today; as it is every day." Lance chuckled and then said, "Which of our members are you guests of?" Lance saw Igor's face darkening and quickly added, "So... so I can tell them you're here."

Vladimir knew why Lance had sped in their direction. There were no vehicles like the Rebel in the parking lot. All he saw were expensive sedans, exotic sports cars, and a single SUV, a gleaming Mercedes GLE that would never leave the pavement. Lance knew they didn't belong here.

Before Vladimir could answer, the Rebel's engine coughed and died.

"I'm sorry, you can't park here."

"You believe this?" Igor said. "Only two thousand miles and trouble."

Igor pushed open his door and hopped to the ground.

Lance was of average size, so when he saw Igor's massive body loom before him, he wondered if he had been a little over-zealous in his parking lot security duties.

Just then a black BMW M3 pulled behind the Rebel, and the driver put the car into neutral and revved the engine, sending all those ponies under the hood racing.

Shit, just who I needed, Jean-Benlipe Crossley. The spoiled son of the club's richest member.

And to confirm Lance's analysis, Jean-Benlipe tooted the BMW's horn twice.

Lance jumped out of the car and started to jog for Jean-Benlipe. But Igor put out an arm, that to Lance looked like a tree trunk and moved ahead of him.

"Excuse me, sir," Lance protested, but Igor acted like he didn't hear.

"Vot fock's your problem?" Igor snarled at Jean-Benlipe.

Jean-Benlipe's senses were shocked: no one ever talked to him like this. His mouth opened to chastise this man who looked like some outcast from the WWE and then took another look, up-close and personal, when Igor's scarred and tattooed hand slammed down on the door sill of his open window.

"You got hearing problem along vit attitude problem?"

"Sorry, sorry, Mister Crossley," Lance said. "We've just had a little engine trouble with our ... our guests."

Maybe it was the word 'guests' or that Jean-Benlipe decided that with Lance there as a representative of the club, he was safe.

"I have a tee time in forty minutes. Forty minutes!"

Igor's hand compressed into an iron-hard fist and traveled the foot between Jean-Benlipe's door sill and his rich, pampered face, shattering his jaw, in a Nano- second of time.

As Jean-Benlipe's head rocked back and he fell into the black abyss of unconsciousness, Igor pivoted, and he backhanded Lance's nose, pancaking the cartilage and splintering his right cheekbone.

"Igor!" Vladimir shouted. "No-no."

Lance howled in pain as he fell to the asphalt and then went silent as Igor's boot boomed into his temple, giving him what the doctors later called a DAI – a Diffuse Axonal Injury - caused by the stationary brain lagging behind the sudden and violent movement of the skull that rips the brain's structures. These injuries usually happen in car accidents or other similar massive external forces applied to the body and head.

In Lance's case, the doctors later determined, that the tearing caused brain chemicals to be released, which resulted in additional injury. For the rest of his life, Lance would have cognitive recognition problems.

Vladimir scanned the parking lot. Luckily, no other cars or people were around. He bent to check that Lance was still breathing.

"Hide the golf cart," Igor ordered.

Igor ran back to the Rebel and got inside the cab. He shifted the lever into neutral and depressed the button that disengaged the transmission. He jumped to the ground and guiding the steering wheel with one hand, pushed the three-ton vehicle into an empty parking slot.

Vladimir drove the cart to the far edge of the lot where bushes and foliage marked the edge of a small pond.

He jammed the accelerator and just before the cart crashed through the greenery, leaped to safety. The cart's momentum carried it through the willows and into the pond. There was a huge and loud spark as the electric motor died and the car tipped over and sunk almost below the water level. It wouldn't be discovered for hours.

Vladimir jogged back and saw that Igor had dumped Lance into the passenger seat of the Rebel and thrown Jean-Benlipe into the pickup's bed.

Igor slid behind the wheel of the BMW. He inhaled deeply.

"Smell this fockin' car. Smells like new wallet. I love smell of money," Igor said, altering Robert Duvall's line from his favorite movie, *Apocalypse Now*, "reminds me of ... victory."

FORTY

"SO MUCH FOR WINNING THE NOBEL PRIZE."

Cole held up J.M. Coetzee's *Elizabeth Costello*, the Nobel Prize winner for Literature in 2003.

"His book ends up as a prop in an open house? Jesus, what a come down."

The book was part of the furnishings and decorations the interior designer had staged for the town's newest and most expensive home.

"That's either an illiterate designer or a sad commentary on the decline of American literature."

"Probably both," said Mollie.

She brushed her hand over the expensive wall fabric that looked like Grasscloth. There was a glossy brochure on the night table by the bed.

"Guess how much this wallpaper goes for?"

"No idea."

"Almost three hundred bucks a yard. Says so right here."

"Isn't that the most amazing material?" An Amazon-sized blond woman boomed as she entered the room. "The developers spared no expense. No expense." She charged up to Mollie, hand extended, "Hello. I'm Amber."

Amber shook hands with Mollie, then Cole.

"You two are just the most darling couple. Honestly. So how soon do you folks need to find a place?"

"We're just looking," Cole said.

"Oh, I know, I know. We have to start someplace. As long as we start, right?

Amber pointed at the bathroom.

"Did you check out the Master Bath? Remind you of a Roman orgy? I mean that tile! Hand-cut and imported from Carrara. In Italy."

Cole smiled at Amber as he moved past her to escape, but she was quicker and moved so he would have to walk around her to exit the bedroom.

"Do you have a home you need to sell first?" Amber said. "Because I can offer you a package deal for both listing and buying with me. Huge savings."

"Neither. When I said we were looking, I wasn't being coy."

He flipped open his leather badge holder.

Amber's eyes bulged at the gold detective's shield. Her head snapped around as if there was a suspect right there in her open house.

"Chill," Mollie said. "No one's in danger. We're supposed to meet a..."

"Person of interest?"

Amber was eager to show she was clued in on the legal terminology word spin, at least the TV version.

"An interesting person," Cole said.

He moved to his left, away from Amber. She started to follow, but he held up a warning palm.

"We need you to remain here for at least five minutes."

"What? I ..."

"Five minutes," Mollie said.

"Oh, my God, you're not going to shoot anybody?"

"Of course not," said Mollie.

Amber exhaled a long sigh of relief. "Thank you, Jesus."

"She seemed relieved," Mollie said as she and Cole left the house.

"A little too relieved."

"What're you talking about?"

"Amber doesn't really give a shit that someone might get shot in her listing, just that they don't die inside it. Because then, according to California Real Estate Law, the seller and agent have to declare that in the listing."

Cole tapped several keys on his cell.

"Section §1102 of the Real Estate Code. Full disclosure."

"Too bad," Mollie said. "That would drop the price; which it needs to be. I mean thirteen million?"

"It's right on the water. Over four thousand square feet, double lot."

"Hey, pitch like that? You could work for Amber."

"No thanks."

"Too tall?"

"Too too."

Cole slid back the window/wall door that led to the mansion's private patio.

He looked at the ocean and the surfers dotting the blue-green water, their shiny wetsuits in every color of the rainbow.

"Just everything about her."

"I guess it's a good thing that Michelle didn't meet us here," Mollie said.

"Because if Amber saw us talking to her, everyone in town would know about it.

And the last thing she or Joelle needs right now is more attention."

"Thinking about buying the most expensive home in history isn't exactly hiding under a bushel basket. Which makes me wonder."

"About what?"

"I thought they were scrambling for money."

FORTY-ONE

"LIFE'S A STRUGGLE."

That was another of Ben Crane's favorite sayings to Cole.

"And while money ain't everything, it sure as hell beats what's in second place."

Cole was driving back home after the aborted meeting with Michelle, listening to oldies music and Journey's *Urgent* had come on right in the middle of that song's sax blow-out; and his mind then jumped to his namesake, John Coltrane, and then, of course, to his dad.

His father was a straightforward, open man. The most black-and-white man, Cole had ever known. Something was either right, or it was wrong. And arguing the fine points about it was a waste of time.

Ben Trane had grown up on a small farm in Pennsylvania just outside of Lancaster. In the heart of the Amish. Little Ben loved roaming through the green hills and fields with his springer spaniel, whom he named, despite his later creativity with Cole, simply Lady. When an Amish buggy would clatter by on one of the countryside back roads, Ben would stop and watch and wave. Not often, but occasionally, one of the Amish kids in their plain clothes and high-sidewalls haircuts would wave back.

Lady had never been spayed and every season when she came into heat, Ben would make sure she never got out. They were always going to take her to the veterinarian but never had the money.

But Nature's calling is always stronger, and cleverer, than mere mortals, and one day, just that one day, Lady got out. And got serviced by the border collie on the next farm.

Ben's mother, Francis, smiled and said she hoped the puppies would be cute. His father, Joe, said whatever they looked like, they would be Ben's responsibility; and he'd better hope she had a small litter.

Ben's grandfather, Micah, who had come to live with them six months before, was furious. He and Lady had gotten off to a bad start when she snapped at him when he'd startled her. Micah had lashed out with a kick that just missed Lady but left an oblong dent in the drywall.

"He didn't mean it," Francis told Ben later, making excuses for her father. "Sometimes older folks get cranky."

But to Ben, his right or wrong principles already in place disagreed. His grandfather had no excuse. You didn't kick a dog; especially when you'd scared the poor creature and she was only instinctively defending herself.

When the puppies were born, just two, both males, that Ben named Bix and Scott, for Beiderbecke and Joplin, his jazz influences also already in place. The puppies were beyond cute. Francis adored them, even Joe would laugh and smile at their playfulness. Only Micah would brood on them, his eyes dark banks of evil fire.

"If I step in another of their piles of shit, there's going to be hell to pay."

Ben would apologize, remove the offending little mounds, and one time even polished Micah's boots. Didn't move Micah's hate needle an inch.

One morning and Ben remembers it for the rest of his life, Bix and Scott were ten weeks old and he was having breakfast with his mother and her father. And Micah stared out the window where there was a little pond, and said, "Oh, how sad, those little puppies have drowned."

Ben's head ripped around to the pond, but he couldn't see anything from here, the tall rushes blocking his view. But he always remembered two things as he bolted from the table: his mothers stricken look of horror, wasn't directed out at the pond, but to her father; and the other sight, Michah's strong hands flexing involuntarily.

Dix and Scott were laying side by side on the slight incline bank of the pond. Their eyes bulged, and Scott's tiny pink tongue lolled out the right side of his mouth.

Ben fell to his knees and cradled the two dead puppies to his chest. Farmer Pryzblowski, who lived a good quarter-mile away, swore he heard Ben's primal howl.

"It was like a banshee. If that's how banshees sound."

Lady whined and whined for days. She had come running to the pond after Ben's cry and nuzzled her lost children. Her whine was so sad and mournful, Francis cried for days, and Joe was quiet and kept to himself. Micah carried on as if it wasn't that big a deal.

Ben carefully placed Dix and Scott in a blanket and put them in the basket of his bicycle and pedaled the fourteen miles to Doc Stofultz's office. Ben brought his piggy bank on the trip. He didn't know how much was in the piggy, but he hoped it was enough to pay the vet's bill; but if not, he'd work for the doc until it was.

"Could they have been choked?" Ben asked Doc Stofultz.

The vet who clearly loved animals, just by the number of pets he personally had, took a moment and didn't answer, but instead asked his own questions.

"I thought you said they'd drowned?"

"No. That's what my ..." Ben stopped himself from saying 'grandfather' and said "what Micah, my mother's father said."

"And you found them by the pond on dry land? Not in the water?"

And at that moment Ben knew his suspicions were right. Micah had strangled them. Because how could Micah see little Dix and Scott through the bulrushes? How could he know, before Ben or even more telling, before Lady?

"No, sir," Ben finally said. "They were laying side by side on the bank."

"Sometimes, water in the lungs cuts off your oxygen, and your eyes can bulge. That's normal."

"If they drowned," Ben said, "there'd be water in their lungs, right?"

"Yes."

"So, can you check?"

"Let me do a preliminary first."

The vet ran through his initial probing and then examined each puppy's mouth. They both had strains of blood in their throats. Their first and second vertebrae were crushed. He didn't need to look in their lungs. Some vile monster had choked the very life out of these poor, innocent creatures.

Ben watched the vet during the examination, and when he saw the doctor's face blanch while he was examining their little necks, that was another weight dropped on his scales of justice – tipping it forever to the guilty side for Micah.

Doc Stolfutz wouldn't take any money from Ben.

Instead, he canceled the last two owners that were waiting, had Doris reschedule them, and advise them it would be a free visit, and then put Ben's bike into the bed of his pickup and drove Ben home. The entire journey Ben never said a word and held Dix and Scott in their blanket-shroud close to his heart.

Ben put the puppies in his bedroom and went to console Lady. He never heard the conversation between Doc Stolfutz and his parents and Micah clearly, but loud words were exchanged, most of them from Micah. And then Ben watched the vet's pickup drive slowly away in the night, its taillights like twin rubies just before he turned on to Lititz Road to drive home.

Ben buried Dix and Scott in a secret place. Not even his parents knew.

And when Francis tried to console him, Ben just asked to be alone. There were at least five or six times at dinner, which was the only time Ben would sit down at the same table with Micah, when he could sense the assassin's eyes on him. A couple of times Ben would look up and stare directly at the old man; his hatred and rage even deeper than anything Micah could muster.

Three months passed, and the deaths of Dix and Scott had softened into a distant pain for the Trane family.

But one afternoon when Micah was playing solitaire by himself on the oak table in the kitchen, snapping down the cards and bitching when he couldn't get a sequence going, Ben waited until the old man had lost another game and was sliding the cards together.

And at the precise moment when Micah's hands were touching each other, Ben held the sledgehammer so its head was sideways and swung it with everything his eleven-year-old body could summon.

It was the perfect blow.

The hammer's wide head smashed index fingers on both hands, the thumb on the left and the right wrist.

Micah careened out of the chair in shock and pain and crashed sideways out of the chair to the floor. His scream of pain startled Francis so bad she nearly tripped on the stairs running down from the upstairs bedroom.

"You killed Dix and Scott," Ben screamed at his grandfather. He raised the sledgehammer to his shoulder, ready to strike again.

"Confess. I know you did. Admit the truth. Or I will hit you again. And not in your hands."

"I didn't..."

And Micah's denial went into a howl of terror as Ben swung the hammer.

But Ben was jerked back when his father Joe caught the hammer's head from behind with both hands.

There was a lot of trouble at the Trane home for a while. Constable Jefferies came out and talked to everyone and convinced Micah that unless he wanted to face criminal charges as well as the wrath of the community for having the stupidity to sue one of his own kin, to just forget it.

Ben had to talk to the school psychiatrist for a few weeks. And although the doctor gave him a clean bill of health, that was the kind of news that went through their little community like wildfire.

And for more than a year after "The Incident" as it came to be called, boys at Ben's school called him "Runaway Trane," "Off-the-tracks Trane," or "Derailed Trane."

But Ben would just smile and not react. He never talked about what happened.

Micah moved to a senior citizen's home in Florida a few months after Jefferies told him what to do. Over time, before Micah stroked out,

Ben would sometimes overhear his mother and father discussing Micah and Francis would say, softly because she didn't want Ben to hear and feel guilty, that the old man had a hard time holding a cup of coffee and that he no longer played Solitaire. His mother thought it was because Micah's hands were so messed up. Ben knew it was because the game would forever evoke bad memories.

Ben did bust open his piggy bank and had Lady spayed. She lived another eight years, eventually passing in her sleep at the ripe old of fourteen.

"Or ninety-eight in dog years," as Ben would say. "She had a long, good life. Not without its burdens. But then life is a struggle."

You were right, pops, Cole thought as he pressed the clicker and waited while his garage door went up.

You're either innocent. Or you're guilty.

Igor and his buddy won't get away with killing Zoey.

Neither will anybody else connected to it.

FORTY-TWO

"JOELLE, MICHELLE, IGOR, AND IVAN."

Cole wrote the names down and said them aloud as he wrote them in a circle on graph paper. He then drew a straight line from each name to the center of the sheet where he'd written Zoey Martine.

"Nat, can't forget you!" He wrote Nat's name inside the others. "You were closest to her, alive and dead."

He looked at the circle.

"Any other satellites? Yeah. Aleksander and Mikhail. And because I'm just not sure how you connect, you get dotted lines. And we can't forget Mr. Slick."

He wrote Boris's name just above Aleksander's and Mikhail's names.

He drew straight lines to each name and then another longer line to Zoey.

"Five Russians. That's not a coincidence." He studied the diagram. "Igor and Ivan rob Zoey expecting a quarter-million in cash. They don't find it and either by accident or rage, Igor kills her. Aleksander and Mikhail come down for damage control, get busted. Boris to the rescue. So, who's pulling Boris's strings?"

Cole dialed Leslie Berkley.

"Stripes, I need you to run a profile on a Boris Yanayev."

"How deep?"

"To the bone."

"Any soft tissue I'm looking for?"

"Connections. Here, Russia, anyplace."

"Got it."

She hung up. No goodbye, no time frame, just the click and gone. But that was Leslie, aka Stripes. Cole called her "Stripes" because in the six years that he'd known her, she'd never worn a top that wasn't striped. Stripes always and forever: horizontal, vertical, angled; in the wildest color combinations, ever.

Stripes' other idiosyncrasy was a messianic devotion to Star Wars. She probably knew more about droids and wookies and the interplanetary machinations of that universe than George Lucas.

Everything else about Stripes was straight-on. Her IQ was stratospheric, her loyalty beyond question. She'd gone to dark or Berserkley side of her family's history of protest and bucking the system. Her grandparents were acid-dropping hippies back in the '60s; her mom a single parent who fought for Proposition 215, the bill for medical cannabis, and who instilled in Leslie a backbone of character, determination and an uncanny radar for detecting incoming bullshit. Pushing the envelope? She ripped it to shreds.

"Why waste time looking for the needle in the haystack? Just burn down the haystack."

Cole drummed his fingers on the page. He knew Stripes would uncover any secret Boris Yanayev might have. But he wasn't looking for leverage on the Russian attorney, just a window into his business.

"Let's see who's pressing you on this."

FORTY-TWO

IGOR WAS PUSHING THE LIMITS.

The speedo needle of the M3 hovered just below the red zone.

"Igor, you going 128 klicks an hour. Slow down ve don't need cops."

"You mean Dudleys."

"Who?"

"Dudley Do-right. Canadian Mountie cartoon. You never vatch?"

"No."

Vladimir didn't want to tell him that he had watched Dudley and all the other inane cartoons that were smuggled into Russia and broadcast on Saturday mornings, and he thought they were idiotic.

"You miss funny stuff. Dudley and Rocky and Bullwinkle. Crazy."

Igor laughed hard in memory. Too hard, Vladimir thought.

"And Rocky and Bullwinkle fight two Russians, Boris and Natasha."

Igor checked his rear view and side mirrors. Nothing. They were clear. So far.

"Natasha, she would be hot fock."

"Igor, she's cartoon."

"I know. I'm just saying if she vas real, vould be hot piece of ass."

The depression that had been overtaking Vladimir settled even deeper on him. How could he have let himself get so far into this? On a killing spree. Speeding over the limit. On what he knew would turn out to be a suicide mission. Igor was addicted to the adrenaline rush of danger, escalating events, daring the law to try and stop him.

"Igor, slow down!"

"Jesus, vot old lady. Only been few hours. They not on our trail yet."

"And I like to keep it like that. If ve don't call attention, ve have chance. Going ninety miles an hour is yelling, 'Arrest me!'"

"Never arrest us." He patted the PSM on the center console.

Vladimir looked at Igor and decided: It ends now. He slowly eased his hand into his right-hand jacket pocket and gripped the Colt .45.

I've just got to find a quiet spot.

As he watched the landscape roll past, he realized it was all quiet along this road. They hadn't seen another vehicle for at least twenty minutes.

"Pull over, I have to piss."

"Fock, you are old lady. You can't hold few more miles?"

"Up ahead where the road curves, see the trees on the side?"

Igor took his foot off the accelerator, dropped the gearshift into a lower gear and steered the BMW for the crest of the curve. The M3's tight suspension transmitted every bump in the dirt road off the highway, as Igor guided the car for the neck of the trees.

"Ah, fock, I think I go too," Igor said as he opened the door. The expensive car rocked as he heaved his hulk out of the driver's seat. Igor didn't bother to close the door or look back at Vladimir.

"You focker," Vladimir said. "You had to go even more than me and you pretend you big bladder man."

Igor's laugh carried through the silence of the wooded area.

Vladimir eased out of the car, his eyes never leaving Igor's back.

I'll wait until your horse cock is out and pissing.

Vladimir trailed behind until Igor was at the nearest tree and his hands on his zipper, then gripped the .45.

He was five yards away when the whoop-whoop of the police siren shattered the stillness of the day.

Vladimir jerked up, and Igor spun away from the tree and sprayed the nearby ferns. Both men turned and stared as a white Chevy Tahoe with the RCMP insignia bounced onto the dirt road, its lights flashing.

Vladimir stowed the Colt automatic back in his pocket. He stole a glance at Igor who'd calmly returned to baptizing the tree.

Vladimir stood ramrod straight, his hands away from his body, showing the lone Mountie who was still in the Chevy, that he was unarmed and not a threat.

The door opened, and Vladimir's first thought was that the Canadians were a little lax on haircuts. Because this Mountie's blonde hair hung way below the tan brim of the Stetson.

And that's when Vladimir realized it was a woman.

A girl, actually, when she stepped out of the vehicle.

"Afternoon," she said in a tight voice.

Vladimir didn't look back at Igor, but he knew he'd turned, hopefully only his head, when he'd heard the feminine voice.

"Sorry," Vladimir heard Igor say and could tell by the chuckle in Igor's voice and the Mountie's face, that he had turned around sideways, so she could get a glimpse of Igor's dick.

"Turn around, sir," the Mountie said. Her hand went to her holster.

"Do it," Vladimir yelled at Igor. "No one cares about your dick, okay."

Igor's eyes blazed at Vladimir, but he turned around, zipped up and then faced the Mountie again.

"Sorry," Igor said.

"Yes," Vladimir said, "we have been driving all day and had, how you say, 'Call to Nature,' so we apologize for..." he stopped and looked back at Igor.

Igor's eyes were narrowed, like a wolf appraising a lamb. He was measuring the distance to the Mountie and if he could pounce before she could reach the safety of the truck.

"I'll need to see some ID."

"Sure," said Igor, his voice all happy-to-do-it, as he took two steps toward her.

"STOP!"

She stepped back and down into a shooting stance, her Glock 35 already out and ready to fire, as she'd stepped to the side, keeping Vladimir and Igor in her field of fire. And while kneeling reduced her mobility, it also made her a smaller target, much lower than the two huge Russians who loomed like hulking twin towers.

"Sorry, sorry," Vladimir said. "We are not vanting any trouble, please."

"Excellent. You, sir," she pointed the Glock at Igor, "sit down."

"In dirt?"

"Unless you want to be beneath it."

Vladimir smiled. She knew her shit. Intimidate them first.

"Do it, Igor."

Igor glared at Vladimir: traitor.

The Mountie's eyes snapped back and forth from Vladimir to Igor. "Now!"

Igor flung himself to the dirt like some defiant child, his ass sending up a small mushroom cloud of dust.

Vladimir didn't wait to be ordered, and calmly sat down, knees drawn up, both for comfort and to partially shield his hands if he was forced to draw the .45.

The Mountie clicked her radio: "This is Corporal St. Laurent. Fifteen klicks north of Quesnel. Caution: Foxtrot. Possible Code 5."

Her radio squawked, and Igor and Vladimir heard the female dispatcher say, "Evelyn, is this 10:33?"

"Negative."

Evelyn St. Laurent's blue eyes flicked back and forth between the two monster-sized men. Godzilla, she decided, for the defiant one, Kong for the one who'd obeyed without having to show his machismo.

For a moment, her mind flicked back to Godzilla who had proudly displayed his manhood. She'd never seen a cock that big and thick. And that was before the tumescent stage. Jesus.

"Repeat," the dispatcher blasted, snapping Evelyn back to the present, "do you request 10:70?"

10:70 was requesting a supervisor at the scene. Evelyn hadn't streaked through the force, becoming the youngest Corporal in department history by asking for help.

"Negative. Will do 10:69. And if needed, proceed to 10:32."

"Copy. On the 10:32, will have two units en route, as precautionary."

"Copy."

"And Evelyn?" the dispatcher said, "be careful."

"Lots of numbers, huh?" Igor said, working a big smile on his face. Evelyn nodded at Vladimir.

"You right or left handed?"

"Right."

"I want you to get your ID with your left hand and slide it to me."

She checked Igor, but before she could ask him, he said, "Left."

Liar, Vlad thought. What fock you doing?

"But ID is in car."

"No," Vladimir said. "It's in your pocket."

"No." Igor barked. "In car." He glared at Vladimir, his eyes black holes.

"You vant me get?" he asked the Mountie.

"No."

Corporal St. Laurent's instincts said to call in radio code 10:30: Danger. Maybe even 10:72: Alarm/Serious Crime. Her boss, Captain Alain Dumont, always told his troops to err on the side of safety. "I would rather have a beer over your caution, then have a whiskey over your coffin."

"10:73," the dispatcher ordered: Advise Situation Status.

"Proceeding 10:69. Checking Vehicle/Person."

She snapped up to her feet, the Glock rock steady.

Vladimir raised his left hand, showing her his wallet. "Okay, officer, uh, Mountie, ma'am, here is my ID."

Evelyn stopped and appraised Vladimir. "Just hold on to it for now."

"Pussy," Igor hissed at him.

"Vot fock you doin'?" Vladimir snarled back. "Show her your ID now."

But the cunning look was back on Igor's face.

"Excuse me," Vladimir said, his voice stopping the Mountie before she took her third step for the BMW. "My friend alvays making jokes. ID is in pocket." He stared at Igor. "Show her."

Igor gave Vladimir the finger.

Evelyn's police training prodded her:

There's something in that beautiful car that Godzilla's dying for me to see, that Kong wants to keep from me. That's a hundred-thousand-dollar machine. That I've got to see.

She took four fast steps and was at the M3. Her eyes took in the technology, the sumptuous leather interior.

And as she sensed movement out of the periphery of her eye, she saw the small, but seriously deadly automatic weapon in the center counsel. She immediately reared back, her thoughts flying – be careful, call this in, where are they?

And it was those multiple signals, information that no one on the Mounties could process as fast as Corporal Evelyn St. Laurent, that still took a second to accumulate, evaluate and designate into a decision that cost the RCMP her life.

Evelyn's second step back, her mind racing, her Glock coming up, her finger already tightening on the trigger, was her last.

She turned towards the movement she'd sensed just a few heartbeats before – Kong rushing forward, low and fast, a Colt .45 somehow in his hand – and she pulled the trigger. Twice.

Two shots, a nanosecond too late.

Because Vladimir had fired first.

The stolen Colt boomed, fire erupting from the muzzle, sending the .452 diameter heavy-grained bullet at 1700 feet per second, right through Evelyn's protective vest, bullet-proof in name only.

Evelyn's two shots, while fired a nanosecond too late, were perfect.

Both 175-grain bullets hit Vladimir with 625 ft-lbs of energy right in the heart.

Vladimir was dead before he hit the ground.

So was Evelyn.

"Fock, Vlad, Vlad… vasn't supposed to go like this."

He cradled Vlad's head in his arms.

"10:72? … 10:72?"

Igor became a tree, rooted to the ground, afraid to move in case the radio mic, somehow still open, could pick up any sounds he made.

The dispatcher, dedicated to the safety of her fellow officers patrolling the endless miles of Canadian wilderness, and especially the wunderkind Corporal St. Laurent was on high alert. She was the mother bear searching for her cubs.

The radio squawked again: "EVELYN!"

FORTY-THREE

"VLADIMIR!"

Pytor slammed the coffee table.

Misha caught the Heineken bottle before it tipped over and spilled beer on the carpet.

"Fock! Pytor yelled. "Wrong focking guy."

They had been watching the news when a special report came in from Canada with the story on the murder of Evelyn St. Laurent and the discovery of Vladimir's body just several feet away. The field reporter gave all the details, identifying both the Canadian Mountie and her killer.

"Authorities believe there was one or two more individuals possibly linked to this brutal ambush and assassination of the Mountie's rising star."

The reporter went on to give details of Evelyn's distinguished and meteoric career, but Pytor hit the mute button.

"Can you believe he gets away again?" Pytor shouted. "God-fockin-damn! He has more lives than cat."

Pytor's cell rang, and he jumped to his feet as if he'd been hit with a cattle prod. He checked the caller ID.

"Fock."

The cell rang again, but Pytor didn't answer.

Oleg and Misha knew who was calling: Nikolai.

Pytor let the call go to voicemail.

"I vant you two on next goddamn plane to Canada."

Oleg rolled his eyes at Misha but made sure that Pytor couldn't see him. This was mission impossible, a waste of time. Misha nodded that he was on it. He faked dialing, then shook his head.

"Damn phone. Ve got to change carriers, Pytor."

Misha walked outside on the patio to see if he could get better reception and motioned for Oleg to follow him. "American Airlines? Yes, I vould like to know next flight to Canada from LAX. ... Vhere? Uh Vancouver. Yes, I vill hold."

He stepped close to Oleg, making sure that Pytor couldn't hear. "Is maybe forty, fifty thousand in safe."

"Yeah? So vot?"

"So, you think Nikolai's happy? No. Pytor doesn't get results, best shot is that Nikolai has himbeaten or killed. I am betting on killed."

"So vot we do, make him give us combination?"

"I know combination."

"Shit."

"Not shit. Seed money. For me and you," his hand waved between them. "Ve use for start our own bizness."

Oleg was so startled at this idea – the audacity of it, the ramifications of what it meant – that he couldn't think of anything to say.

"Yes? ..." Misha said to the phone. "Okay, four-thirty should be perfect. ... Yes, I have credit card. Vill be two passengers ... hold, please?" Misha put his hand over the phone and motioned for Oleg to go back to Pytor. "Try and get him to go into kitchen. I don't vant him hear me."

Oleg shrugged and moved back for Pytor.

Misha couldn't hear what Oleg said, but Pytor put his phone in his pocket and followed Oleg into the kitchen.

Misha's voice was very low, and he covered his mouth.

"Hello? Yes, I am return. Uh, could ask you favor? Possible to tell me flights going to Miami?"

Pytor looked over and for a moment, Misha thought he'd heard him, but Pytor rotated his index finger, telling him to hurry up.

"Hello? ... No. Not round-trip. One-way only."

FORTY-FOUR

"IVAN'S TICKET GOT PUNCHED!"

Cole clicked off the TV.

"Ivan is Vladimir Bezrodney?" said Mollie. "How'd you figure that?"

"Sheer brilliance. Igor and Ivan-Vlad were headed north. There's a kidnapping and stolen car. The father and sons guide team, murdered, their truck stolen. An assault at the country club of an employee and the son of a rich member, where the dead guide's Ram Rebel is discovered, and the rich kid's BMW stolen. And now a dead Vladimir and a dead Mountie. I'm just connecting the dots."

"Big gap between the dots."

"Maybe. But there aren't too many coincidences that link up like this. They're running for their lives. They're taking cars, but no prisoners. And everywhere they go, people turn up dead."

"We take this to Riley?"

"No. He thinks we dodged a bullet with Aleksander and Mikhail. And he's grateful little Boris didn't rip him a new one. And flying to Canada? Way beyond our pay grade."

"And a long way from the beach."

"If they manage to catch him alive, Canada isn't going to extradite him. They've got him for the Mountie. And even if they did let him go, the FBI will move to the head of the class. We're just on-lookers. Pisses me off. Our turf got violated, and we don't get a chance to defend it."

Mollie searched Cole's eyes, saw the anger within.

"You have any sick days coming?" he said.

"Couple of weeks. Why?"
"Maybe this is private serve and protect."
"What?"
Cole's fingers flew across his cell.
"Yes, Detective Trane for Mister Yanayev."

FORTY-FIVE

"MISTER VORONOV DOESN'T NEED PROTECTION."

"We're not offering it," Cole said.

"Then I don't understand," Boris said.

From Stripe's research, Cole and Mollie knew that Nikolai Voronov wasn't just Boris's main client, he was his only client.

"This is the way it looks to us as police officers. You can confirm or deny."

"And if I do nothing?"

"That's an answer, too."

"So I have lost before I begin?"

"No. You've won."

"Now I am really confused."

"It's simple. Mr. Voronov has a private jet, right?"

"Many."

"So, we're proposing he allow us the use of one of his many jets and Mollie, and I fly to Canada to find Igor."

"This is sanctioned by Lieutenant Riley?"

"We're not doing this as official police business."

"So, this is personal?"

"Very."

Boris steepled his fingers together and looked first at Cole, then Mollie. "And if you manage to find Igor, what happens?"

"We bring him back."

"Dead or alive?"

"Alive. But if he's dead…?" Cole left it there.

"Will you excuse me?" Boris said, and without waiting for an answer walked into his inner office and closed the door.

"What do you think?" Mollie said.

"That you don't need to be part of this."

"Up yours."

"We're violating every law and code we know of, and probably a ton we've never heard of. This isn't a career-making move, it's a career-breaker."

"If we screw up."

"Odds are pretty good we will."

"So why are you doing it?"

"Character defect?"

Boris emerged from his office and gave them a big smile. "Would you mind waiting for a half-hour or so for Mr. Voronov?"

"Now I'll have some coffee," Cole said.

"And try one of the tea cakes. My wife made them," Boris said, his face beaming with pride, "from a family recipe that's been handed down for generations."

"Delicious," Mollie said, slightly spraying the sugary powder as she spoke. "Amazing, actually."

Boris's cell trilled, and he smiled as he read the caller ID.

"Speaking of her. Amazing. I think, sometimes, she is clairvoyant."

He pivoted and strode for his office, the little soldier-husband called to uxorious duty.

Cole and Mollie were both into seconds when Nikolai Voronov and Aleksander and Mikhail arrived.

"Comrades," Cole said to the two bodyguards who ignored him and took up positions on opposite sides of the room.

"Mollie Simmons."

She extended her hand to Nikolai.

"My pleasure," he said.

Nikolai turned to Cole, who had stepped over to join Mollie.

"And Detective Trane."

The two men shook hands – neutral, no power trips.

"Wonderful," Boris said. "There is coffee, water, and desserts."

Nikolai had not taken his eyes from Cole.

"So, I am to provide transportation for you into Canada for what purpose?"

"Solve your problem," Cole said.

"I wasn't aware that I had one."

"Igor's a loose cannon. He gets captured by the wrong forces, he could shoot off his mouth and say the wrong things. Sensitive things."

"But this Igor is not in my personal employ; so, he can get caught, he can say whatever he likes, it does not affect me."

"And yet here you are."

The slightest flicker of Nikolai's cheek told Cole he'd hit a nerve with the Russian billionaire.

"To most Americans," Nikolai said, "you say Russian and depending on their generation, they think Krushev banging his shoe, Gorbachov's birthmark, or Putin hacking the election. And yet, throughout history, Russians have played significant roles in the arts, culture, medicine."

"My father was a jazz musician," Cole said, "but he thought Tchaikovsky was the world's best composer. And not just of classical music."

"Yes," Nikolai said, nodding in agreement. "My grandmother used to play *The Nutcracker* at Christmas and *Swan Lake* during the summer."

"Your businesses extend all over the world. But even one bad apple like Igor can taint them."

"Igor does not work for me. I would never employ a cowboy like that."

"Then let's just say it was someone tangentially connected to you or to someone that works for you or to all Russians. Igor is a rock thrown into the lake that's causing ripples."

"And you will prevent him from causing waves? Is that the next line?"

"Tidal waves," Mollie said.

"The only way anyone knows where's he's been is after the fact and the dead bodies he leaves behind."

"Why are you two better than the cops of California, Oregon and Washington? The FBI? And now the RCMP?"

"We're not," Cole said. "We're different."

"And that would be?"

"We find him; your problems go away. Anybody else finds him, no telling what happens."

"You're talking rendition?"

Again, Cole left the question unanswered.

"My question is: Why? What is so personal about this that you would risk your career? Expose your department to legal issues, not to mention ridicule and loss of prestige?"

"High risk, high reward," Mollie said. "This mutt came into our town, blew away the most popular movie star in the world. We catch him, big feather in our caps."

Nikolai searched Mollie's face; then Cole's.

"No. I don't think you want him breathing after you find him. I don't think this is a 'Dead or Alive' mission. I think it's 'Dead. Period.'"

"No," Cole said. "We uphold the law. We will give Igor every opportunity to surrender. He'll deal the play."

Nikolai nodded at Boris; then led him into the attorney's office and closed the door.

Cole looked at Aleksander and Mikhail, but they kept their eyes high, staring at the French molding at the ceiling.

A few moments passed, and Boris and Nikolai came back into the room.

"When?" is all that Nikolai said.

"Tomorrow's Friday," Cole said. "We'll take that as a day sick leave, and that gives us Saturday and Sunday. Worst case we'll take one more sick day and return late Monday."

"With or without Igor?"

"That's the $64,000-dollar question."

"More like $41-million."

FORTY-SIX

"I DON'T THINK THAT'S RETAIL."

Mollie stared at the sleek Gulfstream G450 jet. "$41-million," she repeated.

The luxury aircraft was parked on a private runway at the south end of LAX, the stairs levered out and waiting for her and Cole to board.

"Nikolai Voronov has never paid retail," Cole said.

"So, this could be closer to fifty million," Mollie said as she went up the stairs, carrying a small overnight bag.

A model in a powder blue uniform appeared at the cabin door. Or a woman as beautiful as any model Mollie or Cole had seen.

"Welcome," she said in perfect English with just the slightest burr of an accent. "I am Veruschka."

Even a model's name, Mollie thought.

Veruschka pointed an elegant arm toward the luxurious interior, which was soft, caramel-colored leather and deep fawn carpeting.

"Hello," she said as Cole reached the top of the stairs and gave him her hand.

"Detective Cole, no?"

"Detective Cole, yes."

Veruschka smiled, her plump pinked lips parting to reveal dazzlingly white teeth. Cole took stored his bag beneath his seat and stretched his legs.

Mollie took the seat opposite him across the aisle.

"My butt has just gone to heaven," she said. "Can you believe how comfortable it is?"

The luxury jet moved as the pilot released the brakes and with the barest increase in engine noise, rolled toward the runway. Cole gazed out of the window as the tarmac spooled past and peered ahead as the plane made a slow right turn and headed for the runway.

As it did, Cole caught a glimpse of the V-12 logo on another luxury jet, a Gulfstream IV.

Cole and Mollie settled back as the G450 accelerated down the runway, gaining speed, and then, as Cole had always thought from when he was a child, defied gravity and magically lifted into the night sky.

Behind them, the Gulfstream IV's engines roared and one of Nikolai's many luxury jets, as Boris had boasted, and started rolling down the runway. It quickly gained speed and launched into the air.

Aleksander and Mikhail settled back into their seats and thought of their mission ahead.

So did a third passenger, Sergey Lomovitov.

FORTY-SEVEN

"RAISA!"

Nikolai punched his intercom.

"Yes, Mister Voronov?"

"Arrange a conference call with Timofey and Ilya."

A moment later, Raisa Tankov entered his office.

"It will take a little time."

"Why?"

"Timofey is at the Kusnetskov home in St. Petersburg. And Ilya has found true love."

"Really?" Nikolai said, his surprise slipping through his usually guarded reactions.

"Yes. A Veronika Yaskin. From Moscow."

Raisa waited to see if Nikolai would have any more questions. She didn't think so and would have been surprised if he had.

Raisa had been Nikolai's first secretary. And his last, as she reminded him every so often. She had vetted and directed the hiring of secretaries and assistants for the oligarch's closest business relationships. She had helped some of them move into higher positions of management, all the while ensuring that they knew how much their advancement had been because of her. She also made sure none of them got too close to the throne.

It was a quality she shared with Nikolai, playing the long game, anticipating moves for power, no matter how subtle, from within the ranks, sometimes long before the players thought of it themselves.

Raisa was paid very well by Voronov. Far more than she needed to raise her daughter, Tatianna. And unknown to Nikolai, she would follow up his investments with purchases of her own. Trailing in his wake, she was now her own millionaire.

And like him, it was all held close to the vest.

"I will buzz you as soon as they're both on the line," Raisa said and went back to her office.

Nikolai nodded, his mind now on Oksana Kosar, the Maugham's young sales clerk who was also from Rostov-on-Don. Was she connected to Igor and Vladimir and therefore to Zoey Martine? He didn't like unanswered questions.

And not being able to locate Oksana worried him.

He hit the intercom button, "Raisa?"

"Yes?" she answered immediately.

"What's the situation in the air?"

"According to Veruschka, the detectives are enjoying the chilled Dom with appetizers."

"And the Gulfstream IV?"

"Aleksander is sleeping, and Mikhail is watching a movie."

"And Sergey?"

"Dismantling and cleaning his rifle."

"Again?"

"Compulsive."

"Thank you."

Nikolai clicked off and looked out his office window.

Sergey had come over from the KGB's Komitet Čierna, Black Ops, special group. He'd only been with Nikolai for three years but had proven himself invaluable. He had already taken out four of his enemies with his SV-98, Snaiperskaya Vintovka Model 1998 rifle.

The elimination that pleased Nikolai the most was the disposal of the self- serving bureaucrat Konstatin Zima who'd greedily taken Nikolai's bribes and favors, and women, always the women, and then sat on his fat ass, doing nothing.

Zima's death was good for business both in the bottom line and keeping other politicians in line.

Nikolai also was pleased with the way Zima was killed. Zima was

1,000 meters away when his head exploded like a ripe cantaloupe from the SV-98's 7.62x54R 7N1 sniper bullet from Sergey's rifle.

1,000 meters!

The distance still amazed Nikolai.

Not that Sergey would be so far away when he took out his targets in Canada:

Igor, Mollie, and Cole.

Igor because he had disobeyed.

The two detectives because he didn't like loose ends. Of course, they were only targets if they found Igor. If not, they'd return home and go on with their lives.

Ironic, their success will be their downfall.

But they deserved what they got. Their sheer arrogance that they were smarter than all the combined forces of several states, the United States government and the legendary RCMP. An arrogance that led them to violate their own department's regulations and go rogue.

One of his other men would take care of Pytor. For a man who'd had to flee his country, who had been boxed out in Boston and then had some small success in Los Angeles, Pytor had screwed up badly. He should have done better research on Igor.

And, yes, Nikolai knew of Igor's reputation as an incredibly brave fighter who had saved Pytor's life on two occasions, but that same mentality also caused problems. Why had they attempted to rob Zoey in the first place? What did they expect the movie star to have? Did they have any connection to Oksana?

Nikolai punched the intercom again. "Have Bruno search for Oksana Kosar."

Bruno Campanini was one of the few non-Russians that were part of Nikolai's inner circle. The young Italian who ran his security network out of Milan was blindingly brilliant. He had uncovered vulnerabilities in Nikolai's corporate empire, exposed two secret hackers who had siphoned off hundreds of thousands from V-12 and demonstrated his loyalty to the extent that even Raisa became a fan.

"Anything special he should look for?" Raisa asked.

"Start with Rostov-on-Don, our mutual hometown."

FORTY-EIGHT

"TWO THOUSAND LIGHT YEARS FROM HOME."

Cole sang the Rolling Stones song as the G450's wheels hit the private runway in Canada.

"Feels that way," said Mollie.

"I know. I keep asking myself what the hell did I get us into?"

"Travel, adventure. Maybe ten years."

"You can stay on board, and they'll take you back. No harm, no foul."

"You say that again, and I'm going to shoot you." She looked at him. "With an untraceable .38."

"That's one of the reasons. Think of it: we're in a foreign country, didn't go through customs and carrying drop weapons."

Mollie pulled her carry-on bag from the storage area. "Hopefully we won't have to use them."

"So, we are all okay?" Veruschka said as she pushed open the hatch.

"We're great," Cole said.

Mollie nodded her goodbye to Verushka and went down the stair-ramp. As Cole came up to Verushka, she smiled and shook his hand. He felt a piece of paper against his palm, just as he saw the co-pilot wave from the cockpit door. He slipped his hand and the paper into his pocket then waved back at the pilot.

"Smooth flight," Cole said.

"Thank you," the pilot said.

"You will call, yes?" Veruschka whispered.

"Yes," he said, his voice just as low.

FORTY-NINE

"YES!" MOLLIE'S VOICE WENT UP TWO OCTAVES.

She pointed at a shiny Range Rover that Nikolai had provided for them.

"I'm driving."

After they'd stowed their bags, Mollie started the engine and accelerated for the gate. Cole glanced in his side mirror.

"We might have company," he said.

"What'd you mean?"

"I thought I saw landing lights from another plane."

He turned and looked back out his window, but the cyclone fence along the road was battened down with thin strips of wood in a crisscrossed pattern that blocked his view.

Cole settled back in his seat and watched the dark ribbon of road in the Rover's headlights, set on high, that bounced off the asphalt and glittered the tall tree trunks that lined both sides of the highway.

Behind Cole and Mollie, Nikolai's Gulfstream IV feathered its engines for landing, its lights illuminating the flight crew that raced to chock the wheels and get the stair-ramp in place.

The door opened, and Aleksander stood on the platform and stretched.

"Fock," he said, "it's cold. And this is June."

"Velcome to summer in Canada," said Mikhail. "Don't blink or you miss it."

He chuckled at his lame joke as he followed Aleksander down the stair-ramp.

Behind them, Sergey waited, his hand tight on his gun case. Ilya, the co-pilot, leaned out from the cockpit and gave him a thumbs up. Sergey grunted in acknowledgment; then went down, two stairs at a time, so when he hit the ground, he transitioned into a jog smooth as a Maserati shifting gears.

FIFTY

"PULL OVER."

"What?"

"Indulge me."

Mollie guided the Rover to a curve in the road and braked. Cole was out, flashlight in hand before the vehicle had stopped. As it rocked on its suspension, he bent down and played the light under the chassis. Mollie got out, leaving her door open, the muted ding of the Rover's warning bell loud in the quiet night.

"What're you looking for? A device?"

"Yeah."

He duck-walked back along the driver's side. Mollie clicked on her flashlight and checked her side.

"Let's trade places," Cole said. They came up empty.

"Let's go back, the other way," Mollie said, "together."

The Rover had less than three hundred miles on it, so the transmission, drive train, axles, springs, mufflers and all the other steel and fiberglass and plastic that make up modern machines was still clean.

"There!" Cole barked. "There."

He shone his light right behind the transmission. A small black box pulsed with tiny green lights.

"I'll be goddamned. How'd you know?"

"Something just kept nagging me. Voronov's too much the puppet-master. Likes to control everything and everybody. No way he was going to just let us roam around up here on our own without keeping tabs on us."

"Should we take it off?"

"And put it on another truck going to Montreal? Too Jason Bourne. We see how it plays out."

They got back into the Rover, and Mollie floored it.

Aleksander never noticed that the GPS tracking device had stopped for ten minutes: he couldn't get the software to work.

"Fock, fock, fock! I hate goddamn electronic shit."

Behind him, Sergey sat in the back seat and shook his head. Amateurs. Why did Nikolai send kids to do a man's job?

Mikhail drove a Rover twin to Cole and Mollie's at a steady pace. "You need to get that to vork and fast. Road is straight, but if ve come to a turn, how the hell we know which vay they vent?"

"I'm trying."

"Turn off," Sergey said. "Reboot."

Aleksander was about to tell him don't be stupid, but something in Sergey's voice made him reconsider, and he complied. He waited a minute, then restarted.

After the device went through its process, there was a soft bling followed by the pulsing turquoise light of Cole and Mollie's vehicle moving at a steady pace.

"Hey!" Aleksander said, "it worked. Score one for Sergey."

Goddamn kids.

FIFTY-ONE

"ALEKSANDER AND MIKHAIL?"

Mollie couldn't believe it.

"You're serious?"

"Who else would it be?"

Mollie checked the rearview and her side mirror. The road behind them was black and empty. "And maybe a third."

"A third?"

"Best guess? A shooter."

"For us?"

"Maybe. Depends on how we do at finding Igor."

Cole tapped several keys on his iPad and linked it up to the Rover's Navigation system. After a moment, their route appeared on the panel.

"You think he's got friends up here? Or relatives?"

"I'd bet on it. Unless he and Vladimir ran north because it was safer than going south. What with ICE and the border patrols. Although the flood of illegals are people coming into America, not leaving."

"And two behemoths their size would have a hard time blending in."

But Igor was blending in by moving fast.

He'd taken the Mountie's wallet, then her Glock.

He'd thought about taking Vladimir's wallet, but decided that his cousin shouldn't die nameless. He sprinted to the BMW and roared away. But as he drove, his eyes blurred with tears, filled with shame and hatred for focking up yet again, he glanced at the fuel gauge. The needle was falling. This beast chugged gasoline.

Igor shifted into neutral and coasted the last twenty yards before the BMW's low-profile tires bumped across the uneven entrance to the Petro-Canada station and made it to the pumps before the engine coughed and died. "Fock, vas too close." He flipped open Evelyn's wallet. One focking credit card. Capital One.

Vot's in your vallet?

He flashed on Samuel Jackson talking to camera. You vonder how much money they have to pay Samuel? He makes so many goddamn movies every year, they must pay him fortune to take time away to make commercials.

He looked at Evelyn's photo. Nice looking. Jesus who vould have thought she vas killer-bitch? Igor replayed the scene in his head.

He still couldn't believe how fast the Mountie had drawn her Glock and shot Vladimir twice – twice! – and Vladimir had the advantage, Randall's Colt .45 already out. And Vlad's shot he hated to admit was probably just luck.

The thump on the passenger window startled Igor.

"Hi," a small woman in her forties said through the glass. "Can I help you?"

She pointed to the window and motioned down.

It took Igor a few seconds to find the right button before it slid down with a whisper.

"Hi. I'm Connie," she pointed to the name embroidered on her shirt. "Fill her up, right?"

"Yes."

"Credit or cash?"

Igor had bombed down the highway at over 80; so, it was just about an hour that he'd left Vladimir and Evelyn. The Mountie's radio had been blasting, so Igor assumed the RMCP got there within ten minutes. Another ten minutes to appraise the scene, realize her wallet was gone and call it in.

Fock it, worth a shot.

"Credit." He gave her Evelyn's card. His hand went to his pocket and touched the grip of the Mountie's Glock.

But Connie didn't look at the name; just inserted the card and pulled it back out. She waited for the green accepted light and then handed it back through the window. "Nice car."

"Yes, thank you."

But his answer was drowned out by the overhead thumping of a helicopter flying low.

"Wow," Connie said. "There must be some big stuff back that way. Haven't seen one of those RMC choppers around here in years."

Igor waited for the chopper to circle back, but the roar from the blades faded into the distance.

Going to the crime scene. On the hunt, looking for someone.

Me.

Igor tapped his foot and watched the numbers spin on the gas pump. Finally, it dinged and stopped.

"You need a receipt?"

"No."

Connie had just pulled the pump handle, closed the fuel flap on the BMW before he started the engine. Her thank you never reached his ears because he was already rolling toward the exit.

She was surprised when she saw the BMW's special-issue license plate.

Instead of the usual rectangular shape, this was the left-to-right profile of a running polar bear, all white, with a bluish tint on its feet. It was a limited edition, awarded only to vehicles registered in Canada's Northwest Territories, it's most far- flung and rugged frontiers – land that stretched to the outermost tip of the Northern Hemisphere, the Arctic Ocean touching its shores.

"Northwest Territory," Connie said aloud. "The next chunk of land after that's the North Pole."

Connie watched the BMW disappear around a curve, flying.

"You're a long way from home," she said. "Long, long way."

FIFTY-TWO

"I'M A FEW BLOCKS AWAY."

"But, Nikki, I'm not dressed," Michelle protested.

"Even better." Nikolai Voronov looked over at the legal folder on the soft leather seat of his Bentley Mulsanne. "And I have a present for you." He sniffed loudly.

"Oh, god, you're awful. Give me fifteen minutes."

Yes, there's blow, he thought as he ended the call.

But the real gift is the small concession I made, just for you, in the contract.

"And you will focking sign it!" He slammed the leather-covered steering wheel – the words and anger bursting from him involuntarily.

He glanced over to the other lane to check if a driver had seen him. He wasn't worried that anyone could have heard him cossetted as he was in the $400,000 luxury and silence of the car, just that he'd allowed his emotions to show. But he didn't have time to waste. Things were approaching critical mass.

The Kusnetskov brothers were growing restless. Getting them to heel wasn't a problem, but Nikolai disliked altering his plans once they were ordained; unless there was a better opportunity or an advantage to do so. That's why he had made a small concession in his proposal. A small change that seemed to have greater profit potential for Joelle and Michelle Maugham, but thanks to two other equally small changes deep in the contract, had zero effect on Nikolai's bottom line.

"Oh, Nikki, thank you," Michelle said.

After the sex. After the cocaine.

"For what?" he said, the provocateur.

"For the changes to the contract." She looked in his eyes and reached down for him. She held him for a moment, feeling him start to swell, and then took the glassine bag of pharma-flake and sprinkled the last of the powder on the mushroom head of his penis. "Your cock reminds me of a piece of art."

Nikolai laughed. He had heard a lot of compliments about his penis, but never that it was artistic. "Museum quality, eh?"

"Absolutely. There's a sculpture by the German Expressionist, Ernst Barlach, of a soldier, wrapped in a blanket and his helmet looks just like Nikki, junior here."

"Without the hole in the top?" Nikolai wasn't sure where this talk was heading, but it had definitely crossed into weird territory.

"The Nazis said his art was degenerate."

"Appropriate, no?"

"Yes. Because I'm going to do blow and then blow." She laughed and bent down and inhaled the coke. She ran her tongue over the tip of his glans, teasing him while making sure she got the very last of the drug. Her eyes were already glassy and bright when she looked at Nikolai, opened her mouth and took him so deep in her throat, she gagged.

Later, when Michelle was in the shower, Nikolai Googled the artist. He had intended to find the sculpture Michelle had mentioned but got lost in the artist's oeuvre.

Some of the artist's creations were amazing. His favorite was a sleek, aerodynamic work of a man with a sword poised to strike. He found the soldier in the blanket and did agree that the helmet and his cock did look alike. He was about to dial Raisa and have her inquire about Barlach and if any of his art was for sale when Michelle's cell rang. It was on the nightstand, too tempting not to see who was calling.

He answered when he saw the caller ID.

"Hello, Joelle," he said, enjoying the involuntary intake of her breath, then the quick recovery.

"Oh, Nikolai. I was... expecting my sister."

"Yes. It is her phone. She's in the bathroom. May I take a message?"

"No, I'll call her later."

"I'll tell her. And Joelle?"

He puckishly waited until she said, "Yes?"

"I've made some concessions in the contract. In yours and Michelle's favor."

Another short intake of breath.

"Oh, really? Like what?"

"Michelle can tell you. I'm sure you'll like them too."

He ended the call without saying goodbye because he found that he was engorged.

It's Joelle that you really want.

The water stopped running.

Nikolai grabbed his Derek Rose pure silk boxers, slipped into his trousers. His shirt and shoes were by the bedroom door mixed with Michelle's underwear where they'd thrown them as they plunged onto the bed. He grabbed a shirt, shoes, and socks in full stride.

"Nikki?"

She was still in the bathroom.

He eased open the front door as he heard her call him again, this time a little louder, with a little more curiosity. He raced across the lawn, his shirt half-on, and flung open the door to the Mulsanne. He pushed the starter button with the door not yet closed, the dinging of the warning bell sounding as he put it into gear. He always backed into driveways, an old habit from his early days, always be prepared to leave quickly, and the car was rolling as he slammed the door.

He saw a flash of Michelle at the front door in the side mirror but didn't check to confirm. Better that he could deny it. His cell rang as he rolled through the stop sign. He didn't need to look. It was Michelle. After it went to message, he thumbed a reply:

Emergency. Can't talk. Make sure Joelle signs.

FIFTY-THREE

"YOU MISSED SIGN!"

Sergey almost slapped Mikhail.

"Vot? No fockin' vay," Mikhail said. "Look at the GPS. Turn still ahead."

The tension in the Rover was electric. They had been tracking behind Cole and Mollie for over three hours. And the pressure was mounting.

Mental and emotional pressure.

And for Aleksander, bladder pressure.

He'd had three vodkas on the flight, then tried to balance out the alcohol with three cups of black coffee.

"Pull over, I have piss like racehorse."

"NO!" Sergey's voice bounced off the windows.

Mikhail looked at Sergey in the rear view.

Aleksander snapped his head around, right into the dull metal snout of Sergey's Desert Eagle .50 automatic.

"No time for pissing," Sergey growled.

Aleksander thought of pulling his Glock 20 and shooting this asshole right through the seats, the 134-grain load bullet having more than enough power to do the job. But he had to reach into his pocket without being discovered, then shoot through the seat, while Sergey only had to move his finger a half-inch.

"Piss out door or window."

Aleksander and Mikhail laughed.

"You fockin' crazy?" Aleksander said.

"Ve are not stopping."

"Ve have tracker," Mikhail said. "Alvays know vhere dey are going."

Nothing from Sergey.

"You vould shoot me over pissing?"

Sergey didn't blink, didn't move.

"You should have gone when we stopped for gas."

An hour earlier, their GPS showed the blinking dot at a standstill. Mikhail had slowed down and then pulled into a gas station. He had jumped out and filled the tank, paid and was back behind the wheel in record time.

"Fock it," Aleksander grumbled. He slid down the window. He undid his safety-belt. He glanced for a second at Mikhail and rolled his eyes. He unzipped his pants and slipped them down. He pulled himself out of his jockeys with caution: He had to go so bad the wrong touch would release a flood of urine all over himself.

But the assault of cold air rushing past his penis shocked him at first and he clamped up.

"Like going in ocean, huh?" Sergey laughed. "Dick shrink you piss all over yourself."

Aleksander strained, but that just made it worse. He was cramping.

Sergey hit him in the middle of the back with an open palm, the blow knocking Aleksander up against the window frame and the shock broke the dam. His urine exploded in a gush that hit the chilly Canadian air and flew back past the Rover.

Mikhail hit the power button and slid Sergey's window down and some of Aleksander's piss blew back into the cabin.

"Sorry," Mikhail said. He slid Sergey's window back up, smiling to himself. He looked in the rear view at Sergey.

Damn, he looked even colder and more evil.

Shit, may have focked up.

But Mikhail didn't scare easily. If Sergey wanted to expand his targets to include him and Aleksander, good luck.

Aleksander finished and plopped back into his seat. He zipped up and said, "Okay, piss break over. Put fockin' gun away."

"Sergey's gun," he said, strangely switching to third person. "Sergey decide if gun is in or out."

Aleksander was about to say something, but Sergey cut him off, "Look at screen!"

"Vot the fock?" Mikhail said. "They coming back?"

He couldn't believe what he saw on the screen. The pulsing turquoise dot that was Cole and Mollie's Rover was closing the gap, heading back towards them.

"Pull over," Sergey said. "Up by trees."

Mikhail automatically turned off the road, not caring that Sergey had given him a command. He was too rattled. His eyes, along with Mikhail's and Sergey's, flicked back and forth from the dashboard to the road, waiting for the electronic signal to become a physical vehicle.

"Here they come," Aleksander yelled, his voice rising with tension.

But it was a white Ford Explorer that came hurtling around the bend, not Nikolai's black Range Rover.

Mikhail and Aleksander's heads flipped from the GPS to the Ford as it sped past them.

"Vot the fock? They changed cars?" Mikhail barked.

"No, stupid," Sergey said. "They found GPS." He pointed out the windshield.

"Go, go. They can't be that far ahead."

FIFTY-FOUR

"THEY'LL NEVER CATCH UP."

Cole checked the rearview mirror and smiled because the road was empty and black behind them. No faint glow of headlights.

"And there's no way of them knowing which way we went," Mollie said.

When they'd stopped for fuel, Cole had gone up to a teenage couple and pitched his maneuver as a prank on some buddies.

"We're on a kind of scavenger hunt, except my wife and I are the prizes."

The girl, whose name was Allison, squinted at Cole, not sure if this guy was on the level. The hundred-dollar-bill that appeared in Cole's hand made her eyes go wide and mollified her skepticism.

"What do you think, Mick?" she said to her boyfriend.

Mick was a big, strapping country boy in a Pendleton wool shirt and bib overalls.

"Could be a hoot," Mick said. His eyes kept flicking from Allison to the money.

Cole held up the hundred. "Who's the treasurer?"

Allison snatched the bill from Cole and tucked it into her Wrangler jeans.

Cole held up the GPS tracking device that he'd pulled from the Rover's chassis. "We stick this up under your front bumper."

And without waiting for Mick's permission, Cole bent down to the Ford Explorer and attached the GPS. He made sure it was still sending a steady signal.

"You head out north for about forty miles and then turn around and come back this way again."

"We're doubling back on them?" Mick said, anxious to show Cole that he might be country, but he was slick.

"Exactly."

"But won't they be pissed at us?" Allison said; her skepticism back and clearly the wiser of the two.

"Once they see you go by them, they'll take off north after us because they'll know we've tricked them."

"I don't know," she said. "I'm not sure if we should get involved."

Cole was about to fish out another hundred when Mollie stepped in.

"If they do stop you, you just claim ignorance. 'What device?' 'Wait! How'd that get there?'"

"We'll go out ahead of you," Cole said, "then at Junction 85, we head west."

"And we drive until we're about forty miles out?" Mick said.

"Then turn around and double back."

Mick held out his fist for Cole to bump, then to Mollie. The detectives touched knuckles with the teenagers when Allison gave Mollie a hug. The lovers jumped into the Explorer.

Mick's window slid down.

"Fun stuff, eh?"

Cole drove the Rover north, Mick's Explorer about ten yards behind. The teenagers were having a good time. Whenever Cole checked the rearview, he could see Mick and Allison talking, smiling. Once he saw them bump fists.

Cole kept a steady pace and when they reached the Junction, waved a farewell to Mick and Allison. Mick tooted his horn as they flew past.

"Our rolling decoys," Cole said.

"I hope you're right about not going after them."

"We're their target. They'll be in panic mood trying to catch up and figure out which way we went."

"If they have any brains, they'll head for Ruskin."

"Doubt if they have a brain like Jax's."

"Jax? You're going to use him instead of Stripes?"

"She's busy on Boris."

Jax was the computer hacker that did off-the-books work for the city's police department. As a teenager, Jax was always in trouble. His single-parent mom had to work two jobs and wasn't home enough to guide him. But after his fourth offense, this time for stealing a neighbor's computer system, Jax was facing serious time with the California Youth Authority. Cole got the neighbor to drop the charges by buying him an upgraded system. He also believed that Jax just needed guidance and a direction. And for a kid stealing a computer system? The path was obvious.

Now, eight years later, Jax Robinson was the top computer researcher for a privately-held tech conglomerate. And Jax/Hax, as had branded himself, was the top analyst for a select group of clients who needed black searches.

Cole only used Jax in times of emergency. And no matter what he was working on or who the client was, Jax jumped right on Cole's request.

Twenty minutes after Cole's call, Jax had his report.

"Biggest fact he's heading north? He's got a distant cousin of his mother's living there. Annushka Orlov Beriya."

"How long has she been married?" Cole said.

"Six months."

"So he might still be going on her maiden name."

"I'd say so."

"Why does Beriya sound familiar?"

"Give Cole Trane a kewpie doll. Her husband, Pavel was a distant relative to the infamous Lavrentiy Beriya."

"Who was?" Mollie asked.

"Possibly the most hated man in Russia in the '50s."

"Even more than Joe Stalin?"

"Yeah. Because Lavrentiy ran the Soviet secret police and sent thousands of innocent Russians into Lefortovo Prison. He had them beaten and tortured and if necessary, murdered."

"We're hoping to take Igor alive," Cole said.

"Better hope he knows that," Jax said.

FIFTY-FIVE

"I AM LOST."

The young clerk behind the counter at Tim Horton's smiled at Igor. She couldn't have been more than eighteen, but to Igor looked like she was about twelve.

"Sure," Wanda said. "You want some coffee, too?"

"Sure, sure."

"Our menu's right up there."

Igor didn't bother looking up. "Black, large." He checked the food case. "And two chocolate glazed donuts."

He held up Annushka's address.

"You know vhere is? Some reason, GPS can't find."

Wanda couldn't help smiling. "You're not from around here?"

Igor almost said, "No, shit." But instead just smiled. "Big reason I need help."

His thick index finger pointed at the paper.

"Just give me a second to get your order."

She read the address while she filled a large cup from the gleaming stainless- steel urn. She put a lid on the cup and set it on the counter.

"This is about two hour's drive from here. Straight out the main highway."

"Okay, thank you."

"That'll be four dollars, seventeen cents."

Igor gave her a ten. "Keep change."

"No ... I ..."

"Four-seventeen for coffee, donuts. Rest for travel advice."

Before Wanda could protest, Igor grabbed the coffee and the small bag of donuts and was heading for the door.

There was an Esso station right next to Tim Horton's. Igor cruised through the parking lot and up to the pumps.

The BMW's fuel gauge showed a quarter-tank left, but he didn't want to take any chances. He wolfed down one of the donuts while the pump dinged numbers as the BMW sucked up the premium gas. He took a long sip of coffee as the fueling stopped, replaced the nozzle and got his receipt. He carefully wiped his hands clean of any donut crumbs and folded himself into the cushy leather seat. "Krauts know how to make cars. Fockers."

FIFTY-SIX

"V'AFFANCULO!"

Bruno Campanini thrust his bent right art up as he slapped it with his left in the ancient Italian gesture.

"Fuck! You!" He shouted at the monitor, this time in English.

But he knew he had lost.

Lost? How the hell did that happen?

It had been an intense computer war. A war that comes on suddenly and deadly.

Once he'd tracked down Oksana Kosar, Bruno had a prescient thought:

Maybe Nikolai wasn't the only one looking for the young Russian woman from Rostov-on-Don.

And since ten this morning, when he'd moved his mouse, and the monitor had come to life, his suspicions had been proven right. Some hacker – some goddamn brilliant hacker – was attacking his security blockade; having already penetrated Bruno's fourth level of security.

There were two remaining. Bruno had input data at a furious pace to block the attack and had been successful. So far.

He checked his codes, then launched his counter-attack. The images on his monitor mushroomed out in a red-yellow nuclear explosion.

"Fino culo di tua sorella!"

"Fuck your sister in the ass!"

The hacker was about to get a Trojan horse spyware bomb. If he or she had left the portal open, their system was history.

Bruno sat back and smiled to himself.

He was about to dial Nikolai and tell him how he'd protected the search for Oksana when ALERT! – ALERT! – ALERT! flashed across his screen. Bruno's fingers flew over his keyboard. But he was too late. A putrid vomit green sentence with day-glo orange letters danced up and down as it wrote out on his screen:

You've just been Ha•-Ha•-Ha•-Haked!

Bruno kept typing, throwing every defense and recovery anti-attack software program in his arsenal. Finally, he stopped and stared at his screen. Who was this asshole?

But Jax Robinson had already moved on. His computer pinged as it automatically dialed and connected to Cole's cell.

"Jax? How the hell did you get through up here? I bet there's not a satellite tower for miles."

"Towers? We don't need no stinking towers."

"Hi, Jax," Mollie said to the car's speaker.

"Hey, Molls, how's it going?"

"Cool. What's up?"

"Been an interesting morning. I was working on an assignment and my file on Igor beeps."

"Oh?" Cole said. He and Mollie exchanged looks.

"I still haven't tracked down the connection but turns out Igor knows a young Russian woman named Oksana Kosar. Comes from Rostov-on-Don."

"The same town as Nikolai?"

"Ka-ching! But when I try and run a search on her, I'm blocked."

Cole checked his GPS screen. He had a turn coming up in a quarter-mile.

"Blocked as limited access?"

"Blocked as in 'Don't Even Think About Coming In Here!'"

"That didn't stop you of course."

"Actually, it did. At first. Because I thought it was just a sophisticated personal security barricade. But turns out it's not only an anti-information site, but they're firing back – Trojan Horses, Blitz-Bombs, even a Destruco-5."

Cole shrugged his shoulders at Mollie: WTF is he talking about?

"Sucker counter-attacked and almost got through my first line of defense. So, I knew then, for all you Holmes fans, that the game was afoot. So, this Wopper, and I mean in the nicest way of formidable talent and not just because he's Italian."

Mollie was about to ask how he knew that, but Jax had anticipated the question.

"He's based in Milan. His signal gets bounced about five, six times, but that's its final stop. So we spar around. And he's good, damn good. Just not Jax/Hak good. And he sends out MalKontent Malestrom."

"MalKontent Malestrom?" Cole said, "where do they come up with these names?"

"I think it's pretty cool," Jax said. "And this is a spyware H bomb. It would shut down most everything on the internet, short of NSA or one of the bureaus. But I've got that defended up front. But what he doesn't know is that designed inside within it, provided you know the back-door code, is an automatic ricochet attack. Boom! Guido's no longer in the information game. And I own his system."

"Including Oksana?"

"Of course."

"So why he didn't know the back-door code?" Mollie asked.

"Because nobody does. Except me."

"And why is that?" Cole said.

"Because MalKontent Malestrom is my baby. I created it."

FIFTY-SIX

"DESTROYED? HOW?"

"I do not know, Signore Nikolai." Bruno said. "It has to be the U.S. government."

"The U.S. government?"

"They are the only ones who could get through my defenses. The only ones."

Nikolai held his breath a long moment while his mind raced through everything that Bruno had confessed to him. A confession so contrite and bewildered that Nikolai felt like he was a priest behind the screen.

He was fatherly when he said, "Bruno, the government of the United States or any country is not interested in Oksana. It has to be a private group."

"I... with all due respect, sir, I can't believe that there's another person, another cyber person, who has my knowledge."

Ah, ego. Takes the best of us down. Nikolai nodded his head in frustration.

"None of our information was compromised, was it, Bruno?"

"No. No, sir. Not a chance."

Bruno's answer came so fast, Nikolai knew that his information had been compromised; and that whomever the smarter hacker was, now had everything of Bruno's, and his. It was a staggering loss.

But not a terminal one; because like all his businesses and dealings his entire life, Nikolai compartmentalized.

No one knew the totality of his empire and how it connected. There were some trusted aides, like Raisa, who knew the enormity of its scope, but even she didn't know everything. And there were times when even Nikolai had to review his holdings and make sure they were in alignment.

"Excellent," Nikolai said, "I just wanted to hear you say it. I will be in touch."

But it wasn't excellent. Nikolai knew the breach was serious and that when the other hacker, whether it was a government agency from America or another country or a gonzo hacker, when they came after Bruno, they had to reach a dead end. He had given Bruno his brief note of confidence to buy himself some time and to make sure Bruno stayed in place and didn't run.

Igor was another story. He was running – fast and cautious at the same time.

He had managed to avoid the authorities as he raced north toward Ruskin by darting off the highway, doubling back, hiding in a copse of trees while he slept for over two hours as if he were dead.

At a shopping mall along Donatelli Avenue, he'd noticed the bear plates and replaced them with ones from a beige Nissan.

Igor checked his GPS. He was fifty-eight miles outside of Ruskin. He still hadn't located Annushka Orlov; but he drove on, relentless in his pursuit. I am like shark. I do not stop. I smell blood in vater. Not my blood. As he spun the wheel in a tight turn, he leaned with the motion and felt the watch shift in his shirt pocket. He pulled the shiny Cartier La Dona up by its band, noticing how even now, at dusk, its white gold glinted, catching the last rays of sunshine.

"Focking vatch."

Igor powered down the driver's side window and drew his arm back:

Throw it out. Now!

It was as if the watch wasn't jewelry or a timepiece, but a talisman of evil.

Look at all the trouble it had caused, the lives it had taken.

No. Is only chance for some money. Only. Chance.

He returned the watch to his pocket and drove on.

Sergey, Aleksander, and Mikhail weren't just driving; they were flying!

Aleksander had the tachometer kissing the red line as they hurtled after Cole and Mollie, trying to make up ground that was no longer between them.

Because as the Russians roared east, Cole and Mollie, after heading north, were rolling west at high speed.

"We're about a half-hour from Ruskin," Cole said. "Maybe another twenty before we're at Annushka Beriya's apartment."

"What's the play?" Mollie said.

"Park and wait."

"No, I meant when Igor shows."

"We taser him?"

"Right. And what's our chances of first getting a taser?"

"If we were citizens, maybe fifty-fifty. As foreign nationals? Zero. And finding one means more time and forget the low-profile."

"And forget the taser?"

"That's the way I read it."

"Me, too." Mollie gazed out the window. "You think there's a chance we'll get close enough to shoot him in the knee or foot?"

"Assuming we can take that shot, much less make it.

"And that he doesn't return fire. Or shoot first."

Cole guided the Rover around a long, sweeping turn and glanced at Mollie out of the corner of his eye.

She saw the look and said, "What?"

"We're kidding ourselves."

"What'd you mean?"

"We aren't going to get close enough to take him down physically. Or get answers."

Mollie nodded. "We see the shot, we take it."

"Yeah."

"And that's what we set up from the jump when we get there."

Cole looked in the rearview.

And saw his own eyes.

Pools of dark resolve.

And only a little guilt.

"From the jump."

FIFTY-SEVEN

"IS FINISHED. STOP."

Mikhail was slow to respond, and Sergey slapped the right side of his head.

He did it with an open palm, but the force of the blow knocked Mikhail's head into the side window and the Rover careened hard left toward the shoulder.

"Fock!" Mikhail yelled and yanked the wheel back. He slammed on the brakes so hard the Rover's tires smoked in protest and Aleksander and Sergey lurched against their seat belts.

Mikhail snapped around, his hand going for the weapon inside his jacket. But Sergey had never released his grip on his Desert Eagle and thrust it hard into Mikhail's forehead.

"Turn around, go back. Take side road."

Sergey's eyes flicked toward Aleksander, making sure he wasn't drawing his weapon.

"Americans pull trick. They lose you."

Mikhail wanted to kill this prick, but there was no way to get any advantage.

He pulled back from the .50-caliber pistol and glared at him.

"You vaiting for Christmas? Drive."

Mikhail turned the wheel and put the Rover into a tight 180° turn and roared down the road in the opposite lane. They flew around a long sweeping curve and saw that they'd never get down the side road. Because it was blocked with two RCMP heavy-duty vans. The Mountie vehicles formed a "V" on the yellow line in the middle of the road, so nothing with four wheels, or even two, could get past.

"Fock," Mikhail said and applied the brakes.

"Ne paničarite," Sergey commanded. Do not panic.

"Vot the fock is this?" Aleksander said.

"Ve find out soon enough," Sergey said.

He watched the doors open on the RCMP vans and two officers from each vehicle get out, protected by what he was sure were steel-reinforced doors.

The Mountie on the left raised up his hand and called out in a sharp voice, "Nothing to be afraid of. But I want everyone to vacate your vehicle, one at a time, hands out where I can see them."

"Mikhail, first," Sergey said. "But slip gun back to me." Mikhail eased open his door and stuck his left hand out to the side and with his right, handed his weapon without looking back to Sergey.

"Yours, Aleksander. Look straight ahead."

Aleksander handed his automatic back through the opening between the seats. Sergey took it, then slipped his SV-98, Snaiperskaya Vintovka rifle from its scabbard.

Mikhail got out, both hands raised.

The Mountie pointed at Aleksander. If he were watching Sergey all he'd see was a rock-still man in the back.

But hidden from their eyes, below the seats, Sergey's hands were a blur of motion: He quickly disassembled the SV-98, then eased the barrel to the floor, followed by the stock and sight.

He used his foot to push the stock under the driver's seat. As he undid his safety belt, he managed to slide the barrel under the passenger seat. A keen eye might spot the end sticking out, but Sergey had no other choice.

After Aleksander was out, the Mountie pointed at Sergey. They were in free- fall now. If the Mounties searched the Rover and found just the GSh-18s, they would be arrested. But with the discovery of his SV-98, they might never get out of Canadian prison.

Fock, prison. Ve die here, or they do.

He slipped his Desert Eagle into the small of his back.

Sergey affected a limp as he moved towards them. Two Mounties guarded Mikhail; another two on Aleksander.

The Mountie who gave the commands motioned the last Mountie to cover Sergey.

"Vot is going on, please?" Sergey asked. "Ve are trying to get home. My sister is…" Sergey stopped, shook his head as if all the grief in the world was on his shoulders.

"I'm going to need to see some identification," the head Mountie said, ignoring Sergey. He pointed at Mikhail, "You first. And go slooow." He drew out the word, the threat clear in his voice.

Mikhail held up his index and thumb and reached into his pocket and drew out his wallet. One of the Mounties guarding him took it and put it into his jacket without looking at it.

"Now you," the head Mountie said and gestured at Aleksander. "And do it just like your pal, there."

Aleksander held up his middle finger, held it so the lawmen could see it, then put his thumb next to it and gothis wallet.

Asshole. Goddamn kids never learn.

The head Mountie must have thought the same thing. He said, "How old are you, son?"

"Read for yourself," Aleksander said. He handed his wallet to the Mountie closest to him.

The head Mountie gestured at Sergey.

Sergey pointed back at the Rover.

"Sorry, I left in jacket." Sergey pointed back at the Rover. "I can get?"

"Stop!" the head Mountie ordered. "Stay where you are."

"Prvi hitac, spustiti na zemlju," Sergey said, his voice loud and clear.

First shot, drop to the ground.

No focking vay, thought Mikhail.

"Da," Aleksander said, "focking da."

"Quiet!"

The head Mountie came around from behind the door, so now everyone was out in the open. He drew his weapon.

So, he is first target.

"Sorry," Sergey said.

"MacHenry, you get the jacket," the head Mountie said.

"Vait, I help."

Sergey turned half towards the Rover, which reduced his status as a target to a silhouette, and at the same time pulled the Desert Eagle and in one smooth flowing motion brought it up and shot the Mountie in the head.

Before the retort of the gunshot registered and the senior Mountie's brains were exploding out, Sergey shot the two Mounties next to Mikhail – Bang! Bang!

Mikhail was still fighting the idea that Sergey would shoot, watched the RCMPs collapse in a corona of blood and gore, his mind numb, behind in the processing of events.

Aleksander didn't drop to the ground like Sergey had ordered, but instead head-butted the Mountie closest to him and yanked the man's weapon and spun away.

The other Mountie nearest Aleksander managed to clear his revolver, but never had the chance to fire it when Aleksander shot him three times.

MacHenry, the Mountie that had been sent to the Rover, spun around and yanked his gun and got off a single shot at Sergey that went wide and high as Sergey was diving to the ground.

Sergey hit the dirt and shot MacHenry twice– the first bullet eviscerating his throat, the other continuing the upward trajectory and destroying the top of his head.

The Mountie that Aleksander had head-butted struggled to get to a kneeling position and clear his weapon, but the flow of blood from his shattered nose and head trauma made his movements slow and clumsy. Aleksander stepped to the man's side and shot him in the temple, close enough for a self-inflicted suicidal bullet.

The smell of cordite and blood permeated the air.

Sergey sprinted for the RCMP vehicles, gun ready to fire. But the six Mounties were the entire force.

And now they were all dead.

"Get guns," Sergey said.

Mikhail was still trying to process what had just happened and got behind the wheel of one of the SUVs and drove it off the road.

Aleksander gathered six .357 Magnums, the RCMP's standard issue weapon.

Sergey drove the other SUV to the opposite side of the road.

Mikhail dragged MacHenry, but Sergey yelled at him: "Leave them. Ve go."

"Vot if someone comes?"

"See dead men, so vot? Ve have to catch Americans."

Sergey jumped into the Rover. Aleksander dumped the Magnums on the back seat next to him. He was about to get into the passenger side when Mikhail grabbed the door.

"You drive," he whispered, his eyes pleading.

"Hey," Aleksander said, "my turn behind vheel."

FIFTY-EIGHT

COLE GUIDED THE ROVER TO THE CURB.

They were twenty yards from Annushka Beriya's home. The street was nearly empty. The cars on the street were all older models, some looking like their odometers had rolled past a hundred thousand miles.

"I give us ten minutes."

"Then what?"

"One of two things. A nosey neighbor's going to notice a new Range Rover and stroll past us. Or they'll call the cops and have them do it. And I'd rather not have to answer any questions."

"Especially since we're carrying."

"Yeah."

"So, what's the plan?"

"I'm thinking of knocking on Annushka's door."

"You're kidding."

"No. I'm just trying to figure out the details, how to do it."

"The devil's in the details."

"Yeah. You ever think about that?"

"The Devil?"

"Yes. I mean since we're here, let me ruminate. And the only reason this popped into my head is that I've been following this writer's blog on FaceBook. Guy named Rabih Alameddine."

"And…?"

"And he always has this amazing art collection of paintings, drawings, poems, pictures. I wonder when he has time to write. Most of this art? I've never seen before."

"And?"

"And sometimes, he features a theme. You know, like love or loneliness or war."

An old Chevy rolled past the Range Rover. The driver, a grey-haired man glanced their way and then drove down to the end of the block and turned.

"And the other day, he featured the Devil."

"As in the Bible?"

"Lucifer incarnate. There was an illustration from Dante's Divina Comedia, from around 1480. He had another from Dr. Faust. But the one that got me, and I think relates to Igor, was this art construction on paper, or auf Papier as it was listed, by an artist named Friedrich Schröder Sonnenstern. He's depicted the Devil with this amazing long green tongue that cascades down out of his mouth and wraps around some poor bastard, head to toe, like a boa constrictor."

"Meaning once the Devil gets you in his clutches or like you said, ties you up in his evil, you're fucked."

"Pretty much."

"The Devil made me do it!" Mollie said in a falsetto.

Cole laughed. "Uh…"

"Flip Wilson."

"Right. I remember watching him as a kid. What was the name of that character he played, dressed in drag?"

"Geraldine."

Cole nodded in recognition. "My dad loved her. Or him."

"And how's the Devil connect to all this? And to Igor?"

"People get into shit in their lives. They do something stupid, out of anger or fear or spite or sex. Doesn't matter what emotion or action is the catalyst, they just keep doing it. And they get so far down that road they can't remember who they were before. They only know who they are now. Like Igor. He and Vlad attempted a robbery. It went bad, and he killed Zoey. And it just got worse as he kept killing people."

"He's a psychopath."

"Absolutely. But when these whackos get captured and they're questioned? Most of them say, 'I dunno, something came over me.' So, what if it were true? That Satan really existed? That there was a Devil who whispered in your ear, promised you everything, to steal your soul?"

"Considering how banal and shallow most of humanity is, how hard a job could that be?"

"Just blow in my ear, you little Devil."

Mollie snickered.

"Solves a lot of questions. Fits with Catholicism and a lot of other doctrines."

"And conveniently absolves anyone who refuses to take responsibility for their actions."

"Only in their own minds. Because the law will still make them pay."

"You keep working on that, Cole and..."

A dark blue Toyota approached from the other direction and turned into Annushka's driveway. A woman got out and walked to the house, unlocked the front door and went inside.

Cole held up his cell and looked at the photo that Jax had sent to both their cells.

"Too far away to tell, but it's got to be her."

Cole started the Range Rover.

"We're really going to do this?"

"If nothing else, we'll warn her."

"Wait," Mollie held out her hand. "Maybe we're the ones that should be warned."

"What're you talking about?"

"What if we've miscalculated the timing and Igor's already inside?"

"You make a bargain with the Devil, there's Hell to pay."

FIFTY-NINE

"O MOJ BOZE!"

Annushka Beriya wailed.

"Oh, my God!" she repeated in English. "This monster is coming here? To my house? Why? He is not family."

She stared at Cole and Mollie, wild-eyed.

"Do you remember his mother, Katerina?" Cole said.

"I was eight years old the last time I saw Katerina. If she walked in the door, I would not recognize her."

"He's desperate. And as far as we know, you're the only relative he has in North America."

"Anna," her husband Pavel said, "please sit and try and calm down."

"Calm down? Calm down? Oh sure, Anna, take a seat while the golem from Hell marches toward our house."

She glared at Pavel, her eyes hot with tears and rage.

"We will call the police," Pavel said.

"It's better that you don't," Cole said.

"I don't understand," Pavel said.

Oh, shit, here we go!

"Okay, it's like this," Cole said. "If he sees the police, he'll take off."

"But if they're hiding in our house?" Annushka said, her fear rising.

"That's what we're trying to avoid," Mollie said.

"If he tries to come in?" Annushka said, "they will kill him, or he'll try and kill them. And then we have blood all over our house." She wagged her finger at her husband. "No, Pavel, you are the one who needs to calm down.

"Your wife is right," Cole said. "You don't want him inside."

"So what then?"

"Do you have any friends you could stay with for a few days?"

Pavel and Annushka looked at each other. She shrugged. "I have a friend, but it would be difficult to explain." She thought about it for a moment. "No. It will not work."

"What about a hotel?" Mollie said.

"Even motels are expensive," Pavel said. "And my work hasn't been..." he stopped, embarrassed to continue.

"Let us take care of the cost," Cole said.

He looked at Mollie, "I'm sure Nikolai will cover it."

Two hours later Annushka and Pavel were tucked away on the top floor of the Granville Island Hotel in Vancouver.

"I have never been in such luxury," Annushka said to Cole when she called his cell. "I am laying in the bed on sheets that aren't silk but feel even better. After I hang up, I am going to take off all my clothes and just feel the cotton against my skin." She laughed when she realized what she'd just said. "Oops, I did not mean it that way."

There was some noise from Pavel, which sent Annushka into peals of laughter. She covered the phone with her hand and Cole couldn't make out what Pavel was saying, but when she came back on, she was quieter in tone, more serious.

"Please be careful," she said. "And while it is very strange circumstances that Pavel and I are here, thank you. This is even better than the hotel where we stayed for our honeymoon."

Cole heard Pavel grunt something, followed by Annushka's raucous laugh and then the dial tone as she hung up.

"If nothing else," Cole said, "Pavel loves Annushka."

SIXTY

"I HATE THIS SHIT!"

Sergey was goddamn loud.

Aleksander steered to a shoulder on the side of the road without a moment's hesitation. He didn't want his head slammed into the glass again. He put the gearshift into park and stared ahead.

Suddenly he was jerked forward when Sergey punched the back of the driver's seat!

"Fock!" Slam.

"Fock!" Slam.

Sergey's fists pummeled the seat, his anger and rage penetrating the steel frame, springs, padding, and cushion.

Aleksander and Mikhail kept quiet.

"Call Nikolai, then give me phone."

Mikhail pressed the auto-dial button for Nikolai and passed his cell over his shoulder to Sergey without looking at him.

"Hello? Hello? Nikolai, can you hear me? Hello?" Sergey listened, the cell compressing his ear into pancaked flesh, but there was only the empty void of white noise. "Hello? Fock. No goddamned reception."

Aleksander's eyes flicked to the rearview and saw Sergey's red-faced rage, he glanced at Mikhail out of the corner of his eye, but the young Russian was staring straight ahead.

"Drive," Sergey ordered. "Find place without all trees. I need reach Nikolai."

Aleksander put the SUV into gear and accelerated, the fat tires spewing dirt from the road's shoulder. He flew through another long turn and there on the left was a field of pure white, unblemished as far as the eye could see.

"Stop!" Sergey commanded.

"Stop, go. Vot the fuck?" Aleksander said.

"Hydrangeas," Sergey said, his tone reverent and quiet. "Look at them. Beautiful flowers like white cotton candy on stick, no?"

"Hydrangeas?" Mikhail said. "How can you tell that from this far away?"

"Because Sergey knows flowers."

"Yeah?"

"Of course. My grandfather vas gardener appointed Big Joe."

"Big Joe?"

"Stalin! Joseph Vissarionovich Stalin. Leader of Russia from 1920s until he die 1953. You don't know anything of Motherland's history?"

Sergey thrust Mikhail's phone back at him.

"Here. Google. Find out."

"Okay." Mikhail tapped his phone.

"After Stalin, came Khrushchev," Sergey said. "My father works alongside main gardener. Then when dada Fyodor retire, my father inherits job. He keeps through Joe, Nikita, all way to Gorbachev, who was best leader, also Secretary of Agriculture."

"Stalin was tough," Mikhail said, his eyes focused on his cell phone screen.

"No shit," said Sergey. "Focker killed people by thousands, maybe millions."

"Millions," answered Mikhail. "'A single death is a tragedy; a million deaths is a statistic.' That's one of his quotes."

"Then my father, not long after Gorbachev appoints him First Deputy Gardener, he trips on tree root, gets big cut on arm from tea rose, develops infection that attacks nervous system and three weeks later, dead."

"Sorry," said Aleksander.

"Yeah, is focking life and medicine in Russia."

Sergey tapped Mikhail's shoulder, which without anything behind it, still hurt like hell.

This guy's an animal.

"Give me phone."

Mikhail handed him the phone.

"And you never wanted to keep up the family tradition?" said Aleksander.

"No. But I still love flowers."

"A secret side to you," Alexander said.

"Vot the fock? You saying I'm fag?"

"No, no." Aleksander shook his head to emphasize his words. "I just meant that…"

"Shut up," Sergey snarled. "Call is going through."

Nikolai only heard parts of what Sergey said; the connection drifting in and out.

"Have Aleksander pull over."

"Pull over, now!" he heard Sergey bark.

There was a sharp squeal of brakes.

"Okay, ve stopped."

Nikolai listened to Sergey's recount of how Cole and Mollie had duped them, their efforts at recapturing the trail and their frustration.

But there was something else; something Sergey was hiding.

"Vot else?"

For a long moment, silence; then "Vot you mean?"

"I mean there is something you are not telling me."

A few more moments passed of just the empty, tinny sound of the electronic silence. "Ve ran into trouble."

Nikolai listened to Sergey's unemotional telling of the annihilation of an entire RCMP patrol, reporting the massacre with passion and boastful pride – how his faster, deadlier marksmanship had saved them.

"Vot is situation?" Nikolai snapped.

"Situation?"

"Yes. Mounties are looking, they find you…"

"They vill not find us," Sergey interrupted. Nikolai was surprised for a moment. He couldn't remember the last time an underling had done that.

"Stay vhere you are. I vill contact Cole and Mollie, find out their location and call you back."

Sergey had another question, but Nikolai had ended the call. He put the cell on the seat and gave a new order: "Ve vait here."

Fock, boss pissed at me.

Sergey looked out of the window and back across the small valley and the white field of flowers, snowy, pristine.

I vish I vas laying down in middle.

SIXTY-ONE

"I AM IN DEEP SHIT."

"Ya," Oksana's reflection in the mirror answered back.

"How did it go so bad? And so quick?"

"That focking, crazy Igor," the mirror said.

"How do dresses become money?"

She felt like the wicked witch in Snow White, talking to the mirror. But it seemed to help, or at least make things a little easier to understand.

Not that there was any way to understand Igor's senseless murder of Zoey. That was bad enough. But she'd had no idea that they were behind the killing spree.

Not until the news was broadcast of Vladimir's death in the shooting of the woman Mountie, Evelyn St. Laurent.

She'd been watching it in the lunch room with two other sales girls at her job at the J.C. Penny's out in the valley at the Northridge Fashion Center. The two other sales girls that were sharing the table, Margo and Nell, had asked her if she was okay, since she looked pale.

"I... I'm not sure," Oksana had said. And her stomach had clenched, and her bowels turned liquid, and she'd had to use the Men's Room, which was closer to their table, before she'd exploded from both ends of her body.

She'd rushed, embarrassed and sick, from the room, ignoring Margo's and Nell's anxious calls, straight to her car and sped back to her dingy one-bedroom rented apartment.

She watched the TV again, flicking through the channels before leaving it on CNN, absorbing as many details as possible. Then she wasted no time, threw the few clothes and toiletries she had into a small suitcase and backpack and headed north on the I-15; not stopping until she'd reached Las Vegas late that night.

She'd been holed up in a small hotel that was so far away from the main action, she got it for sixty dollars a night. She was desperate, frightened out of her mind. Her mother, back in Rostov-on-Don, always said she had a rat's instincts for survival: squeeze through the narrowest of openings and get away. Sharp teeth helped.

Oksana liked Vladimir and was sorry he was dead. Too bad it hadn't been Igor. He was the only link now left that could connect Zoey to her. She hoped he would get killed, too. She made the sign of the cross after the thought had blossomed in her mind. Of course, it was a long shot: All she'd done was tell Igor that she thought – *thought* – that Zoey would be coming to the store with over a quarter-million dollars.

She didn't know it was in dresses and not cash.

Even so, that didn't mean she'd told Igor and Vladimir to rob her. Much less kill her.

Circumstantial. His word against hers; which, from all the TV shows she'd watched, wouldn't lead to anything.

The bang on the door scared the shit out of her.

She stayed quiet.

Another knock.

"Hello?"

Oksana tiptoed to the side of the window away from the door and eased the thin curtain away from the glass.

Two men.

Shit, shit.

Another bang, this one harder.

"Nancy? Goddamnit, I know you're in there. Open up."

Oksana was going to tell them there wasn't any Nancy in here.

But then she heard one of the men say, "Wait. Fuck, this is the wrong room."

"What?"

She saw the man touch the room number and heard the metallic sound of the number being moved.

"This is room six, not nine. The nail at the top's gone, and it rotated down."

Both men laughed. Definitely drunk.

"Sorry," one of them said.

Oksana watched them walk away.

She sat on the edge of the bed and sucked in deep breaths.

"So ve are safe," she said to her reflection across the room.

"You think so?" the mirror said back.

"I think ve need to get moving."

SIXTY-TWO

"STUCK IN THE MIDDLE WITH YOU."

Mollie was singing the Stealer's Wheel tune to herself. But louder than she thought.

"As long as I'm not the cop and you're not Michael Madsen."

"Oh, yeah, Reservoir Dogs. I wasn't thinking of the movie. More like our situation right now."

Cole's cell buzzed. He checked the ID and let it go to voice message.

"Nikolai again? He's going to be furious with you."

"Sorry, Nikolai, I never got the calls. Reception up there was terrible." Cole deleted this call like the others. "He's just trying to pinpoint our location, so he can send his thugs after us."

Mollie nodded and checked that her 92-FS Beretta was close by.

"This all could go FUBAR," Cole said. "Igor shows up at the same time as the three comrades."

"Meaning who's our target?"

"That. And who's targeting us."

"We're doing Nikolai a solid, taking care of Igor. But Nikki didn't get where he is by owing people. And he doesn't like loose ends. We do our job; his boys do us."

"You really think so?"

"Better to think it and not be true, then the opposite. Trust is an elastic principle. Your mileage will vary."

Cole's cell buzzed.

"Again?" Mollie said.

"No, it's Jax."

"Holy shit!" Jax said. No hello, no hey, no Cole. Nothing.

"And hello to you, too, Jax."

"Sorry, but this Nikolai? He's amazingly rich."

"I told you he was an oligarch."

"There's rich. And then there's RIIICHH! This guy's a billionaire. Like Bill Gates, Jeff Bezos class. His stuff's very compartmentalized, so it's taking some work to get around his firewalls, and I've got a lot more to go, but he's mega bucks."

"I don't remember asking for this data."

"You didn't. But once I started checking, you know me and info."

"Anything stand out?"

"Just your usual gold, oil, commodities, etcetera, etcetera. But there's some dark ops too. I think he's into paramilitary arms trading, stolen weaponry. And…"

Jax hesitated, "the poppy highway. Opium, heroin."

"You can prove that?"

"In a day or so. But the signs are there. And Cole?"

"What?"

"There were some people that opposed him – both in business and politics, that … all died."

"They were murdered?"

"Can't prove it, and most of Russian news is just manufactured information slanted so you can only agree with them or be in conflict."

"Pretty much like it is here, in the Age of Trump."

"Yes. But, I mean …"

Cole could hear the tattoo of Jax's keyboard as he typed like a madman.

"Konstantin Dronin. Third tier Minister of Energy; meaning he's small potatoes and really had no influence or power. But Dronin opposed some regulation regarding oil pipelines in the Russkies' Priobskoye field, which is freakin' Siberia. An opposition that delayed approval for one of Nikolai's drilling companies. And even though Dronin's opposition gets blown away and Nikolai's deal goes through, five weeks later, Konstantin Dronin's discovered in a cheap motel hanging from the shower head. Suicide the local police say."

There was more keyboard clicking.

"Arkady Lokhionov. Was a vice-president at Voronov Technology. Didn't deliver on a new kind of software. Two days later, brakes go out on Arkady's new Mercedes and he hits a bridge abutment, at 75 kilometers an hour. Brand-new AMG E63 S sedan."

More clicking of Jax's keyboard.

"And there are about another half-dozen men, and one woman, who disagreed with him over the last five years and, as Grigory Azarov, his version of Sarah Huckabee Sanders, says, 'suffered unfortunate events.'"

There were several long moments of silence while Cole digested this news.

"Cole? You still with me?"

"Yes. Just trying to process it all."

"Lot to process. Gotta go. I'll update you as needed."

Cole clicked off. Mollie looked at him, waited for an explanation. Cole relayed the results of Jax's laissez-faire research.

"So, we're definitely targets," Mollie said.

"Definitely."

"How do you want to handle it?"

"We could wait for Mikhail, Aleksander and the assassin du jour to show up, then call the police using Annushka's landline and then hightail it out the back door."

Mollie looked at Cole and laughed.

"Definitely not Trane and Simmons style."

"No, but I thought I'd throw it out there. It's a way to cut our losses before they're losses."

"And it does give us a cover for Nikolai. We say the cops showed up and we had to get out there or else spend the next decade as guests of the Canadian government."

"So, what do you think?"

"Fuck them! We ambush the ambushers."

SIXTY-THREE

"YOU'VE BEEN LED ASTRAY."

"Vot?" Igor said.

The tall man ruefully shook his head, then smiled. "Led astray. Someone has sent you in the wrong direction."

Igor stared at the man who was Annushka's neighbor. "Annushka does not live here?"

"Not anymore. She moved."

"Vhen?"

The neighbor, Charlie Ruggles, flinched at Igor's tone. He wasn't sure, now, whether to convey any information. After all, this guy might be some whacked-out Russian killer like they were talking about on TV.

"She's your cousin, you said?"

"Yes. Third cousin. Through our mothers."

"So, you didn't know she was married?"

"No."

He caught the caution in the man's eyes.

"It's been many years since I see her. Ve played together as children. Back in Russia. And my mother," Igor bowed his head and crossed himself, "just before she passed, asked me to find Annushka and give her this."

Igor held the watch in his massive palm. "Family heirloom."

It didn't occur to Charlie that for an heirloom the watch looked brand new until he was inside watching TV and Igor had gone. All he could do when he first saw the watch was marvel at its graceful design and shimmering beauty. And all those goddamned diamonds. Jesus, that watch had to be worth a couple thousand bucks.

"Yeah, she married some guy," Charlie said, "I think his name was Peter?"

Charlie turned back into his house and called to his wife who was making dinner, "What was Annushka's husband's name?"

Igor couldn't hear her response. Neither could Charlie.

He held up a finger, "Be right back."

Igor looked around at the houses. Not much to them or the street. His cousin wouldn't know anyone with the kind of money he expected for the watch.

"Beriya," Charlie said as he came back to the door. "Pavel Beriya. They invited us to the wedding."

He held up a buff-colored square piece of paper.

"Nice, since, I mean, we didn't really know them all that well."

"She was very sweet," Helen said, appearing behind her husband. "I hear it was a nice wedding. At St. Barth's."

"We didn't go," Charlie said. He shrugged and declined to say anything else.

Probably too focking cheap to buy present.

"May I see?" Igor held out his hand.

Charlie hesitated – a chill running through him - but gave Igor the invitation.

Igor read the engraved printing – Saint Bartholomew church ... honored by your presence... holy matrimony... celebration and joyful union.... Reception to follow.

"This ..." Igor pointed to the Reception's address, "...is far from here?"

"Across town," said Charlie.

He reached to take back the invitation.

Igor stared at him, held it just out of Charlie's reach.

"It's... a souvenir," Charlie said.

Igor held on to it for a few seconds, just to show him who was in control.

"Thank you," he said and gave it back.

Charlie watched Igor's broad back all the way to his car, his shoes heavy on the road.

Guy was a monster.

SIXTY-FOUR

"YOU'RE AN ANIMAL."

Cole is lost in memory, thinking of Amelie as he sits next to Mollie while they wait for Igor.

"An animal?" he asks.

"Yes," she laughs. "A beast."

She then kneels over Cole, exposing her secret self to his eager, upturned face.

And then their animal lust consumes them now as it has the morning and night before. And as the scenario plays itself out in his silent reverie, he guiltily looks at Mollie.

And his mind jumps to when they were lovers. Before San Francisco.

Does she ever think of those times?

It is a reflective strategy: think about anything else but the upcoming encounter with Igor. He should be thinking of firing lines, of defensive and offensive strategies for when the Russian shows, but he also knows those will come automatically, the training and practice kicking in, and to dwell on them too long might confuse him.

Or so he tells himself.

That deluge of passion with Amelie – of romance and love and affection and sex... and sex... and sex – was their zenith.

And then ... nothing.

She was gone.

And she would not return.

He would never see her again.

If she had been a spy, Amelie would have been the perfect foreign agent, exposing him for all his secrets, rounding up his network, and then vanishing to some faraway country.

"You think he's going to show?" Mollie said.

Before Cole could answer, his phone rang.

"Nikolai, again."

"You should answer it."

He nodded and hit the button.

"Nikolai. Finally."

"Yes, finally."

Cole could hear the frost in the oligarch's voice.

Fuck him.

"I tried calling you back when I saw your ID, but couldn't get any bars. I'm surprised it came through now."

"Where are you?"

"Up the street from Annushka's. Twenty-eight, seventeen."

Mollie looked at the address of the house where they were parked and started to correct Cole, but he waved her off.

"Yes," Cole continued, "north side. We'll be watching." Cole listened for a few moments, then hung up

"You gave him the wrong address on purpose."

"I'm betting that when Aleksander and Mikhail and probably one or two more comrades arrive, they'll circle around and come in from the south, so they'd have an advantage on us."

"If we were on the north side," Mollie said.

"You catch on very quickly, grasshopper."

Cole looked ahead, then suddenly threw his arms around Mollie and kissed her.

"Cops!" he said just before their lips met.

It wasn't a real kiss but coming so soon from his memories of Amelie and then Mollie, her soft lips sparked an incendiary flare in his loins that he quickly stopped and pulled away, keeping his mouth still close enough to feel her breath.

"Fake it," he whispered.

The harsh white-hot glare of the 215,000 lumens spotlight hit them and lit up the interior brighter than daylight.

Cole moved away from Mollie, put his hands on the wheel, nodded in the direction of the police car.

The spotlight went off.

Cole's eyes were still reacting to the shock of the spotlight, so the darkness of the night seemed even blacker. He shut his eyes tight, then opened them to see the driver's door open, and the RMCP officer get out of the car. He powered down the window.

"Sorry, we were just leaving."

The Mountie held up his hand. He scanned the area, checking to make sure that his spotlight hadn't awakened anyone other than the busybody who'd called in the "suspicious car."

The Mountie's flashlight was pointed at the ground and in the reflected light, Cole could see that the Mountie was a veteran, so he'd seen his share of furtive lovers locked in an embrace or even further along the sex trail.

The flashlight came up and washed over Cole and then Mollie. They both shielded their eyes.

Then Mollie put her other hand over her face and sobbed loudly.

"Please, please," she moaned through her hands. "My husband ..."

Freakin' brilliant.

Mollie had always amazed Cole with her ability to process any situation and make an instant decision that seemed to always be the very best decision.

"Okay," the Mountie said, his voice baritone and stern. "Move on. And next time, get a motel room."

"Thank you, officer," Cole said. He started the engine and drove slowly away from the scene. He kept the car in his rear view until they reached the corner and stopped. He signaled and made the turn. Then floored the Rover.

"Good job, Mollie."

She stared at Cole for a long moment.

"What?" he said.

"You have nice lips. I'd forgotten."

SIXTY-FIVE

"YOU REMEMBER ME?"

"Feliks Krakoer," Pytor said. "Of course."

No one ever forgets an assassin.

Pytor's bowels had gone watery when the sallow-faced thin man had appeared at his office door, somehow getting past security without any alert to him. That meant their loyalty was to Nikolai and not him. If he got out of this – How much money would it take? –Pytor would take care of those traitors.

"And vhy has Nikolai sent you to see me?"

"We should talk about it someplace else." Feliks tilted his head towards the door, the fluorescent lights highlighted the deep acne scars that ravaged his face.

"I am comfortable here. Besides, I have work to do."

"You remember Dimitri?"

Pytor nodded, his mind racing back to the power show that Nikolai had put on for all his younger associates. It was a decade before when Pytor was just starting out as a street organizer back in Moscow.

Dimitri had tried to go around Nikolai, siphoning off a small drug shipment for his own, but Nikolai, even then, had amazing control over his expanding empire and learned of the betrayal.

Pytor and the thirteen other organizers were escorted into a dark, mildew- smelling room, the dank odor assaulting their noses. Then suddenly a spotlight illuminated the center of the room, and there, hanging crucifix-style from the raw ceiling beams, his feet just inches above the floor so his arms were being pulled, slowly, excruciatingly, from their sockets, was Dimitri Sorokin. Or what was left of him.

His nose had been smashed so grotesquely that he had to breathe through his mouth, long, raspy gasps that sounded like stones rattling down a drainpipe. His eyes were swollen purplish slits. Pytor could see that several of Dimitri's fingers jutted out at impossible angles.

"Please," Dimitri pleaded. "Please."

"Please what?"

Nikolai's voice cut through the room as he stepped from the shadows. "Let you go? Forget that you tried to cheat me? Is that what you are asking, Dimitri Sorokin?"

Dimitri shook his head.

"No." He inhaled a painful, harsh breath. "Kill me."

For several long moments, there was only the grim sound of Dimitri fighting for his next rattling breath.

"Oh, that I am going to do for sure. It is only when."

Nikolai had then nodded at Feliks.

Pytor closed his eyes to shake off the horror show that Feliks Krakoer performed that night. A long descent into hell not just for poor Dimitri, but for the young associates who were forced to watch, too afraid to turn away since Nikolai had commanded them to look at what their future would be if they acted so foolishly as Dimitri.

Feliks Krakoer – ringmaster of the macabre, of torture, of sadism that went beyond monstrous.

Feliks Krakoer who asked Pytor again, "You remember Dimitri?"

"I have never forgotten him or that night."

"So, you leave with me, without any trouble, which of course would be useless, and you accept that which you cannot change, and I promise you there will be no pain."

"But I did not betray Nikolai. I am not Dimitri."

Somehow, in a move so subtle and fast that Pytor didn't comprehend it until it was a fact and the black snout of a small revolver was pointed at him. Pytor knew his weapons and recognized the Smith & Wesson Model 60 instantly – which explained Feliks's subtly: the S&W .357 Magnum's barrel was 3-inches. Its stainless-steel body was 23 ounces, and its synthetic grip was a sleek four finger platform.

"I am going to call Nikolai," Pytor said.

He reached for his cell on his desk, but Feliks' speed at covering ground was even more impressive than pulling a weapon. He clamped Pytor's wrist and the phone firmly to the glass top of the desk.

"I do not want to shoot you here, Pytor. But I vill, if necessary."

Pytor nodded and released his grip from the phone.

Feliks took away his hand and grasped the phone instantly. "Latest model iPhone. Nice."

Feliks gestured to the framed painting. It was an abstract of the ocean with wild turquoise and navy blues, splashes of white to represent the surf.

"Open safe."

"How did...?"

It was silly to ask. Nothing was secret with Nikolai.

"Do combination, but do not pull handle."

Pytor lifted the painting away from the wall and leaned it against the baseboard. He spun the dial to set the sequence, then rotated through the numbers:

10-31-1999. The first two numbers his birthday, followed by the year he came to America. Anyone with the basics of tradecraft could have figured it out.

"Turn around and look at me," Feliks said. He waited for Pytor to obey. "Now reach back and pull handle and open safe."

Pytor tapped behind him until his hand found the handle. He pulled it up instead of down, a small deterrent to thieves.

"Move."

Feliks kept Pytor within his side vision and glanced into the safe.

"Vhere's money?"

"Vot?"

Feliks thrust the Smith & Wesson at Pytor.

"Focking money, vhere?"

"Fifty thousand, right there. Take it."

Feliks grabbed Pytor's face and shoved it by the safe.

It was empty.

"Fock, fock." Pytor couldn't believe it.

Feliks had figured it out, too.

"Misha and Oleg. They took your money."

"I vill kill them."

"First you would have to find them."

"Help me, Feliks, I will pay you."

"How much?"

"Anything, just tell me."

"And this money? Say a million? You think that is enough to hide from Nikolai?"

Feliks stepped away and gestured with the gun.

Pytor stepped towards the door. Feliks was to his right. His best kicking leg side. He shifted his weight as if to take the next step, but instead pivoted and launched a vicious kick that caught Feliks in his heart.

It was the best kick of Pytor's life.

Feliks thundered back into the wall, his head bouncing off the edge of the safe door, opening a head wound that spouted blood all over Pytor's painting.

But Pytor didn't see it, he was sprinting for his life. He catapulted through the door, racing for the elevator.

And felt like his head had been taken off at the neck, his feet flying out from under him, as he was clotheslined by a massive forearm.

Pytor looked up, gasping for air, at two mammoth men. Russian thugs, back- up.

One of the men lifted Pytor up by his jacket as easily as picking up an infant.

"Ah, fock, Pytor," he heard Feliks say behind him. "Now, ve got do this hard vay."

"No, no. Please, please."

The other thug clamped a beefy hand over Pytor's mouth and nose.

He saw Feliks dial a number on his own phone.

Feliks chuckled as Nikolai answered.

"No, is not Pytor."

Feliks listened for a few moments.

"Nyet."

SIXTY-SIX

"NO, I AM SORRY."

Father Dominic smiled and handed Igor back the invitation.

"Do you think anyone at the church might know, Father?"

"I can check with Arthur, he's the church's Custodian of Records."

"Thank you."

"Arthur will be back tomorrow, and I can have him contact you. Is there a number where we can reach you?"

Igor shook his head. He didn't have time to wait, and he wasn't about to give the priest his cell number.

"No, I vas just passing through. I am heading to Brandon. Perhaps on my vay back?"

"Sure, but why not give me a number and he can call you and maybe save you having to double all the way back."

"My phone is from America, and I have been having trouble." He pointed to his ear, "Bad reception. I am thinking of getting pre-paid from local store."

Father Dominic nodded. He had heard confessions at Saint Bartholomew for more than two decades, so could tell when someone was lying.

And the brain inside this shaved, bullet-headed giant of a man was working at a feverish pace to spin a story that he thought he would accept.

"Good idea," Father Dominic said. There was a soul-gripping chill that emanated from this man, the kind that spoke of depravity and sins that no one in his church, he was sure would ever have committed.

"Thank you," said Igor and turned back for the M-3.

"In nomine Patris et Filii et Spiritus Sancti."

Father Dominic made the sign of the cross and waited on the church steps until Igor's car was gone.

The door behind him opened and his second in command, Father Michael, came up to him. The younger priest looked at his benign leader.

"Are you okay, Father? You look like you've seen Lucifer himself."

"Or one of his minions."

SIXTY-SEVEN

"TO SERVE AND PROTECT."

"What about it?" Mollie asked.

"Redundant when you think about it. Because if you're a cop, protection is your job. It's what you do. Serving is part of protecting."

"Unless you're serving coffee and donuts at the church bazaar."

"More like eating donuts and drinking coffee."

"You're as bored as I am."

"Yeah. Jesus, how long's it going to take them to find this place?" Cole checked his watch. "It's been two hours."

"I'm getting squirmy myself."

Cole looked at Mollie.

"Gotta pee." Cole started the Rover. They had parked up the street for fifteen minutes, then driven off. Parked in a different spot and repeated the maneuver.

They didn't want another busybody to call the RCMP again.

"There's a Tim Horton's about a mile back. Where they'll serve us coffee and donuts."

"And let me use the loo, too."

"Koo-koo-kachoo!"

"What?"

"Jesus, I'd never make it in prison."

"Because you're the law?"

"No, because staring at all that time ahead of me would drive me whacko. I mean, look at me, nonsense rhyming to your words. And this has only been a couple of hours."

"It isn't the time."

"What, then?"

"We're looking at a firefight. It's nervous energy. We're burning it off."

Five minutes later, they got out of the Rover. Mollie didn't close her door and looked at Cole.

"When I ran track in high school? Just before the meet, every stall in the rest room was occupied non-stop. One girl does her business, flushes. By the time she's at the sink to wash her hands, another girl's already sitting down. Their bodies were reacting to the upcoming competition and were preparing for fight or flight."

"Guess we better check our weapons again. Because we ain't flighting, so that means we're fighting."

SIXTY-EIGHT

"STOP ARGUING!"

Sergey's voice bounced off the car's glass.

"I'm not arguing," Aleksander said. "I'm driving."

"You driving wrong way. Follow GPS." Sergey held out Mikhail's cell that showed their vehicle and the route.

"I am!" Aleksander pointed at the Range Rover's impressive display. "The car's GPS. 2817 south."

"South? This says north. Fockin' Canucks, they have been hit with hockey pucks so much cannot even give straight directions." He thrust the phone back at Mikhail. "Here, piece of shit."

"Not all Canadians play hockey," Mikhail said.

"So then they just stupid naturally?"

"No, I'm just saying they couldn't all have been hit with a hockey puck."

"Hit with puck, are fockin' puck. Who gives shit?"

"There vas American comedy guy," Aleksander said, "who called people hockey puck. Don Rickles."

"Oh, vait. I remember this guy," Sergey said. "Vould insult everybody. Your vife, mother, vay you looked. Nasty focker. Said those things to me, I vould shot him in back of head."

"Well, you're too late," Aleksander said, "he's dead."

"Shit," Sergey said, "too bad. He vas funny guy."

"Your destination is ahead on the right," the GPS guidance voice intoned.

"Drive past," Sergey said, "ve make sure."

Aleksander slowed, and they checked out the house.

"Lights on," Sergey said. "They home."

Mikhail didn't see a car in the driveway, and it was a one-car garage. So, unless Annushka or Pavel parked on the street, it was more likely they weren't home. But he wasn't about to contradict Sergey. No telling what he might do.

Aleksander found a place to park several houses away and pulled to the curb.

Ten seconds later, Cole turned on to Annushka's street and saw the other Range Rover.

"There they are."

He nipped behind a Toyota Land Cruiser on jacked-up wheels. "They won't be able to see us behind this beast."

Mollie tilted her head to check the sight lines.

"And we won't be able to see them." She switched off the interior overhead light switch and opened her door. She held on to her safety belt and leaned out of the car. She kept her head just below the window sill and counted heads inside the Range Rover. "Looks like two ... no, three of them."

"Just like we thought," Cole said.

The interior light went on inside the Rover and confirmed Mollie's count.

"Three... and... one of them is getting out."

Cole stood on the door sill of their Rover and leaned on the roof.

"Big bald-headed tank. That ain't Alexsander or Mikhail."

The Rover's headlights came on and the vehicle reversed into the driveway and went back to the small garage.

In the reflected light, they saw Alexsander yank up the garage door.

"That's Alexsander," said Cole. "So, Mikhail's driving."

"Where's Mt. Baldy?"

Cole scanned the home.

"There, he's going in the back door."

"Let's go back to Horton's," Mollie said. "There's a phone booth with a landline outside Tim's."

Cole turned the automatic light switch off, so the Rover stayed dark as he backed away the Toyota.

He stayed in reverse around the corner, then spun the steering wheel, sending them in a tight 180° and floored it. The Range Rover's big wheels chirped and by the end of the block when they were doing 60 mph, he turned on the lights.

At Tim Horton's, Mollie was shouting hysterically into the phone before the dispatcher on the other end had a chance.

"Police? This is an emergency. There are men outside my home, twenty- twenty-eight south Farmington. In a black Range Rover. With American plates.

Hurry, please. They have guns!"

Before the dispatcher could say anything, Mollie hung up. She spun out of the booth and jumped into the passenger seat. "Go-go."

Cole rammed the Range Rover out of the lot and heard the squeal of brakes and a strident horn behind him.

He glanced at his rearview, but the angry driver was just a pair of rapidly diminishing headlights.

SIXTY-NINE

"FLASHING LIGHTS! FOCK!"

Sergey stood to the side of the window in Annushka's living room and kept his Desert Eagle ready. "Maybe neighbor saw us put Rover into garage."

"Three cars," Mikhail said.

The red and blue lights flickered through the blinds, throwing eerie shadows on the walls. There was just the single table lamp, so most of the house was in darkness.

"Here comes trouble," Sergey said. "Be quiet."

There was the loud rap of a heavy fist or a nightstick on the door. A few moments of silence, then the rap again -- stronger. "Hello. Police. Hello."

Sergey pointed at Mikhail and Aleksander to go and guard the back door.

He waited until they were in position, then stuffed the Desert Eagle behind his back, switched on all the living room lights, mussed up his hair, pulled his shirt out, then turned on the porch light.

"Vot is going on?" he said to the two burly cops that had stepped back from the door. He rubbed his eyes as if he'd been sleeping.

"We got a call of armed men from this house."

"Goddamn fockin' kids."

"Excuse me?" one of the cops said.

Sergey pointed across the street. "Neighbors' kids, twin boys. They think funny to play tricks, cause trouble. Goddamn delinquents."

"Are you Mister Pavel?"

"No. That is cousin. I mean, Annushka is cousin, Pavel is husband. They are at dinner. I am visiting. From Russia. Sorry for trouble, officers."

"You see a black Range Rover parked around here?"

"No. I vas asleep. Still little jet lag." He blinked at the cops. "I can go back to bed now?"

The two cops looked at each other. Something was hinky about this, but there wasn't a black Range Rover, no signs of violence, and his explanation seemed reasonable.

"Sorry to bother you, sir."

"No, thank you. Police in Canada much nicer than back home."

One of the cops smiled.

"I vill have Annushka talk to neighbors."

Sergey watched the cops stride back to the other men and women in blue and then softly shut the door. He waited a moment, then turned off the porch light and all the other lights in the house.

The strobing lights from the street disappeared and then he heard the acceleration of the police engines whine down the street.

"Okay," Sergey said, "volfes have gone, three little pigs are safe."

SEVENTY

"THIS IS DANGEROUS," COLE SAID.

"We've got to warn Annushka and Pavel," Mollie said.

She and Cole had scrambled around the corner from where Cole had jammed the Range Rover beside a fire hydrant, not risking parking behind the jacked-up Toyota a second time.

They'd watched the two cops go up to the door, waited and watched the discussion, then stepped back into the shadows as the flashing lights were extinguished.

"I didn't see the Rover," Mollie said.

"They backed it into the garage. Then broke into the house."

"They'll bivouac there all night, waiting for Annushka and Pavel."

"Or Igor."

"Or us."

"I'll call the hotel, leave a message at the front desk, tell them to have Annushka to call me in the morning."

"Might be better to call them now."

"Break into their second honeymoon?"

"Better that than their last holiday."

Cole nodded in agreement.

"I'll do it," Mollie said.

Cole jogged back to the Range Rover, started the engine, then drove to get Mollie.

"How'd it go?"

"I didn't tell her there was a break-in; just that they should stay an extra night.

And to not answer their cell or any calls from the front desk."

"And…?"

"She giggled and said both she and Pavel were going to call in sick tomorrow at their jobs."

"I hope she put out the 'Do Not Disturb' sign."

"Hit the Nav button," Mollie said. After the GPS voice came on, she said, "Find the nearest 7-Eleven."

She held up a finger before Cole could ask what was going on.

Three different locations appeared on the screen, and Mollie touched the first.

"Setting destination," came through the overhead speakers. "Make a legal U- turn and proceed to the Highlighted Route."

Cole turned the Range Rover around.

"7-Eleven?" he asked.

"I have an idea."

Fifteen minutes later she and Cole were stealth shadows on the side of Annushka's garage. Cole watched their backs, his weapon ready. Mollie carefully opened the side door of the garage and slipped inside. She kept her hand over her Maglite so the beam only shone down on the floor. She listened for any sounds, but the night was silent.

She eased away the door handle and jumped into the Range Rover and killed the interior overhead light fast enough so there was just the briefest flash and then the garage was black again except for her Maglite.

She withdrew a thick, plastic-encased chain from her jacket and looped it around the steering wheel and up through the overhead grab bar. She held both ends of the chain together in her left hand, then hooked a heavy-duty lock through them and slammed the lock shut. She yanked on the chain to make sure it was secure, then slipped beneath it and out of the Range Rover.

"They want to make a run for it," she said to Cole after they were away from the house, "that's exactly what they'll be doing: running."

Mollie's cell chirped. She checked the ID, and her face went white. "How … how is she? … Okay … okay, I see … yes, thank you … No, call me instantly."

She hung up and looked at Cole, her eyes bright with tears.

My mom went into cardiac arrest. She's alive, but in intensive care."

"Shit. I'm so sorry."

Cole fired up the engine, and the Range Rover screamed into a U-turn.

"Where you going?" Mollie said.

"Airport. You've got to go back."

"Cole! No. I've got to stay here."

"Bullshit. This is just a fucking job. And not a great one, either. Your mom is way more important, trust me."

"Jesus, who's gonna cover your back?"

"I'm not planning on doing anything that needs it."

Cole dialed Nikolai's cell.

"He's going to be pissed, you calling him this time of night."

"Fuck him. We need that plane ready."

Mollie reached out and grabbed Cole's hand.

"God, Cole, I can't lose you, too."

Cole powered the Range Rover around a curving on-ramp to the highway.

"I didn't come to Canada to die."

SEVENTY-ONE

COLE NEVER FELT MORE ALIVE.

"Take a deep breath," he told himself, his voice loud in the Range Rover.

But he couldn't deny it.

He was vibrating with energy.

He felt guilty for the way he was feeling, but being alone out here on edge, had heightened every one of his senses.

He loved and had loved, Mollie. But in every partnership, there is always that small part of you that is worried about the other. Your partner is your responsibility.

You have his or her back. Your partner gets hurt, you take the blame. He was sure Mollie felt it too: Is Cole okay? Where is he?

But now, alone against the four Russians, Cole was playing Texas Hold 'Em for keeps. And he was all in –he had to be. His life depended on it.

They're absolute stone killers. Total assassins. They'll take me out in a heartbeat; the last heartbeat of my life. Cole had told Nikolai everything about Mollie's mom and then demanded in no uncertain terms, that a plane be ready by the time they arrived at the airport.

Nikolai quickly agreed, then talked to Mollie and offered his condolences and all his resources.

After Mollie handed the cell back to Cole, Nikolai asked about the mission.

"This isn't the time," Cole snapped. "I'll fill you in later. Thanks for the jet."

He hung up and left Nikolai with far too many questions and no answers.

Why was Igor still in the wind? Why hadn't Sergey taken care of business?

Cole didn't know about the "Whys?"

He only knew about the Now and the When.

The Now was that the situation had changed: Nikolai certainly had told Mikhail, Aleksander and the bald-headed killer that Cole was all by himself.

The When was still ahead of him.

I've just got to get them outside.

SEVENTY-TWO

COLE SLIPPED INSIDE THE GARAGE.

He kept his fingers over his Maglite so there was just a soft, muted glow that extended three feet. How to bait the trap?

He checked the garage: Pavel was highly organized.

He had a large selection of tools mounted on pegboard, each outlined in white paint. Below them was a shiny red Craftsman toolbox. Cole opened it and took out a thick roll of duct tape.

Cole eased open the Range Rover's door and unwound a long ribbon of tape.

Then he wrapped it around one of the horn buttons. He went back, made sure the side door was open. He went to the Rover and slammed down the tape.

The horn blared. And kept blaring. Cole sprinted around to the back of the garage.

Jesus, that horn was loud.

"Vot the fock?" Sergey yelled. He grabbed his gun. "Mikhail, go check on Rover."

Mikhail moved for the back door. He took one of the .357 Magnums they'd captured from the RCMP and peered through the back door.

"Fockin' horn must have shorted."

Mikhail ran to the garage door and hauled it up. The blare from the horn, not blocked by the door seemed to triple in volume. He saw the duct tape and the chained steering wheel and pulled on the door handle. But the door was locked.

"Fock!" he shouted.

That moment of anger and distraction was followed by the most intense pain of his life as Cole shattered Mikhail's wrist with a tire iron.

The momentum from the powerful blow carried the tire iron down to the garage floor, where it bounced and then continued up as Cole backhanded it up into Mikhail's groin.

Which was a level of pain even beyond that from the wrist.

All this screaming through his mind.

And then … nothing.

A pool of darkness that he fell into as the butt of Cole's weapon smashed against his temple.

Cole dragged Mikhail's limp body out through the side door and rolled him into the plants behind the building. He ran back and got into a firing stance that allowed him to see anyone coming through the garage entrance without them being able to get a clear shot at him.

The horn kept bleating. Cole saw the next-door neighbor's light go on in their kitchen.

Crap. He hadn't counted on that.

"Hey! Pavel!" the neighbor yelled from his back porch. "Pavel!"

Cole saw the neighbor stomp off his porch, heading for the Beriya home. Just as he saw a tall Russian slip out of the back door, a nasty-looking weapon held down low by his thigh.

And from around the front, the same bullet-headed thug he'd seen talking to the police. This one had what looked like a machine-pistol.

There was a sudden squeal of tires on pavement and the white-red-blue flash of police lights as two squad cars slammed into the driveway.

The young Russian spun around and dived back for the house.

But the bullet-headed thug raised his weapon towards the police.

Cole didn't hesitate.

BAM!-BAM!

All hell broke loose.

One of Cole's shots grazed the bullet-headed man in the shoulder. He roared like some prehistoric animal, so loud he didn't hear the first two cops who'd taken cover behind their car's doors and were shouting, "DROP YOUR WEAPON!

DROP YOUR WEAPON!"

But the only thing Sergey dropped was his body. He dove to the ground and sent a burst of fire at the first cops.

They never had a chance.

Cole couldn't believe the firepower of the weapon as the bullets pierced the steel and then the cops' bullet-proof vests. They both were dead before the two cops in the squad car behind them could raise their weapons.

Sergey spun on his back in Cole's direction – where the shots had come from.

Cole cranked off three shots. The first two missed. So did the third, but it ricocheted off the concrete and creased Sergey's skull, opening a bloody divot across his shiny dome.

Cole sprinted around the garage and saw the neighbor scrambling back to his house on all fours.

The second squad car burned rubber in reverse as the cop riding shotgun yelled for back-up and officer down into his radio.

The driver slammed to a stop behind two cars. The cops jumped out and launched a hail of bullets at the man who'd killed their fellow officers.

But Sergey wasn't on the ground.

He was in the first squad car, behind the wheel.

He didn't wait for Aleksander, just floored the big sedan in reverse. The car catapulted out of the driveway and thundered into a neighbor's parked car.

As the Ford Crown Vic bounced away, metal shrieking, Aleksander flew from the house and sprinted for the squad car, shouting for Sergey to "Vait! Vait!"

The two cops opened fire. Sergey spun the wheel and flung open the door.

Bullets shattered the driver's side window.

One caught Aleksander's carotid artery.

Sergey floored the police car and wasn't ready for its massive torque. Its rear end fishtailed and slammed into a parked car. The car ricocheted off and shot ahead, hurtling for the stop sign. Sergey roared through it, lights flashing, siren wailing.

To his left, he saw three squad cars racing to the officer down call.

He stomped his foot and screamed down another block. He saw the turn and buried the brake pedal; fighting the wheel as the car's tires shrieked in protest and he blasted through the turn, caromed off another parked car and flashed through the next stop sign over 70 mph!

Cole had vaulted over the neighbor's back wall, cut through another yard and just as he made the front lawn, saw the stolen police car hurtle through the stop sign. He saw the flashing lights of the other approaching police cars, then heard the sirens.

Instead of going north to the Rover, he jogged south away from the on- coming law enforcement. He slowed down at the next intersection and saw two more cop cars roaring at him from this new direction. He dropped to the lawn of a small house and waited for the cops to pass in a flurry of light and sound.

He walked due east at a fast, controlled pace away from the crime scene. Two blocks later, he went north, then west until he had run an escape 'square,' and saw the Range Rover.

SEVENTY-THREE

IGOR SAW THE SIX COP CARS.

"Vot the fock?"

Then he saw three ambulances and two dark blue detectives' cars.

The local affiliate of CBC News had sent a single media truck and a small crew. The cameraman was trying to get better video, but the yellow crime-scene tape blocked the street at the corner, so he was over fifty yards away. The radio and newspaper reporters paced around, drinking coffee, bullshitting. The street was clogged with neighbors who stood in little groups up and down the block.

"Excuse me, officer," Igor said to one of the young cops standing guard, "vot happened?"

"Shooting incident. Do you live here?"

"No, I vas going to …"

Igor stopped because he saw that the squad cars and the other vehicles were in the middle of the block, close to where he thought Annushka's house would be.

"I usually take this street on vay home. Okay, thank you."

He turned to go: Vot if vas Annushka?

Igor sidled closer to a tall man with a beard and a clipboard. "Excuse, please. Do you know if anyone vas killed?"

The man glanced at Igor and said, "Rumor's that it was two cops."

"And a civilian," a thin man who was within earshot said. "But nothing's confirmed. We're still waiting for their PR guy to make a statement."

"But no voman?"

"You know somebody there?" the bearded man said, sensing

maybe a story.

"No. Just guessing. Vhen man shot at home, maybe vife is dead, too."

"Domestic violence," the beard said. He smiled and pointed at Igor, "You're not a reporter?"

"No fockin' vay. I hate reporters."

Before the two men could react, Igor had turned and was jogging to his car.

"Not a reporter?" the bearded reporter said. "No shit. Guy that huge? Looks more like a WFC wrestler."

"Either way, he's still an asshole," another reporter said. "We need tighter immigration laws."

Igor wasn't familiar with 'domestic violence.' A woman obeyed, or she was beaten until she did. Sometimes, the women struck back, usually with a gun.

Maybe cousin Annushuka has hot temper.

As he got to his car, Igor overheard a man talking on his cell: "Some terrorist shot two policemen." The man listened, then said, "Yeah, no shit ... yeah, I think he's dead. Fucker. I bet he's an illegal immigrant."

So not domestic violence.

Igor didn't turn on the M-3's engine. He leaned back in the dark interior, resting his back against the plush leather seat and tried to figure out what had brought cops to Annushka's house? And who had shot them? And who was the dead man?

Rotten focking luck. And to make things worse, his stomach clenched.

He had stopped to gas up the BMW and use the bathroom. As he went to pay, he felt his stomach growl with hunger. The station had a selection of enchiladas.

"Those any good?" he asked the clerk, who was Indian and looked like every computer geek that Igor had seen in the movies.

"Sure. Try the tuna. I'll nuke it for you."

"Okay. Add Coke, too."

Igor was tense as the clerk ran Evelyn St. Laurent's card, but it went through.

"Anything else?" the clerk asked.

"I am trying to find cousin. Have not seen her long time. She got married."

Igor held out the invitation.

The clerk, Ganesh, rapidly typed on a wireless keyboard and a few seconds later said, "Bingo."

He turned the screen around, so Igor could see through the glass of the cashier's window. It was a newspaper article showing a radiant Annushka and a beaming Pavel. Holy shit, too bad ve not kissing cousins. She is hot.

"2028 South Farmington," Ganesh said, interrupting Igor's incestuous thoughts. "Right there in the newspaper."

Big break, he'd thought as he drove for their home. She has big wedding, must have rich friends. Get some good money for vatch.

But now this: Cops everywhere.

Shit, hope immigrant vasn't Pavel.

Goddamn, vhy nothing is ever easy?

SEVENTY-FOUR

NIKOLAI'S VOICE WAS HARD.

"Americans not around. Rover not around. So how the fock police come?"

Sergey checked his mirrors and wiped the blood from his eyes. He was bleeding like the proverbial stuck pig. Head wounds were always bloody; even minor ones. He squeezed both sides of the gouge in his skull together.

Fock, going to need stiches. Vhere vas that guy shot him?

"Sergey!" Nikolai barked.

"Sorry, I am trying to stop blood."

"Blood? Are you hurt?"

"Is nothing. Head wound, lots of blood."

There was a pause from Nikolai, as if the oligarch was trying to calculate his next move or his possible losses.

"Should stop in vhile."

Stopping his head from bleeding was even more difficult because his left shoulder was on fire. The bullet had only grazed him, but it burned like hell.

"I need you there, Sergey. I'm sorry, but you can't go to an emergency room."

"Vasn't going to."

He didn't like taking shit from anybody, even someone as powerful as Nikolai Voronov. He wanted to tell this rich Russian prick that he shouldn't have sent kids to do a man's job. But Sergey hadn't outwitted or outgunned a long line of dead men by letting his emotions show.

"So vot is situation? Vhy you call?"

It took Nikolai a moment to process Sergey's question. He couldn't believe the gall.

"I don't need a reason."

Shit, fock up.

Right, sorry, boss.

"You trust two cops?"

Fock, keep mouth shut Sergey.

"I trust nobody. Vhy I have them monitored. Vhy I control action."

Things getting out of control.

Sergey put the Rover into a hard-left turn, the tires protesting, and accelerated down a long street in a business district. That thought, of Nikolai losing control, bothered Sergey. If things went sideways, it wouldn't be Nikolai's balls in the legal vice, it'd be his. Nikolai had so much power, legal and lethal, backed by his billions, that he couldn't be touched. It was men like Sergey who took the fall.

"Sergey? Are you listening?"

Fock, he'd been thinking.

"Sorry, must be bad service. Say again, please."

"Even more important now you take out this mad dog Igor. And voman cop is on vay home, so you only have Cole to execute."

"I don't need to vait see if cops take out Igor?"

"No. I am wiping slate clean. Mollie, that is his partner, is on my jet. I vill have someone meet her, offer ride from which she doesn't return."

Fock, Nikolai was in kill mode.

"And I vill send Cole to you. Both in picture and in person for set-up. Here is picture."

Sergey waited for the ding and opened the photo of Cole that Nikolai had sent.

"Focking pretty boy."

"Don't let looks fool you," Nikolai's voice snapped.

Fock, he'd voiced his thoughts out loud.

"I understand, boss."

"And Sergey? Vhen you see him? Don't vait. Shoot him on sight."

SEVENTY-FIVE

"WHAT'S HE LOOK LIKE?"

Cole was testing Nikolai.

"He is tall, dark brown hair."

"And his name?"

Nikolai hesitated just long enough to know this would be a lie, too.

"Dimitri. Dimitri Smirnoff."

"Like the vodka?"

"Yes."

"And why do I need him?"

"It's nothing personal. I think you and he vill vork vell together. Especially now that Mollie von't be around."

"Got it."

Cole ended the call and said to the phone.

"Sorry, Nikki-baby, I don't do AM-FM. I'm single channel. And Mollie is my partner. So, as you Russkies say, 'Fock you!'"

Annushka's house was two blocks away. He slowed down. Something was clicking in his head, but he couldn't pinpoint it. Something that Nikolai said or the way he said it. He replayed the message. Then a second time. What was it?

Working with an 'associate'? That wasn't Cole's style. And the associate sure as hell wasn't tall with brown hair. He was bald-headed. And a tank of a man. A man that had assassinated those policemen. The same associate that Nikolai had sent to kill him. Kill Mollie, too. And that's the part that's bothering me: Mollie.

"Now that Mollie von't be around.'

Not isn't around.

But won't be around.

Not present tense, but future.

Am I going 'round the bend, here?

Reading too much into it?

Alright, Cole, back to earth.

He started to text Mollie a message, but then remembered that she didn't want to use her cell because she didn't want the police to be able to track her. And what had Nikolai said when Cole had ordered the jet for Mollie? After he'd agreed, he'd asked what was going on, and Cole had said the cops were about to swarm Annushka's house.

And what had Nikolai said?

"Did you call them on cell?'

Why the hell would he ask that?

Because he's monitoring our phones. Mollie, you are smarter and more instinctive than you even know. Cole made a hard turn away from Annushka's house and raced for the 7-Eleven.

He had to get a prepaid cell phone.

Nikolai's monitoring would see the text message, but he wouldn't know who sent it. At least not right away.

And Mollie would be safe by the time he figured out the message.

Ten minutes later, Mollie's cell beeped.

How the hell did she get reception through up here? Must be Nikolai's special electronics on the plane. Of course, oligarchs didn't play by any rules but theirs.

She checked and saw it was a text message. But from a number, she didn't know. A Canadian number.

She opened the text:

Be sure to drive to the hospital and Nancy is safe.

Nancy? Who the hell sent this? Had to be a wrong number. Wasn't intended for her.

But she looked at it again.

Hospital. That's too close to be a mistake.

Nancy. Not her mother's name.

Shit! Cole. He was sending her a warning.

Something was up or would be when she landed and drove to the hospital.

Goddamnit, had to be Nikolai.

Repercussions from the cops at Annushka's? Or maybe he was tidying up loose ends. No. Nikolai had planned to take them out from the beginning. That was the only possible answer.

She started to text Cole. Then stopped. No. If Nikolai was monitoring her cell, he might not understand the message; or it would take him a while. But if she immediately contacted Cole, Nikolai would know that he had warned her. He would know they were on to him. And that they were on to him.

The stakes just went up. Nikolai had all that money and all those nasty men.

But she had Cole.

And Cole had her.

Damn, I should be back there.

She called the hospital and got through to her mother's room.

"This is Marilyn."

"Mom!"

"Oh, darling, how are you?"

"Wait, I thought ..."

"Oh, dear, did the doctors call you and set you worrying?"

"Yeah. And, yes, of course, I worry. Mom, are you... I mean."

"I had a little blip in the old pump. And that's really all it was, a little blip."

"The doctors said a myocardial infarction."

"I think it was just that tamale I ate."

"Tamale?"

Marilyn giggled. "And probably those three margaritas from Pancho's. Janice and I were celebrating her birthday, and we overdid it."

"I'm flying down to see you."

"Flying down? From where?"

"Canada."

"Mollie Simmons, you will do no such thing. I am perfectly fine."

There was some noise in the background, then Marilyn said, "The doctors are here. From the looks on their faces, I think they found out about the tamale."

Someone was talking to her mother, but Mollie couldn't make out what was being said.

"Okay, baby," Marilyn said, "These people stick and poke me. Bye. Love you."

"I love..." but Marilyn had hung up.

Mollie undid her belt buckle and stood up.

The hostess, Galina, who could have been Verushka's twin sister, smiled at Mollie. Then jumped to her feet as Mollie strode past her toward the cockpit, but she was too late. Mollie threw open the cabin door.

"Change of plans," Mollie said. "We're going back."

"Sorry, ve have orders," the pilot said. "Direct from Mister Voronov."

"You have new ones," Mollies said. She chambered a round in the automatic.

"Direct from Mister Beretta."

SEVENTY-SIX

"THANK YOU MISTER STRONSKIY."

Sergey thought Vladimir Stronskiy, the man who designed the SC-98 sniper rifle, was a genius. He loved the weapon. The claim was that it could hit a target 1,000 meters away. Sergey knew this to be true because he had shot Konstatin Zima, the greedy oil baron's head exploding like a cantaloupe, from just that distance.

"Time to feed baby," Sergey said.

He snapped the 7.62x54R 7N1 bullets into the 10-round magazine. He checked that the ammo was secure, then slammed home the clip. He had found the standard-issue first-aid kit in the police car's trunk. He'd cleaned his shoulder and head wounds; then put a large gauze pad on the shoulder and taped it tight. There was a needle and thread in the kit, so bellowing like a wounded ox, he'd stitched the head wound closed.

Fock, look like Frankenstein's neck.

The needle was a 5/8 circle, so its piercing and suture thread was thick. Sergey didn't know how to tie a surgical knot, so he jabbed the needle through two flaps and pulled the thread through, looped it over the wound and repeated the process like he'd seen his grandmother sew a pair of pants.

It was grueling and the most pain he'd felt in years, but the bleeding stopped.

Doctor Lomovitov.

He laughed. Once this bullshit job was finished, he'd have one of Nikolai's expensive Beverly Hills doctors do the job right. Maybe even get a plastic surgeon to tidy it up.

Fock, don't vant to have to grow hair.

Sergey checked his watch. Nikolai said he'd call him with the meeting set-up, but that was an hour ago. He had wedged the police car between two huge dumpsters at a construction site. From all the noise and garbled reports on the police radio, he knew it was only a matter of time before the car's GPS gave up its location.

The suppressor stretched the SC-98's length to 53", so there was no way to conceal it. He'd slung it over his shoulder and picked up the thick mesh bag that held the collection of weapons that he'd taken from his victims.

He started to jog, but the guns clanked against each other, so he had to walk down a dark side street away from the site. He looked for a passing motorist, but this street had zero traffic. Then his luck turned. A newer Lexus pulled up to a dark house, and the back door opened.

"Thanks," a man said, and got out of the car. "Here this is for you."

"Thanks. Much appreciated," the driver said. "You've got my number."

"Yeah, first time I used Uber. But for sure I will again."

Sergey had sprinted ahead to the stop sign, cut across the street so he was on the driver's side.

He laid the SC-98 and the bag on the grass so the driver wouldn't see it.

When the car pulled to the corner and stopped, Sergey had waved his hands and yelled, "Vait, vait! Please. Emergency."

The Uber driver squinted at Sergey, not sure whether to run the sign or be a good Samaritan.

The Samaritan, and commerce won out.

"Can I help you, sir?"

"Oh, thank you, thank you. My sister, she... I need to get to hospital."

The driver saw Sergey's monster stitches, and there was still some residue of blood on his skull, and he went hyper: "Hospital? Shit. Which one? Are you okay?"

But by then it was too late.

Sergey yanked open the door and smashed the butt end of the Desert Eagle into his temple. Sergey pulled him out of the car, checked the street.

Leave him here? Or put in trunk?

Sergey looked at the guy's face. He was young, maybe early 20s.

Okay, focker, you get break.

Sergey dragged him to the passenger side of the street and laid him on the sidewalk. He couldn't be seen from a passing motorist. By the time he regained consciousness or was discovered, Sergey planned on being out of Canada.

Sergey drove back to Annushka's street. Things had quieted down.

There was one squad car and the two detective vehicles. The reporters had gone back to file their stories, and the yellow crime-scene tape was gone. The street was again open to traffic. Every light was on in Annushka's house. As he drew even, he saw two men in suits, detectives, on the front lawn.

Sergey was startled by a bang on the car's body. He turned and saw an overweight man who'd just slapped the front fender of the Lexus.

"Hey! Uber. Stop."

Sergey was confused: How did he know this was an Uber. Then he noticed the sticker on the passenger side of the window.

The man flashed a badge, a detective. He motioned for Sergey to roll down his window.

Fock. If he looks on floor in back seat and sees rifle and guns, I am dead man.

"Sorry, off duty," Sergey said.

"This is police business. And stop rolling."

Sergey braked. His eyes bored into the detective's.

"I need to get back to the station, pronto. The city will pay you, no problem."

The detective kept his hand on the car, dragging it over the hood and then the panel as he went around to the passenger side.

So, I von't run him over.

The detective yanked open the door. "And don't worry about a ticket."

He laughed and dropped his fat ass on the seat. He gawked at Sergey's head.

"Jesus Christ, what the hell happened to you?"

"Accident."

"Not driving I hope?"

"No, sorry. I am not from here."

"So?"

"So I do not know vhere is station."

"Where'd you say you were from?"

I didn't focker. Nice try.

"Moscow."

"Moscow. Oh, right. That's about a thousand miles from here,"

"No. Moscow is halfvay around planet."

"I know. I'm talking about Moscow, North Dakota. Bet you didn't know that there was a town named Moscow in the US."

"No."

The detective chortled, smug in his lame joke.

"So, where I go for station?"

"Jesus, you weren't kidding. It's over on Fraser Highway. Go three blocks then make a left on 280th; that'll get you on the main road."

He checked out the Lexus.

"Nice ride."

He pushed down on his seat.

"Real leather. I like it."

He pulled down the visor and looked at his face in the mirror. He rubbed his cheek, his thick, rough hand scraping against his two-day-old beard.

Just as he reached to close the mirror, he stopped and peered at the corner.

"What the fuck's that?"

Sergey glanced at the mirror. The SC-98 rifle was on the floor, but the suppressor stuck up into the passenger corner of the back seat.

The detective tried to move around to get a better view, but his seat belt prevented any movement, his bulk overflowing the seat. "Stop the car."

"Vot?"

"Stop this goddamn car. Now!"

The detective unbuckled and shifted his fat ass to look in the back seat.

Sergey yanked on the emergency brake.

The Lexus nosedived, its tires screaming in protest, and it fishtailed wildly across the road. The detective, unbuckled and vulnerable, lurched forward and his face thundered into the windshield.

As he rebounded, his head thrown back, his neck exposed, Sergey's massive right fist backhanded into his throat.

The force was so powerful, it crushed the detective's larynx. He gasped for air, flopping like a fish on land. Those gurgling sounds, Sergey knew, were the last gasps of his life.

Sergey released the emergency brake and slammed the Lexus to the curb.

The detective clawed at his throat for air that wasn't coming. And then the stench of the detective's bowels flooded the car.

God damn! He just shit pants.

Sergey ran around the car and yanked open the passenger door. The poor bastard was really suffering, his eyes bulged, his face purplish with engorged blood as he fought to get air that would never come. Sergey grabbed him by the lapels and yanked. The detective went airborne for a few feet, and his left cheek slammed into the curb. He flopped back into the street and twitched several times. He gasped one long rasping breath. And then was quiet. Dead.

Sergey checked the area. No one around. He slipped out the man's wallet, his badge and weapon.

"Senior Detective Carl Percy. You have early retirement. Better go this vay, then die of heart attack from super fat ass."

He slipped Carl's money from the wallet.

"Three hundred American, fifty Canadian."

Sergey pocketed the American cash, dropped the wallet and

Canadian money to the street.

"Holy shit. This Smith & Wesson M&P9 Shield."

He worked the slide, correctly assuming the detective always had a round chambered, and caught a thick bullet mid-air as it ejected the live round.

"Centerfire laser? Nine-millimeter? And hollow-points? Canadian police don't fock around."

SEVENTY-SEVEN

"GAME FACE TIME, COLE."

He exhaled slowly.

He was hunkered down in the bushes of the neighbor's yard.

From here he could see the squad car's headlights shining on the street. In the quiet, now that the horn had been silenced, he could catch snatches of the detectives at the front of the house.

They'd found the Russian Cole had clubbed with the tire iron. Poor bastard wouldn't be shooting anybody for a long time.

Maybe never. Not with that wrist. Had to be broken in at least six places.

Cole heard the back door open, and two men came through and walked down the two steps to the driveway. They both lit cigarettes.

"Forensics about done?" one of them said.

"Another ten minutes is what Wilson said," the taller man answered.

The other man exhaled a long plume of smoke. "Be nice to get home early for a change."

"They ever get hold of the owners?"

"Not yet. Like they ghosted away."

Good, Annushka and Pavel were safe in the hotel.

"You think they took that Russky out? Then split?"

"Don't know. Supposedly, they're a real quiet couple. Newlyweds. Least that's what the neighbors say."

Another cop appeared at the back door. Cole could see the silver bars on his uniform reflect off the porch light.

"Lieutenant?"

"Brantley? You and Harrison got the short straw."

"What? Shit."

Cole assumed that was Brantley complaining.

"You're to secure the premises and wait for one of two people to show up."

"Who's that?"

"The owners. Or your relief."

The Lieutenant stepped closer to his men.

"Are we clear?"

"Yes sir."

"Because for a moment there, it sounded like you were complaining."

"No. No, sir."

"I didn't think so. Who would whine about sitting in your patrol car, drinking coffee and collecting overtime?"

"Uh... no one. No one, sir."

The Lieutenant turned and went back inside. Cole saw Brantley give the finger to his commanding officer. The two cops waited a minute or so, then followed back into the house.

Cole heard the front door slam shut, followed by two pairs of heavy shoes on the driveway. There were twin thumps as two car doors closed hard. A powerful engine roared to life; then a set of headlights pierced the night. The cop car shot forward, then braked hard. The rear yard was bathed in the harsh white backup lights as the car reversed into the driveway. A bright aura of red flashed as the driver hit the brakes; then there was only silence as the cop turned off the engine and he and his partner settled back to wait.

SEVENTY-EIGHT

"HOW LONG YOU FOCKERS STAY?"

Igor's spirits had risen when one after another of the squad cars – two, three, four and five – drove away. But when the sixth car reversed back into the driveway and killed its lights, he knew it was going to be a long night.

"They vaiting for Annushka come home. Or vaiting for shooter come back."

He checked his watch.

"Only half-hour? No vay!"

He flexed his legs against the floor and pressed the button on the seat frame.

The electric motor hummed impotently, the seat at the end of its track. There was no place to go. The small PSM pistol jabbed his back. He slipped it from his pants and tucked it into his jacket.

He'd parked the BMW in front of a small house with a neat, trimmed lawn and a driveway bordered by roses on both sides. The house was dark when he'd first arrived. The people living there were either extremely sound sleepers or too afraid to check out what was happening.

Or maybe they not home?

And suddenly, that thought – that the occupants were gone – became a fervent hope. He was getting kickback from the tuna enchilada. And his bladder was ready to burst. Tension and the anticipation of upcoming violence did that to him.

He didn't want to risk getting out of the car.

Then his bowels spasmed and his stomach rumbled.

Goddamn tuna. I knew tasted funny.

His stomach clenched like a fist.

Fock!

He moved the overhead light switch, so the interior would remain dark when he opened the door and staggered out, holding his abdomen.

It was very dark here, the neighbor's two-story house blocking the thin moonlight.

Please, no dog.

He held his Desert Eagle in his right hand and put his left hand on the handle. He turned it slowly, expecting resistance. But there was none.

Holy shit! Not locked.

Which meant the owner was probably home.

Igor eased open the door, which was weathered and cheap: the center panels where the paint had peeled was thin plywood. He could have put his fist through it. He eased open the door. The dim light that shone on the old linoleum floor was from the huge porcelain kitchen stove.

Arrgghh. His bowels spasmed hard.

Igor closed the door and took two steps into the kitchen. There was an old Formica table with chrome legs and four chairs with thick red cushions. His grandparents, Egor, for whom he was named and Irina, his beloved grandmother, had a set just like it.

Igor turned from the table and heard, just as he saw, a tiny brown and white dog come into the room, its nails clicking on the linoleum.

Don't bark, don't bark.

Igor stood motionless, clenching hard against his bowels.

The dog breathed hard several times, then cozied up to Igor. It sat at his feet.

Slowly, Igor reached down and brushed the dog's head. He moved to the dog's right. The dog moved with him, staying close but not interfering. Igor looked out the kitchen entrance. Down the hall, he could see the black-and-white tile floor of what had to be the bathroom.

How old is this house?

Igor tip-toed to the bathroom, went in and closed the door. The dog whimpered. Igor's pants were halfway down, but he opened the door to shush the dog, and it went quiet and sat down and watched.

Igor couldn't wait. He slid down his pants and boxers and just made the porcelain before his bowels exploded. It was so rude, so loud, Igor couldn't believe that those sounds could come from his body. The dog squeaked at the sound. Then shook its head at the stench that permeated the room. Igor put his hand over his nostrils. He should flush, get rid of the mess, but he knew he wasn't finished.

He waited, anticipating the next violent attack, and realized he was still holding the Desert Eagle. He reached behind him and put the automatic on the porcelain tank. His bowels clenched, and he gripped the towel bar on the sink next to the toilet.

Ohhhh!

He winced silently, his eyes closed to fight the pain and the burn. Jesus Christ, the burn. He kept them closed while the waves of fire roared through his rectum and intestine. He took deep breaths, fighting to not cry out. This was worse than any of the bullets he'd suffered during his life of crime.

Finally, the pain subsided. He opened his eyes.

And was staring at the twin black tunnels of a double-barreled shotgun.

"Son, what crawled into you and died?"

Igor was speechless.

The man holding the shotgun looked to be in his late seventies. His thin grey hair was spikey and sleep-tousled.

"This here's a Stevens 555 over and under. And I'm hoping I don't have to use it. But for a man that breaks into my house and takes what is easily the foulest dump it has been my misfortune to smell, I'd have a good cause. So, just stay calm and don't make any sudden movements."

Igor's gun was behind him. There was no way to get it and shoot this old geezer. Besides, he didn't want to alert the cops.

"I am sorry," Igor said. "I thought this was ..."

His bowels flexed again, and a sudden watery rush splashed into the bowl.

The dog whimpered and shook his head at the smell.

"For god sakes, flush the damn toilet."

"Okay. I vill."

"Slowly."

Igor kept his eyes on the old man and reached behind him, found the handle and pushed it down. The toilet flushed, and he could feel the water splash up on his ass. He was surprised that it helped.

"I am sorry. I am here from Russia and vas going to see my cousin, Annushka ..."

"Annushka's your cousin?"

"Yes, yes. You know her?"

"They haven't lived here that long, but yeah. I make it my business to know everybody on the block."

Igor shifted a little on the seat. Jesus, his ass was on fire. But the old man's shotgun moved with him.

"Vhen I come, they not there and... police."

The old man's eyes narrowed.

"You don't like the police?"

"No, no. I mean, yes, I like them. In fact, my father vas policeman back home. But if Annushka and Pavel are having trouble, then I do not vant to make more."

"Yeah, I could tell. You show up with that little noisemaker you've got sitting on my toilet tank, I'm sure the police would be very interested."

The old man moved into the bathroom and to Igor's right.

"That an Eagle?"

Igor was impressed at the man's knowledge.

"Yes. I keep for protection."

"What's your name?"

"Igor. Igor Petrak."

"Okay, Igor. I want you to raise your ass-cheeks and sit on your hands."

"Vot?"

"Do it."

Igor nodded, raised his right buttock and slid his right hand under it, then did the same with his left. The old man stood as far away from Igor as possible, then reached in and snatched the Desert Eagle.

"Now, you're going to get up, wash your hands and then tell me what the hell's going on."

"Can I vipe first?"

"What?"

"Vipe. My ... my ass."

The old man nodded.

"Yeah. Sounds like you might have a case of red-ass anyway. What the hell'd you eat?"

Igor freed his right hand, then his left.

"Tuna enchilada."

"Tuna? When'd they make it?"

"I... I don't know."

"That's your problem, right there. You can't eat tuna that's been sitting out for even a couple of hours. Shit goes rancid in no time."

"I thought tasted funny, but vas very hungry."

He reached across his body and pulled a long ribbon of paper from the roll.

He looked at the old man.

"What?"

"Is embarrassing. Not just sit here, but to clean up."

The old man nodded again and moved back into the doorway.

"Close door, just little? Please?"

The old man pulled the door shut just enough to give Igor some privacy.

There was a small wicker basket on the floor with several new rolls of toilet paper still in their wrappers. Igor slipped the small PSM pistol from his front pocket and picked a roll from the basket. He jammed the PSM into the thickness of the roll. He stood up, making sure his jeans didn't make a sound. He reached back and flushed the toilet.

The old man pushed open the door.

Igor pulled the trigger.

Fire belched through the fat roll of toilet paper, slightly muffling the sound as the heavy-grained bullet streaked on its fiery trail into the old man's heart.

He flew back to the opposite wall of the hallway, his head thudding so hard it dented the drywall.

The little dog howled in terror and bolted down the hall for what Igor thought was the old man's bedroom.

Fock, vhy you had to be home?

Igor listened. The little dog was whimpering from under the bed.

Igor didn't hear any other sounds. He looked down at the old man. Up close, his features sagged in death, he looked closer to ninety.

Vell, hope you had nice life.

Igor went back into the bathroom and cleaned up. He found some lanolin lotion in the medicine cabinet. He spread that on a square of toilet paper and tenderly patted his rectum. He took more lotion and spread a thick layer of it on a new square of paper and gingerly slipped that between his cheeks. He washed his hands again.

He retrieved his Desert Eagle; then picked up the Savage 555 shotgun. He checked the weapon.

Nasty. Better they call this 666. It's beast.

He moved to the living room and peered through the Venetian blinds at Annushka's house. The squad car was still there. Didn't look like they'd heard the shot.

Things looking up.

SEVENTY-EIGHT

"STARTING DESCENT."

Captain Aaron McSwain looked at Mollie. "And once we land you are in some serious shit."

Shut up," Mollie commanded.

"I'm not talking about the law. I'm talking about Voronov. What the hell you think he's going to do to you when he finds out you hi-jacked his plane?"

"Actually, it's what I'm going to do to Nikolai. Now, squelch this chatter and land this hunk of tin."

Captain Aaron McSwain looked like he came from an airline commercial: tall, handsome, with a full head of glossy black hair and chiseled cheekbones.

And that was Aaron's problem: he'd gotten by all his life on his looks. He wasn't used to a woman talking back, much less ordering him around. He didn't want to do it, but his hand casually moved for the distress/mayday signal.

But Mollie knew about planes and flying and hi-jacking.

"And don't even think about it."

"What?" But his hand kept moving.

Mollie slammed her Beretta into his ear.

"Code 7-5-0-0. Don't do it."

"Vait," Galina said from behind Mollie. "You cannot shoot."

"Aaron's charms got to you?"

"Vot? No vay. But if you shoot him, ve lose cabin pressure and ve all die."

Mollie slowly withdrew the nine-millimeter.

"How long before touch-down, Joe?" Mollie said.

Joe Hancock was the co-pilot. And while he didn't like what Mollie was doing, he liked living better.

"Six minutes. Take a seat, buckle yourself in."

"Sorry, no can do."

Joe glanced over his shoulder at Mollie. "You can trust me on this. I will land us safely."

"I do trust you."

"Then please take a seat."

Mollie went to a knee and held fast to the door frame.

"ETA?"

"Four minutes, thirty seconds." Joe said.

SEVENTY-NINE

"THEY'RE LATE."

Nikolai checked his watch again.

"Perhaps they had turbulence," Raisa said.

"Call the FAA."

Nikolai hit a button on his cell.

"Nothing," Grigory said as he answered Nikolai's call. "I checked with tower, and they have no plane coming in from Canada. In fact, no plane at all."

"Something has happened. Something bad."

"Mister Voronov?" Raisa called from the reception area.

"Hold on, Grigory."

He held his hand over the cell and strode to Raisa's area.

"Nothing. They have no flight plan that was registered. And no planes."

"Vould they tell you if there vas crash?"

Raisa crossed herself. "God forbid." She shook her head. "No, they wouldn't tell us unless we were family."

"How about my focking plane?"

Raisa cringed. She hated it when he cursed in her presence.

Nikolai saw Raisa's expression. "Sorry," he said.

"No problem. I will check again."

Nikolai went back into his office. "Grigory, you still with me?"

"Yes, boss."

"Tower tried radio contact?"

"Many times. Nothing."

"And no mayday call?"

"No."

"Shit."

"Maybe they had engine trouble and had to turn around."

Nikolai hadn't considered that possibility.

"Good idea, Grigory."

He made a mental note to give Grigory a raise.

"I vill check and get back to you."

EIGHTY

COLE WAS WORRIED.

Nothing from Mollie.

She's busy, or she didn't understand the message.

He started to text another message to her, then stopped.

Nikolai's tracking our cells. If she gets another from this cell, he may get suspicious.

Cole leaned so he could get a better look at the police car. The two cops were motionless as cardboard cut-outs, silhouettes in the soft moonlight.

Back door's open. I can use Annushka's landline.

Cole slipped from his hiding place.

What if Brantley or Harrison has to use the toilet?

He left his safe place and scurried towards the back door, keeping his profile low and angled away from the police car. There was a wrought-iron railing on the far side. Cole put both hands on the black-painted metal and vaulted over. He cleared it easily but didn't see the empty clay pot tucked into the corner. His foot came down on the edge. He lost his balanced and careened forward. There was a loud crack as the pot shattered.

Goddamn, my foot.

But there was no time for the pain.

He scrambled up as he heard the cop car doors open.

Back or inside?

No time to hide.

He turned the door handle and slipped inside the door. He hunkered down below the window level and limp-walked for the front of the house. His foot hurt like hell.

"What the hell?" Brantley's voice came through the screened back window.

Cole saw the reflected glow from the cops' flashlights as they moved towards the garage. Cole grabbed the Beriya's cordless phone and moved to the front door.

Just as he heard the back-door open.

And officer Harrison's voice: "Hello? ... Hello?"

Cole turned the handle and opened the front door just enough to slip through sideways and didn't shut it.

Right or left.

Left was the cop car.

He hobbled over and checked the ignition.

Keys were there.

Jesus, two stolen cop cars in the same night.

Now that's gotta be a record.

Cole inched door open enough so he could slip into the driver's seat.

Then in one continuous motion, he started the engine and slammed the gear shift into first.

He spun the wheel hard as the front tires cleared the driveway. The rear end of the car swung around as he floored it, the tires screaming.

EIGHTY-ONE

THE GULFSTREAM'S WHEELS SMOKED THE RUNWAY.

"GS-Roger-David," said the Tower flight controller, "touch-down successful at nine-thirty-seven."

"Roger. Proceeding to corporate hanger."

"Damnit," Aaron whined, "the night crew's gone. We'll have to do this ourselves."

The sleek jet rolled to the Voronov hanger. Joe checked the gauges, wrote in his flight log and killed the engines.

After they'd rolled to a stop, Mollie pushed Aaron. "You go into the head."

"What? No way."

"We're not flying, Aaron. So, I can shoot you."

He glared at her as he went past, then stumbled. In that moment of distraction, he pivoted and hit Mollie with a slashing back-fist right on the point of her chin. "Bitch!" he yelled and followed that with a straight right heel punch that Mollie managed to slip even as she was falling against a seat.

Aaron moved to destroy Mollie.

And felt the most intense pain of his life as his left leg collapsed like it had been severed from his body. He crashed into a seat and flopped into the aisle.

"Asshole," Galina snarled at him. She was ready to strike him again.

Aaron howled and writhed in pain.

Mollie struggled up from the seat; her pride hurt more than her

255

body.

"I... thank you."

"He has that coming for long time."

"You cunt! I'll kill you."

Galina pivoted into a strike position. "No-no, please."

"Christ, you aren't just a pretty boy," Joe said. "You're a goddamn pussy."

He looked at Mollie.

"Let's put that pile of crap where it belongs. In the toilet."

He grabbed his Aaron's shoulders.

"No, you're helping her?"

"Shut-up."

Mollie undid Aaron's belt buckle. "I'm sure this used to be a rush for you," she said. "A woman undoing your pants. But not tonight, Romeo."

She slid the leather strap out through the loops, yanked his arms behind him and while he yelped, bound his wrists together.

"You tore my knee to hell," he growled at Galina.

"Probably interior and exterior cruciates. Lateral too. And forget meniscus. I think total knee replacement."

"Goddamnit. I won't be able to fly for months."

"I'd say never," Galina said. "Not for Nikolai for sure."

Aaron's eyes betrayed his fear and bewilderment.

Mollie motioned for Galina to step up front with her. Joe just sat in a leather seat and looked out the window at the empty hangar area.

"My knee's on fire. Please, I need help."

Mollie and Galina came back.

"Here's the plan, Aaron. You go along, you keep your job with Voronov. You don't, you're..."

"Focked!" chirped Galina.

"What do I ... god, my I'm hurting so much."

"First, you shut up," Mollie said. "If you can do that, you can stay out here. We'll even put you on a seat, stretch out your leg."

"What's the plan?" Aaron said.

"You and Joe tried to save the Voronov aircraft, but you were unarmed. In your heroism, I hit your knee and..."

"No! Galina kicked me. Fucking bitch!"

Galina's palm slapped Aaron so hard it sounded like a gunshot. She grabbed his shoulder and pulled him towards the bathroom.

"He vill never cooperate."

Galina shoved Aaron into the bathroom so hard his head smacked into the toilet, his skull making a dull thud against the porcelain. He yelped in pain.

"You are focking pussy."

She grabbed a hand towel off the rack, stuffed it into his mouth, then tied it with her designer scarf. She slammed the door, muting Aaron's whimpering.

"I'll need your cell, Joe," Mollie said.

He handed it to Mollie.

"Galina will give it to you when she gets back."

"Where's she going?"

"I am being kidnapped," Galina said. "Makes for better story."

Mollie looked at Joe. "I'll need an hour."

Joe nodded. He undid his belt and looped it around one wrist.

"It'll take me about ninety minutes to make a brilliant escape. I mean, I'm only the Co-Captain."

"For now," Galina said. "But I see you flying high."

He smiled and nodded his gratitude.

"Do you know how to drive?" Mollie asked Galina.

"Does Bear know how to tap-dance?"

"It's 'Does a bear shit in the woods?'"

"I know. But mine is funnier, no?"

EIGHTY-TWO

"I DON'T UNDERSTAND QUVESTION."

Mikhail waited while the nurse adjusted the sling that held his left arm and the thick cast on his wrist. His right arm was handcuffed to the arm of his wheelchair.

Major Albert Baeten shook his head. He was born in Amsterdam and had carried his Dutch traits of pragmatism and direct speech with him when he'd migrated to Canada more than two decades ago. But this Schurkenstaat, this possible terrorist, was trying his patience.

"So, this Aleksander Prokhanovich. You saying you don't know him?"

"I am sorry, who?"

The nurse stepped back. She scanned Mikhail's eyes. She held up her index finger.

"Follow my finger."

She moved it left, then right. Brought it toward Mikhail's nose, then back.

"You have suffered major head trauma. We will need to keep you under observation for the next twelve hours."

"Not in this room," Albert said.

The nurse, Greetje Groeneveld, who was also Dutch, but born in Canada, was about to protest, but the Major's big palm held up like a stop sign, gave her pause.

He glanced again at her name tag. "This man is Schurkenstaat. You understand?"

Greetje glanced at Mikhail, her face paled. She took a deep breath, then answered in Dutch.

"Boef."

Albert nodded and smiled that they'd communicated without Mikhail knowing.

"He is a danger to every one of your patients."

"I see."

"Is there an isolated area of the hospital?"

"On the top floor."

"I vant Russian Consulate," Mikhail said. "I am political prisoner."

"Right. Next, you'll be claiming diplomatic immunity."

"You saw I vas tied up, like hostage."

"One more time, who is Aleksander Prokhanovich?"

"Vhich one vas he? Big bald guy?"

"Two local police officers were gunned down in cold blood. One of the assassins got away. But the brave Ruskin police ..."

"Vait! You are not from Ruskin?"

"We ask the questions," Albert snapped.

"No. I understand now. You do not act like cops. More like... secret service.

Show me badges again."

Albert thrust his badge at Mikhail.

"CSIS," he said. "Canadian Security Intelligence Service."

"Now for sure I demand Consulate. No more quvestions."

"Nearest Consulate's in Ontario," Albert said. "And I hear he's out of the country. Visiting the Fatherland."

Mikhail glared at Albert.

He's focking with me. Okay, I vill shut up.

"Vhen he comes, I talk." He made the child's pantomime of locking his lips and throwing away the key.

Albert stepped out of the ER and waved down the hall. A few moments later, two RCMP Mounties entered.

"Escort our distinguished guest up to his room. Ms. Groeneveld will show you the way." He smiled at Greetje and said, "Dank u wel."

"Geen dank." Then she said it again, in English, "You're welcome."

An orderly in scrubs came in and stood behind Mikhail's

wheelchair.

"Just position him outside the door," Greetje said. I'll be right with you."

The orderly rolled Mikhail into the hall, the two Mounties on either side.

Greetje made sure Mikhail was out of earshot before she whispered, "Will they need to draw their weapons?"

EIGHTY-THREE

"I HAVE FOCKING ARSENAL."

Sergey surveyed his cache of weapons.

"Six .357 Magnums. Thank you, Mounties." He shifted the RCMP's standard- issue automatics to the floor on the passenger side.

"Thank you, second time, Mister Vladimir Stronskiy."

Sergey knew the SV-98 wouldn't work for what he needed to do next – get in close, make sure he took out the right targets. But he wasn't going to leave the sniper's rifle.

A car had turned the corner and was coming down the dark street where Sergey had parked. His hand slid to his favorite gun, his Desert Eagle, and he turned his face away from the headlights as they got closer. The car passed, its speed never changing.

"Not cops. Or maybe smart ones - don't slow down."

He watched in his side mirror as the car continued down the street and turned a corner. He looked at the fat detective's Smith & Wesson M&P9.

"Powerful bullets, but too short killing range."

He placed the small automatic on the deck with the other weapons. He took one of Aleksander's and Mikhail's GSh-18s nine-millimeters and put the other on the slush pile.

"Eighteen shots. Never know when might need."

He thought of the two young men and shook his head.

"I vas right, boys in over their heads. Aleksander gunned down, Mikhail caught by cops."

He started the engine.

"They not survivors."

He checked his reflection in the rearview.

"I look like shit. But, I am survivor," he thumped his chest. "From very first. From Alfio. That focker."

And he remembered his mentor.

Alfio Zuberi is a rising star in the firmament of the Moscow mafia.

Sergey is sixteen; already a bruiser, well over 87 kgs.

He has been expelled from the private academy near Sergiyev Posad, the small town, 70 miles northeast of Moscow. As he boards the ancient steam engine train that will take him back to the capital, twin emotions wash over him.

The first, guilt, rises with the knowledge that his father Taavi, will be disappointed; appointments to the academy, even for the son of Gorbachev's official First Deputy Gardener, are hard won.

The second, anger, is more intense and all-consuming. He knows that his expulsion is retaliation cleverly disguised as academia. Edvard Adin, the son of the academy's largest contributor had enlisted the two biggest boys in the senior class to beat Sergey for what Edvard thought was disrespect for the Adin name.

Sergey had broken one boy's arm, gave the larger boy a concussion. He does not harm Edvard, but instead strips him naked and hangs him by his ankles upside down in the school commons. Edvard screams and cries as his classmates roar and point fingers. It is a twenty-minute long humiliation that does not end until the headmaster realizes that not one boy is in a classroom.

Sergey is made to listen to a dressing-down by the headmaster and two teachers that had constantly given Sergey extra homework and disciplined him daily.

The phones to Moscow do not work, so Sergey's father has no inkling of what has happened; only that a telegram has arrived informing him to be at the train station that evening at 7:00 pm.

When Taavi and his wife Ida see Sergey disembark they are apprehensive and confused. Sergey's explanation that this is a putsch for standing up for himself is accepted without comment by Taavi, but Sergey knows he has hurt his father deeply.

His mother lovingly accepts his story and takes him home for a hot meal and his room, which is exactly as it was when he left two years before.

A year later, Sergey is working for Alfio. He starts as a runner, becomes an enforcer and is now one of Alfio's three bodyguards. Sergey is awash in the mafioso life of easy women, fast cars and revenge.

And of course, the money. Jesus, the money. Sergey can't believe how much and how often Alfio sits with stacks of banded cash, showing off, laughing. Sergey also knows that Alfio, for all his swagger, is one of the lower masks on the Solntsevskaya Bratva Mafiya totem pole; and the profits rise as you move up.

Sergey will turn eighteen in two days when Alfio orders him to go on a special meeting with Semion Ivankov. Ivankov is a treacherous rival, who tells Alfio they should join forces and get a bigger slice of the pie. The meeting will be on neutral ground, and they will each bring one man as protector.

"Ve are vory v Jaxone, no?" Semion says. "We are thieves-in-law."

Which in Semion-speak is: "You can trust me."

The neutral place is a small coffee shop on the north side of Moscow. The meeting is scheduled for three in the afternoon. The shop is empty except for the very nervous owner who rattles the cups and saucers while he's serving.

Sergey doesn't take coffee; neither does Konstantin, Semion's bodyguard.

The two rising gangsters are seated in the rear of the shop. Konstantin faces the shop's front window, Sergey faces away, his eyes on the rear entrance.

Sergey is not sure what galvanizes his counter-attack and saving Alfio's life on the attempted assassination. He thought, later in the safety of his house, that it was the narrowing of Konstantin's eyes. Or maybe the way the owner spun back for the kitchen.

It doesn't matter.

Sergey is moving.

He pulls his CZ-75 Compact and shoots Konstantin twice while

Semion and Alfio are still reacting to the noise. Sergey swings the Czech automatic and puts a single round between Semion's eyes and grabs Alfio by his jacket as his boss's mouth hangs open.

Sergey shoves Alfio through the back door as the wall next to them is ventilated by machine-gun fire. Sergey hears the plate glass window explode and vanish in a hail of bullets from what Alfio and Sergey learn later are three sedans filled with Semion's hoods.

Sergey spins around and drops to his knee at the back door and blows the first Semion assassin off his feet with three shots.

"GO-GO!" Sergey bellows at Alfio. "Red Lada. Josef driving."

Alfio still doesn't grasp what Sergey has accomplished until they are out of the parking lot and roaring away towards the highway.

"How did you...? I don't understand," Alfio says, his eyes wide.

"I did not trust Semion, boss."

"You realize vot fock you have done?"

Sergey can't believe it.

"Save your life."

"Fock you. You killed Semion, now Oleg vill come after me."

Alfio is in the back seat and reaching for his cell when Sergey's massive fist crashes into his nose. The gangster's blood explodes down the front of his once brilliant white shirt.

"Fock, Sergey!" Josef yells.

Sergey hits Alfio again.

This blow shatters his cheekbone. He sags against his seat-belt. Incoherent, concussed.

"Turn around," Sergey orders. "Go back to shop."

"Vot? No, you crazy."

Josef sees the look in Sergey's eyes and turns back to the road, finds an opening in traffic, then slams the Russian sedan into a 180° screaming turn. He accelerates away from the cars and trucks behind them – horns blaring and tires shrieking – and slaloms through traffic well over the speed limit.

"Slow down," Sergey says as the coffee shop comes into view.

Sergey surveys the area. The police have not arrived.

And Semion's men have gone.

"Go around back."

As they pull into the lot, Sergey yanks Alfio from the car and drags him toward the rear door of the coffee shop.

He turns the moaning Alfio around, so his back is to the restaurant, as if he is running away. He stands him upright, balances him against gravity, then shoves him forward.

As Alfio stumbles, Sergey shoots him three times.

"Go," he yells as he jumps into the Lada.

Josef can't speak.

"You vere hero," Sergey says.

"Vot?"

"Hero. Ve both vere. Ve tried saving Alfio's life, but too many Semion's men. They kill our boss."

EIGHTY-FOUR

"YES, BOSS, I AM PARKED UP STREET."

Sergey gave his cell and Nikolai the finger.

"Vhy are you whispering?" Nikolai asked

"Vindows open. Don't vant anyone hear."

He had opened all the windows and the sunroof, then turned on the air conditioning. That had helped get rid of the stink when Carl Percy had lost control of his bowels. Sergey thought Percy's trousers had leaked and his feces were smeared into the seat or floor, but he didn't want to check.

"You can see the house and anyone that comes or goes?"

"Yes."

"Cop are still around?"

"Only one car. Parked in driveway."

"Any sign of Cole?"

Stupid focking quevestion.

If I see pretty boy, I kill him.

"No, boss. He has not shown up yet."

Nikolai drummed his fingers on his desk.

His Gulfstream was missing; which meant Mollie was also missing. And she was too much the firebrand to be out on the loose. Cole, wasn't returning his calls.

And Nikolai got the sense that Cole unchained was even worse than Mollie.

Aleksander was dead.

Bruno Campanini, who he liked very much, would have to be eliminated.

Mikhail was in police custody.

This focking animal Igor, where was he?

FUBAR. Definitely FUBAR.

"Boss? Boss? You there?"

"Vot?"

Nikolai realized he'd been thinking about his problems and hadn't heard Sergey. "Yes, I am here. I am thinking."

"That's vhy you boss. You great thinker."

Nikolai wasn't sure whether Sergey was complimenting him or insulting him.

And that was definitely FUBAR. If you don't know what your workers are going to do before they do it, you are in trouble.

"I vill call you back. Be ready."

"No shit," Sergey said to the cell after Voronov ended the call.

I am alvays ready.

But he wasn't ready to see the police car rocket out of the driveway and hurtle down the street.

The front door of Annushka's house flew open and a cop ran after the rapidly-disappearing squad car. A moment later, the other cop came sprinting around from the back of the house.

Somebody stole car? No vay.

The smile broke across Sergey's face, then turned into a loud guffaw.

Who did this? Vhere vas he? He vas hero.

Both cops were on their radios.

Shit. Street vill be crawling vith them again. Twice in same night.

Sergey started the Lexus. The headlights came on automatically, but he snapped them off. He checked to see if the cops had seen the lights, but they were too busy flapping their arms and yelling at each other. He slowly pulled away from the curb, the car dark. He kept the wheel cranked over and turned the sleek machine in the opposite direction. It was a narrow street, but the car's tight lock-to- lock steering made it in one smooth turn.

Sergey let the car's idle speed carry it away from the cops while his eyes stayed focused on the rear view. When he reached the corner, he stomped on the accelerator and hit the lights as he accelerated into the turn.

Igor also saw the police car barrel away from Annushka's house.

Now I go inside.

Then he saw the two cops running after the car.

No! Somebody stole it?

He almost missed the Lexus gliding down the street in total darkness and was thinking that the driver must be an idiot. But when the Lexus turned the corner, hit its lights and roared away, his curiosity peaked.

Doesn't vant cops to see him. Vhy?

The Lexus hurtled north. Sergey saw the red and blue flashing lights of police car rolling towards the crime scene coming from the south and took the first turn heading east. He wanted to approach and observe Annushka's house from the opposite direction; just in case a neighbor or the cops had seen him.

Igor heard the sirens before he saw the flashing lights.

Then the street was filled with three black-and-whites.

He watched from inside the darkness of the house.

The cars all slammed to stops, and the six cops erupted from the vehicles. Igor could hear shouts from the two cops whose car had been stolen but couldn't make out the words. He hustled to the front lawn and went down a couple of houses. Now the words carried to him loud and clear.

"Jesus Christ, Brantley, you know how this makes the department look?"

Before Brantly could answer, a black SUV cruised to a stop. The driver got out and opened the rear door. A tall man in a dark suit stepped out of the Lincoln Navigator.

Must be Chief.

Igor couldn't hear a word. Men in power didn't need to raise their voices. The two cops that had lost their vehicle stood at attention and nodded their heads, silently taking the dressing-down. The Chief pointed up the street. The two cops who'd lost the car went to Annushka's neighbor and knocked on the door.

Fock, they going door-to-door.

Igor hustled back and locked all the doors.

I von't answer.

There were eight houses between Annushka's house and the old man's, four on each side of the street. The cops would be here in five minutes. Igor made sure the back door was locked, then leaned against the wall in the hallway. He racked the Savage 555 shotgun and waited.

EIGHTY-FIVE

COLE HELD OFF GOING DARK.

He kept the siren and lights on and roared through the streets. Just another two blocks. He scanned the side streets. There!

He went to silent and dark mode, took a turn at speed and slammed into the driveway of a business center.

"Jesus!"

He didn't see the speed bumps and the car hit them so hard his head thumped the ceiling. He stepped on the brakes but still hit the next speed bump hard enough to rattle his teeth. The rear tires smoked, and the car finally stopped.

He turned for the back of the section, looking for the dumpsters.

There were two big green ones. Unfortunately, they were behind a locked gate. He put the car broadside along the gate. That way he'd blocked the gate but kept the car's profile difficult to see from the street.

Cole turned off the engine.

There was a Colt C8 assault rifle locked in the upright position. These were lethal weapons that Canadian police and now the RCMP used. It was a defensive move that barely kept them even against the increase and intensity of violent crimes from Yukon and British Columbia all the way to Quebec and even Prince Edward Island.

Cole checked the keys on the ring and inserted the smallest one into the rack lock holding the C8. It snapped open and he took the rifle with him as he stepped out into the dark lot.

His cell rang.

"Mollie! You can't be in L.A. already."

"No. We're... I'm heading back to you."

"Wait, how …?"

"I'll explain when I see you. Where are you?"

"Ditching a police car."

"No, Cole, what're you doing?"

"I'll explain when I see you."

He ran to the front of the lot and looked at the sign, its neon flickering on/off.

"I'm at the Knowlton Business Centre."

"I know vhere is."

"Who was that?"

"Galina. You'll like her."

"Hello, Cole," Galina's voice on Bluetooth came through loud and clear. "See you in five."

EIGHTY-SIX

THE COPS WERE THERE IN THREE.

"Fock!" Igor hissed under his breath.

Bang! Bang!

"Hello! Police. Open your door please."

Breath in, breath out. Don't vorry.

Two more hard knocks.

"Police. Open the door, please."

Igor could hear the cop talking to someone, but the other person's words weren't loud enough to understand.

"Hello. Leo?" a woman's voice shouted.

There was another double-knock, these not as loud.

"Hello, Leo? It's Brenda."

Bang-bang. Loud and hard. Had to be the cop.

"Maybe he's gone," said the cop.

"No. He would have told me, so I could look in on Joshie."

"Who's Joshie?"

"His dog." She said it as if the cop should have known that.

Joshie? Vierd to call dog man's name.

Igor looked towards the bedroom. Joshie had stopped whimpering but was nowhere to be seen.

"I've got a spare key," Brenda said. "I hope nothing's happened to him."

"Hold on a second, ma'am."

The cop's radio squawked, and he spoke into it.

"This is Jennings. I'm at twenty-eight oh nine. Owner isn't responding. Neighbor believes he is at home. Entering premises for visual confirmation and to check on ..."

"Kalogerakis," Brenda said. "Leo Kalogerakis."

"Leo Kalogerakis."

More squawking.

"Negative on Code five-seven-nine. He's in mid-eighties according to neighbor ... Roger."

Jennings and Brenda moved away from the front door.

Igor could hear their footsteps going down the driveway. He hustled to the kitchen and squatted by the door.

"Here's the key," Brenda said. "Under the plant."

"Not the safest," Jennings said.

"We live in a very safe neighborhood." She turned the lock. "At least we did until..." She came into the kitchen. "Leo...? Leo...?"

Brenda started for the hallway. Jennings was right behind her. As he moved to shut the door, Igor jammed the Savage into his face.

"Not a fockin' sound."

Brenda turned and saw Igor and gasped.

EIGHTY-SEVEN

COLE INHALED SHARPLY.

"Galina? You could be Verushka."

"I know, ve look like sisters."

"Not just sisters," Cole said, "more like twins."

He turned to Mollie.

"I gave you the heads-up for L.A., not to come back."

"Nikolai wanted to separate us," she said.

"Easier to take out one at time," Galina said. "Vhere ve going?"

"Back to the party," Mollie said. "Annushka's house."

She buried the accelerator and the big sedan flew down the street.

"You really ditched a police car?" Mollie said. "Where's your car?"

"It *was* the police car."

"Wait, run that by me again."

Galina put the big sedan into a power slide around a corner. She smiled at Cole in the rear view.

"My father vas Formula One driver. Back in 'eighties. Before I am born. He crashed several times, so my mother, who vas only girlfriend at time, said 'Lose cars or lose me.' He chose visely. Then, vhen I vas fourteen or so, he teach me how to drive."

Galina stomped the gas and the car leaped forward.

"You two talk, I drive."

Between grabbing the overhead handle several times and bracing his feet against the floorboard, Cole told Mollie and Galina everything that had happened and what his game plan was to take down Igor and what was left of the team that Nikolai had sent.

"One guy's still out there," Cole finished.

"That vould be Sergey Lomovitov," Galina said.

"How the hell do you know that?" Cole said.

"Ve know Nikolai Voronov and companies very vell."

"Who's we?" Cole said.

"You don't work for Nikolai," Mollie said.

Galina slammed the Genesis around a turn. "I do."

"But you also work for someone else." Mollie said.

Galina nodded, her eyes on the road.

"My government has been hunting Comrade Voronov for long time."

Cole and Mollie looked at each other.

"KGB?" Cole asked.

But Galina didn't answer.

"It fits" Mollie said. "You wiped out pretty boy Aaron on the plane. You're an ace driver. And I'm sure you're armed."

Galina smiled.

"And dangerous."

EIGHTY-EIGHT

"YOU DO NOT VANT FOCK VIT ME."

Igor's eyes were red with rage.

"You don't want to do this." Jennings said.

"Oh, my god, my god," Brenda wailed.

"You shut up." Igor said, not taking his eyes off Jennings.

"On knees. Now."

Igor stepped back so Jennings couldn't attack him and to include Brenda in his field of fire.

"You too, Brenda."

"How did...?"

"Do it, ma'am." Jennings said.

"Now, Jennings," Igor said, "you lie on stomach, hands behind head."

Jennings stared at Igor, calculating the distance, what were his odds. Then, wisely, obeyed.

"Brenda, you handcuff his right wrist."

She pulled the handcuffs from Jennings' belt. She attached the bracelet to Jennings' wrist and clicked it down.

"Now put other on your right wrist."

She hesitated, and Igor took a menacing step toward Brenda, to scare her, but more to get her ass in gear. She did as ordered.

"Don't move."

Igor pulled on the cuffs. They were cinched down to the last notch.

"Now give me keys."

"I don't know where..."

"In my right pocket," said Jennings.

Brenda was squeamish about going into a man's pockets so near his crotch; and she wasn't adept at using her left hand. But after a moment, she pulled out the key.

"You take long time, Brenda. You feeling Jennings' dick?"

She gasped, but Igor's lewd laugh stifled that.

"Okay. You get vote on vot happens next. I can hit Jennings and you, in head, knock you out. Or I put you in bathroom, take your vord that..."

Jennings' radio squawked.

"Don't fockin' answer."

A few moments passed; then the radio squawked again.

"I don't respond, they'll come and check. Then it'll be not good for anybody."

"I die, one guy. How many cops you vant me take vith me?"

Jennings stared up at Igor, the hatred evident on his face.

"Let me just say everything's okay."

Igor nodded. "Tell them Leo is sleeping."

Jennings fumbled with his left hand, pressed the mic button, "Negative on Code five-seven-nine. Mr. Kalogerakis was asleep ... Roger."

"Good vork, Jennings. You save lives tonight."

Igor gestured with the shotgun.

"Both into bathroom."

Jennings used his left hand and got to his feet. He used his right hand to help Brenda up. They started down the hall and then Brenda staggered.

"Oh my god, my god. Leo."

Leo was an island of sagging skin and bones in a bloody sea of crimson.

"You're under arrest for murder," Jennings snarled. "You bastard."

Igor jabbed Jennings hard in the ribs. But the barrel bounced off the cop's bulletproof vest.

"Take off your blouse, Brenda."

She looked at Igor, horrified.

"I don't vant see your old saggy tits, okay? You are going to stuff blouse in Jennings' big mouth. Then tie sleeves in back, so it stays."

Igor waited while Brenda removed her blouse, revealing a lacey pink bra. She wadded up her blouse and put it in the cop's mouth.

"I'm sorry, really."

Jennings nodded his head that he understood.

Brenda gathered the sleeves of her blouse, but Igor threw her to the floor, the motion unbalancing Jennings because of their handcuffed wrists. Igor moved fast and yanked the sleeves together himself. He pulled so hard, Jennings head snapped backward and by the time the officer had recovered, Igor had tied off the blouse.

Before Jennings could plan any play, Igor yanked the cop's Smith & Wesson 9 mm automatic. He took a washcloth from the chrome rack on the sink and handed it to Brenda. She didn't hesitate and stuffed it into her mouth, grimacing at the taste. He grabbed a hand towel, wrapped it around her mouth and secured the gag.

"You remove gags in ten minutes. You do before, and I vill kill you. I may vait outside see if you obey."

EIGHTY-NINE

"FOCK YOUR ORDERS."

Sergey didn't answer Nikolai's third call.

"All that money and you act like pussy. You have vagina instead of dick?"

Sergey had doubled back towards Annushka's house going up a hill. He rolled past a small mini-mart mall, then hit the brakes, did a tight U-turn and drove back into the lot. All the stores were closed. But if Sergey was right, the elevation of the mall, being on the tallest park of the hill might be perfect for his job. He parked the Lexus in the back. He bounded up on the lone dumpster, then unto the roof of the car. He hated to scratch the metallic paint, but it wasn't his car. He eased the barrel of the SV-98 rifle over the edge of the flat roof, making sure the sight didn't get damaged.

Then he jumped up, caught the edge of the rough stucco and pulled himself up and over the ledge. He looked in the distance. About a quarter-mile away he could see the red-blue flashing lights of the cop cars on Annushka's street. He put the scope to his eye and dialed in.

"I am right."

In the yellow-green moonscape of the night vision scope, the heads of the cops were dark green silhouetted targets in the scope. He shifted from one to another.

They were standing around, jawing at each other.

"Can't blame you sorry bastards. Have a police car stolen right under noses."

His cell chirped again. Nikolai again.

He turned off his cell "That's it. No more."

Officer Karim Shikir also said "No more." He pointed at the green-shuttered neat home. "That's the last one."

"Okay, Kev, let's go."

Karim's partner, Tom Hansen, had trouble with Islamic names and always butchered his pronunciation of Karim, so had just defaulted to calling him Kevin.

And then had shortened that to just Kev.

It annoyed Karim that Tom, whose duty was to cover his back, like Karim did Tom's, couldn't expend the small effort to learn a simple thing like his name. But Karim was the first Muslim on the force and knew that he was always under scrutiny, so had let it pass.

Hansen's radio squawked. He listened and said, "No, sir; haven't seen Jennings... Twenty-eight-oh-nine... Roger."

Before Tom could relay the message, Karim had already started for the house.

"Hey, we're supposed to ..."

"Check on Jennings. I heard."

"Oh, yeah. Right." Tom caught up with Karim.

"Jennings hasn't reported?" Karim asked.

He didn't wait for an answer and marched straight for the house.

"No. He's probably lollygagging around."

Karim looked at Tom, his brow furrowed.

"Lollygagging?"

Karim hated to admit that his phenomenal learning of the English language in so short a time still required someone to explain certain colloquiums and idioms to him.

"Yeah. You know, screwing around."

Tom moved his fist up and down; as if Jennings were masturbating.

Igor heard the cops' footsteps on the porch as he looked over his note he was leaving for Annushka.

He whispered the words in English as the read the Russian:

Аннушка, Привет, мой кузен. Привет из Москвы. Я присутствую для вас. Я позвоню вам через два дня после того, как все эти проблемы прекратятся. Игорь

"Annushka, Hello my cousin. Greetings from Moscow. I have present for you. I will call you in two days after all this trouble has stopped. Igor."

He propped the note against the salt and pepper shaker set that was on the kitchen table. The cops would find it and get it to her. He listened. No sound from Jennings and Brenda. But then came the double-bang on the front door.

"Yo, Jennings. Open up."

Igor eased open the kitchen door and went out into the night. He propped the Savage 555 against the back wall, then vaulted over. He then reached back into the yard and carefully pulled the gun to him. He'd made sure the safety was on before he'd gone over the wall, but you couldn't be too careful. He clicked off the safety and bent down as he ran through the neighbor's yard.

I have maybe five minutes.

Igor sprinted down the narrow cement path along the fences between the houses and bolted into the front yard. The street was empty. He needed to find a car, but not around here. His footsteps sounded loud to him as he pounded up the block and spun around a corner. He ran faster as he saw a big black sedan heading for him.

A black Genesis G90 sedan.

Cole, Mollie and Galina all saw the bald burly man running their way.

"IGOR!" Galina shouted.

But Igor didn't react. He cantilevered his body out, the Savage at an angle and let loose both barrels.

The noise was deafening. Twin booms of death.

But the Genesis was traveling faster than he'd calculated. And going in the opposite direction.

And the loads were birdshot. Not buckshot or slugs.

Which saved their lives.

Still.

The small No. 10 lead pellets, 848 of them per ounce, launched from the twin barrels in a subsonic cloud. Travelling at 1600-feet-per-second, they disintegrated the body panel, penetrating to the door pillar. The driver and passenger windows vanished in an explosion of glass that cut Galina's shoulder, Mollie's neck and Cole's left cheek.

Fock, birdshot. Goddamn old man.

Igor stumbled two steps, the recoil throwing off his balance. He dropped the Savage and fought to stay upright. But his momentum was too much. His left foot caught a rise in the sidewalk and sent him sprawling.

Galina slammed on the brakes and put the Genesis into a tire-smoking 180° U-turn ... that didn't quite make it. The big G90 rammed a parked car and bounced into the road, the impact killing the engine.

"Goddamn!" Galina shouted.

Cole was already out one door.

Mollie was out the other.

Cole took the sidewalk, Mollie the street.

Igor scrambled up and looked back. The SV was still in the small of his back, but Jennings's S&W had more stopping power and greater range. He pulled the 9mm automatic and snapped off two shots at Cole.

Cole felt the air sizzle just past his right ear. Two inches to the left and he'd be a dead man running, his momentum carrying him on several steps while his brain brain and heart would have stopped.

Cole jumped to the right, landing on a lawn slick with water from a nighttime running of the sprinklers. He skidded and almost went on his ass but managed to stay upright. He pulled the trigger on his Beretta four times, moving the barrel slightly with each shot, hoping a wider shot disbursement would strike Igor.

It did.

One of the 9mm bullets grazed Igor's shoulder, bouncing off his clavicle, shattering it.

Igor roared against the pain and cut left hard into the street.

Mollie saw him and steadied her Beretta with both hands. She pulled the trigger as fast as she could, her steps as she ran, bouncing the muzzle of the weapon up and down. It wasn't anywhere near her training, but she didn't care.

That son-of-a-bitch needed to die.

Her wild spray of fire ...

Exploded car windows ...

Blew an SUV's tire to shreds ...

Ricocheted off the asphalt and hit Igor ...

The first shot blew out his left knee, scything him down like the proverbial shaft of wheat.

The second shot destroyed his right kidney as he fell.

The S&W clattered from Igor's hand as he crashed to the asphalt.

Cole had Igor's bald head square in his sights as he approached from his blind side.

Mollie angled to her left, keeping Igor in her field of vision, so they had him centered in their field of fire. She ejected the clip, not sure how many were left, and rammed home a fresh magazine.

They heard a car approaching.

Cole glanced at it: Galina and the battered Genesis.

Igor didn't moan in pain, he roared in anger.

"FOCK YOU! FOCK YOU!"

Galina approached Igor, her H&K 9mm trained on his head.

"Do not move, Igor," she said; first in English, then Russian.

Hearing his native tongue confused Igor. He peered at Galina. Slowly, he eased his hand to the small of his back for his trusty SV. He wouldn't get out of this alive, but he could take this bitch with him; maybe even one of the others.

Head shot for this whore.

Then Igor's head exploded.

"Get down!" Cole yelled.

Because the shot hadn't come from him or Mollie or Galina.

It had come from a distance.

A long distance.

Sergey had stopped using the scope since that only gave him a narrow field of vision. He'd been scanning the surrounding blocks after the cop car was stolen.

When he saw the distant twin flashes from Igor's shotgun, he pulled the sniper rifle up and zeroed in on the area. It took him a moment to locate the action.

There in the yellow-green moonscape he saw – A man with a gun... and to his left... A woman slamming home a magazine.

Sergey moved the scope and saw...

A black car jerk to a stop and another armed woman emerge and march forward, her weapon out. He moved the scope ahead to where she was walking and saw– a bald man in the middle of the street.

That is focker!

Sergey dialed in his scope.

Igor was centered on the cross-hairs.

Sergey inhaled slowly, then timing it with the slow release of breath, squeezed the trigger.

Igor's head exploded in a dark green aria of bone and blood and matter in the scope.

Sergey looked for another target.

The man had ducked behind one of the cars, Sergey couldn't tell which one.

Same for the woman that had been to his left.

But he woman from the automobile was at the front of the black car.

Sergey zeroed in on the hood of the automobile. He didn't need to be so careful with these shots.

He shot, snapped another cartridge into place, shot, snapped another cartridge.

Three shots so fast it was hard to comprehend.

Galina's ears were buffeted by the thunderous explosion of the Genesis's hood. She felt part of the car's grill disintegrate as the bullet cored through the sheet metal and steel.

She went prone on the ground just as the windshield vanished in an eruption of glass and metal.

The third bullet went wide, gouging a chunk of asphalt three feet past her head.

There was silence.

"He's waiting for one of us to move," Cole said.

They heard the first of the police sirens approaching.

"We've got to get out of here," Mollie yelled. "Now."

"Mollie, run on the lawn. We'll meet you at the corner."

Cole leaped to Galina and pulled her upright. He shielded her with his body.

But there were no more shots.

NINETY

SERGEY WAS DONE SHOOTING.

For now.

"They von't know vot car I am driving."

He ran to the edge of the roof.

But it was too dangerous to jump down to the Lexus and take the weapon.

Fock it. I can't use, no one else either.

He gripped the rifle by the stock and hammered the barrel down on the concrete ledge. The metal collapsed 30° and twisted skyward. He propped the rifle against the ledge and went airborne and thundered down squarely on the trigger assembly.

The wood cracked. Sergey stomped the rifle once... twice... three times. The trigger guard was bent, the trigger a twisted sliver of metal.

He picked up the battered weapon and flung it across the flat roof. It clattered and bounced and finally came to rest in the far corner.

Be days before they find. Maybe not till roof needs repairs.

Sergey hung his legs over the edge of the roof and jumped down. His weight shattered the sunroof as he landed on it dead center, then bounced down to the hood.

The shiny sheet metal collapsed into twin dents from Sergey's shoes.

Cheap Japanese shit.

He started the engine and rolled out of the lot.

Cops come from south. Fockers went north.

But he was wrong.

Because Cole, Mollie and Galina were running east.

"To the cop cars?" Mollie said between deep breaths as she flew down the street.

"It's closest. The Rover's about a half-mile north."

"Not cop car, Rover," Galina said. "Cops vill be looking for their car, if haven't already found."

Cole nodded in agreement and slowed down.

Mollie and Galina caught up and the three of them walked together.

"How far away was the shooter?" Cole asked.

"Least quarter-mile," Galina said.

"No way," Mollie said.

"Story goes that he took out one of Nikolai's competitors from thousand meters away."

Mollie reflectively looked behind her. She started running again.

"The sooner we get into a car and on the road, the safer I'll feel."

Cole and Galina fell in behind her.

Sergey's path took him past Annushka's street. It was still jammed with police cars and, once again, TV crews. He gave the Lexus more gas and focused on the road ahead. His eyes searched for anyone on the street.

Maybe they split up.

"Go right," Cole said. "It's in the next block."

The Rover was still fifty feet ahead when Cole saw the Lexus turn the corner.

"Bandit at eleven o'clock."

He slowed down and walked into the street.

Mollie and Galina stopped and hunkered down behind a parked Chevy Tahoe. The SUV's bulk offering the most protection.

Cole could feel the car picking up speed as it rushed toward him, but he forced himself to act like he was going to his car.

Sergey saw Cole.

Doesn't look like in hurry.

Sergey gave the Lexus some gas and accelerated towards Cole.

He not looking at me?

Sergey lowered the passenger side window as he saw the man reach for the door handle of an old car. He raised his automatic, ready to fire.

Cole counted... three... two... one.

And dove over the hood of the Lexus.

Vot the fock!

Sergey's trigger finger jerked automatically. The shot blew apart the car's window.

He stomped the brakes to go back and kill the focker.

But the car's momentum carried him directly into a fusillade of bullets as Mollie and Galina opened fire.

The 9mm slugs pierced the Lexus's body panels and windows.

He floored the car.

Just as two bullets hit him: One in the left shoulder, the other creasing the back of his skull.

Neither wound was life-threatening.

But the impact threw Sergey off and he plowed the Lexus into a parked car, grazing the fender.

He shook off the impact and threw open the door.

He brought up his weapon. And was stunned to see the man. Right there.

Cole's first shot pierced Sergey's sternum, the bone fragments exploding like shrapnel into his lungs.

Cole's second shot blew out Sergey's throat, his spinal column shredding through his skin and out into the dark, chilly night.

Cole went to make sure Sergy was dead, but Galina saved him the trouble by ventilating the assassin's body until the breech of her H&K stuck open. Cole counted ten shots.

"Bastard!"

She spit on Sergey's body, then launched a vicious kick that shattered the dead man's jaw.

"Focker killed my brother."

She pulled out her cell phone and snapped a photo. Then she jumped behind the wheel of the Lexus.

"You think this will make it? All shot up?" Cole said.

"Ve find out soon enough."

NINETY-ONE

"AIRPORT HALF-MILE AWAY."

Galina had finally broken the silence.

It had been a quiet ride.

They were all three still processing what had happened and how many times they'd come close to death.

And survived.

"Why the picture of Sergey?" Cole asked.

"Bargaining chip."

"For what?"

"Nikolai cannot be in public spotlight. He is like vampire vith daylight. He vithers. So, we don't show his man and he gives us vot ve need."

"What's that mean?" Mollie asked.

"Nikolai has haute couture designer company in Milan. NV for envy? You have heard of this, yes?"

"Who hasn't?" Mollie said.

"To avoid spotlight, he gives us NV and ve run it."

"Are you kidding?" Cole said.

"No. Makes sense. Ve need funding, NV is very profitable."

"Why would he do that?"

"He has no choice."

"This the way they do business in Russia?"

"Vay business is done all over vorld. Rich bastards alvays get avay. Alvays has been, alvays vill be. Money buys you freedom."

"What about the law?" Cole said. "And justice?"

"Oh, there is justice. Sometimes is Butyrka prison, sometimes losing home, sometimes freezing Swiss banks accounts. But very rare that justice is bullet. Bad for business. Need long-view. By keeping asset in play, you still in game."

Galina parked near the hangar.

Nikolai's sleek jet was parked nose out from it. A crew was finishing fueling the plane.

Cole saw a tall woman approaching them.

Verushka peered into the car. She saw Galina and Mollie and smiled. Then she saw Cole and gave two thumbs up and a big warm smile of promises to come.

She opened the door for Cole.

"Hello, Cole. So nice to see you again."

He looked at Galina, then at Verushka.

"You two?" he said, waiting for an answer.

"Ve are..." she gave a high-five to the air. "Tag team."

THE END

Thank you so much for reading one of our **Crime Fiction** novels.
If you enjoyed the experience, please check out our recommended title for
your next great read!

Caught in a Web by Joseph Lewis

"This important, nail-biting crime thriller about MS-13 sets the bar very high.
One of the year's best thrillers." –*BEST THRILLERS*